THE HAUNTING
of the
ANTIQUE BROOCH

THE
HAUN

TING

of the
ANTIQUE BROOCH

HINA ANSARI

MILL CITY PRESS

Mill City Press, Inc.
2301 Lucien Way #415
Maitland, FL 32751
407.339.4217
www.millcitypress.net

Printed in the United States of America

ISBN-13: 978-1-6312-9055-8

For my niece and nephew
Eyshal Noor and Ilhan Syed

AUTHOR'S NOTE

ANY PERCEIVED OR ACTUAL LIKENESS found in this novel to real people or places is purely coincidental. I have a vivid imagination and am terrible at pairing names and faces.

CONTENTS

ONE

I'M MOVING MUCH FASTER THAN MY mind can keep up with as I am hurled through a window, what little glass left shattering on impact. Across my line of sight are flashes of the dining room—a splintered table and broken chairs—a ceiling that is falling in, remnants of a kitchen in the distance—and then I hear and feel a loud crash as I roll through the winding walkway and stop outside an abandoned—and possibly haunted—house. I'm staring up at the night sky. It looks like the inside of a stuffed animal. The stuffing is gray and worn, holes everywhere. The stuffed animal was loved once, but not by me. My back is aching; my neck is tight. The chain on my necklace caught on an errant thread on the back of my shirt, nearly choking me. My senses are out of whack. My skin tingles all over. There is a mix of battery acid and rotten eggs wafting through the air, making me gag.

I ease up on one elbow, then the other, doing my best to assess the damage. No broken bones, but I'm going to be bruised all over. This was supposed to be a quiet hobby, one that didn't involve anyone getting hurt, one that kept me busy through the summer months until school started again. It should have been fun. Truthfully, it isn't a hobby at all, but a mission to discover where people go, where my grandmother went, when she died. I still think she's there, at home, or around, somewhere. I just know this place is haunted. I should be able to find proof on one of the cameras I brought that ghosts do exist.

When I try to get up, I tumble over sideways, feeling the dry grass poking me. The summer heat has everything wilted. I've never been graceful, but this is worse than usual. Get your bearings, Roni. Just then I see there's something, or someone, moving in front of me. The old house is isolated, the neighborhood abandoned, three miles away from my crowded cul-de-sac. No one should have heard anything. I came here alone. Or at least I didn't tell anyone. What was I thinking? I stumble to one knee, the dry grass crunching under me, and wait for the world to snap back into focus. This is taking too long. Sound is starting to penetrate the stupor in my head. Something is howling—maybe shouting, given I feel like I'm in a box, the air closing in around me. No, it isn't howling. Those are sirens. Crap! I better move, and fast.

I groan. "Ow, move it, girl."

Willing my limbs to respond is a much harder task than anticipated. I'm practically crawling, grabbing fistfuls of dirt and grass as I finally find my legs and balance has returned. The sirens are closing in, but I can easily get lost in the adjoining neighborhood, even if it is a mile away. A car would be nice right about now, but I don't have my driver's permit, let alone a license. It's good I run for the track team at school, sort of. It's not like I win races. The goal is to just keep moving the feet until I cross the finish line. I'm huffing and puffing after just a hundred yards, the loose gravel on the unfinished road scattering at each step. I should probably start training in another month or else that first run in the fall will be murder.

It feels like something is still right behind me, watching me. I think about the prayer my grandmother used to recite in Arabic. It autoplays in my head without my having to speak the words. Though even if I say it, I don't speak the language. My mom always told me it was spoken to ward off evil things. In Sunday school, we were taught classical Arabic to read the Quran. The feeling is fading, but the sirens are getting closer. I'm out of gas. Breaking into the abandoned house was tiring enough. A few more feet and I stumble behind an abandoned van. The vehicle has been gutted. All that's left is a metal husk.

The sirens turn the dark night a mix of red and blue. The sound is now deafening. What am I even doing out here? What happened in there? I fumble for the pocket in my pullover, finding the tiny video camera and handheld audio recorder. Both look like they're still intact. I need to get the files back to Matty. He'll know what to do, and how to decipher all of this. I wince. My ribs are aching. I probably shouldn't have sprinted like that, but the last thing I need is a run-in with my brother. Awkward.

The cops are walking the perimeter. I hope I didn't leave anything. Right now, it probably looks like just a bunch of kids messing around. The cops are so blind. If it isn't standing right in front of them, it doesn't exist—unless you're not white, then they see you. Ready. Aim. Fire. Hence my running.

The momentary break lets me catch my breath. I can't believe I just did that. The surprise isn't receding in my mind. My brother says people are the worst witnesses, that they remember things all out of order. After what just happened, I think he might be right. Am I completely losing my mind? Did anyone hear that crash? My hands are shaking as I bring the camera up. There isn't enough light to see clearly and my eyes are jumping. I can barely make out my own disheveled reflection: frizzed-out ponytail, high cheekbones, red lip balm, and the darkest eyes ever.

I stay put for another ten minutes, my heart finally slowing. Lucky me, no one lives anywhere near here. My eyes flow across the scene as the cops leave. The neighborhood just stops. At first, it's a slow fade, like a bald guy's receding hairline, but then an abrupt stop. My house is in your average neighborhood. We have a playground and a man-made lake that's more like a pond. If you go west, there is a neighborhood that's empty, which is where I am. There are about ten, maybe twelve houses. It looks like someone thought this would be a great location, but no one moved in. There's no grass, no trees; the houses are just shells now. A few gangs used to hang out here, but a couple years back they vanished. It's like light just disappears in this place. I feel that sense again and the hair on the back of my neck stands up. It's time to get moving for the long walk home.

This time I take a slower pace. The cops are gone. The sky is clearing, or at least the clouds are staying put while I continue forward. They always stay put, like they're locked into place over that dilapidated old neighborhood. I turn around and the moon is shining brightly, paving the way home. I can feel an ache in my side, in my knee. I must have hit something besides the window on the way out of the house. I'm still not sure what I saw. Was it real? Did I imagine it? My mind is kind of hazy.

It takes a lot longer to walk home than I'd expected. My feet are aching as the ground turns from gravel to grass. The lights, thankfully, are off in my house as I approach. I stop in the shadows between two houses, staring at our name emblazoned on the mailbox—Khan—making sure there's no movement in my house. The driveway is packed with my dad's car and my brother's truck. My mom's car is in the garage. The lawn is spotted with brown patches, a few bushes scattered about. After five minutes of silent waiting, I try to hurry across the empty street and then round the

4

corner, hopping the low fence into the backyard. I stop for a second, closing my eyes, listening. Nothing.

I climb the ladder that doubles as trellises outside my window. The room's dark, but that's how I like it. I can get lost in the dark, and so will anyone else. I do my best to step carefully, hoping my feet aren't making any noise. I hold my breath for a few moments. It sounds like a freight train is coming through the front of the house. Mom and dad must be sound asleep. I turn on the nightlight, sliding the window shut and loosening the curtains. I pull my phone out and message Matty. He's not awake, but when he gets up, he'll have a lot of stuff waiting for him. My laptop is sitting on my desk and I download the files, knowing I'm too tired and beat up to review them now. Normally I'd never work in silence, but I can't risk making any noise. I'm dead tired as I set my glasses on the desk before changing into my pajamas. When I empty my pockets, I find a rock or something. It must have gotten in there while I was doing acrobatics out the window. I toss it into a drawer, not thinking much of it. I flip the light off once I've sent the files and hope to get some rest. The clock displays two a.m. It is going to be a long day tomorrow.

Two

THE ALARM IS GOING OFF. IT'S BLARING through every last fiber of my being, the vibrations shaking me awake. My eyes feel glued together as I see the sun pouring into my room. There's a lot of sound around me. Music is playing (louder than it needs to be) from down the hallway. My perfectly perfect older sister, Sara, is obnoxiously doing this while getting ready. She always has to look perfect. God forbid that perfection shouldn't be noted daily, if not hourly.

My neck was tight before, but now it's like a vise is locked at the base. If I dare to sit in bed for too long, I won't ever hear the end of it from my parents for daring to waste even a second of time on doing nothing. My knee is burning. I push my pajama pants leg up (when did I change?) and see there's a massive bruise. To the side of my knee, it looks like there are teeth marks. I trace the marks with my finger, feeling a slight pulse of pain as I press down. My heart is racing and I can feel a cold sweat sliding down my back, dampening my t-shirt. There are scratches down the back of my arm. When I try to sit up, I can feel a pull. So I reach back, feeling another trio of marks, like claw marks, running diagonally across my back. How did I get so many cuts and bruises? Everything hurts. Did I get all of them from being thrown through the window? That doesn't seem possible.

7

I'm still trying to do a full assessment of all the injuries when my sister, in all her glory, bounds into my room, my private sanctuary, glowing and smelling of roses, bringing the beginnings of the day with her. "Roni, you better get moving. Mom's leaving for work and wants to make sure you're not sleeping the day away."

"I'm not." God, would she just go away so I can go back to sleep?

Her eyes rove across my most hallowed items and prized possessions. "You're disgusting," she says.

With that, she's gone. I sigh in relief. I look across my disorganized room. The desk is overflowing with papers and books. My laptop is sitting precariously on the edge of the desk. There are still quite a few boxes strewn across the room. The closet looks like it imploded, clothes hanging on for dear life. I ignore all this, seeing my phone blinking. Matty must have been able to process everything. Relief washes over me as I stare at his responses. There aren't really words, just strings of letters, like he's developed some type of secret code that I'm not clued into. That's either a really good sign or Matty's having a tough day. The latter is not desirable. It happens a lot during the school year—never ends well for anyone, least of all poor Matty.

Adults describe his being transgender (even though he's biologically a girl) as an emotional problem, a byproduct of being a teenager. We've never really talked about his choice to be open about his identity. I don't really think about it too much. We've been friends for years. When we were younger, he was always a tomboy. Now that we've grown up, his parents, I think, have accepted that it wasn't a phase. Given that both our families are Asian, I'm amazed they allow him to be himself. In my house, everything is about tradition and appearances. I barely go outside without being attired properly, my parents wouldn't allow me as much freedom as his parents accept, even encourage. Considering we live in a pretty conservative state, Illinois, but a progressive suburb of Chicago, the school allows him to be who he is too. Lucky for everyone, the days of changing for gym are long passed. I don't dare ask Matty about those years. He had a variety of bullies. Somehow he powered through it. I'm proud of him, but more than anything, I'm scared. I don't want anyone to hurt him because he's different. That's the world we live in now. Difference is bad.

I pop open my laptop, collect my thoughts, and focus on the task at hand. He's already there. The silly icon of a raccoon staring up at me. His name is blinking: Matty Walker.

I turn the video chat on. Matty's been up for hours. The elapsed time on his icon is at four hours. The screen is filled with a sea of books. The bookshelf is bulging, as if it couldn't possibly eat one more volume and is going to vomit books out in all directions. There are a couple posters on the wall, lined up perfectly. I love Matty's precision, but it can drive me nuts when we're doing projects together, like enough already. Everything has a place, and if it isn't in the right place, then we have to start all over again. Maddening.

"Matty," I smile as I speak, even though my hair's a mess and I haven't brushed my teeth. Even if I'm not attracted to him, he's still a guy.

He doesn't make eye contact. That isn't something Matty does. His forehead is really all I can see. "You okay?"

"Sore," I admit, rubbing my neck. "Anything of value? We need something."

At this Matty sits up, his dark eyes, like obsidian, stare up at me. "Are you kidding? You definitely caught something."

"Or something caught me," I quip, trying to be cool about the fact that we might finally have proof. "I could have used backup."

"I would have come if you'd told me you were going," Matty replies, lowering his head again. "I printed the images. You have to see it for real, not digital. We have to go back."

"Back to the house? I think I might need to rest before trying to break in again." I'm yawning, though my hands are shaking at the thought of going back and finding more proof. "I had a late night and the cops showed up."

"What? Are you okay? How did they know you were there?" Matty asks this all in seconds.

I wince. "I guess someone called or something. I don't know how they knew, but I got out of sight quick."

"Maybe we should take a cop with us next time." Matty's mumbling the words together.

"No."

"It couldn't hurt. He is your brother."

"Are you kidding?" I spit the words out, almost jumping up. "If I tell him, he'll tell Mom, and then the whole world will know. We're doing this to prove there's something, but we don't need to prove anything to any of them."

Matty doesn't reply. This is his usual response, his version of the silent treatment. He just gets super quiet. He's too polite to disagree. That's how we Asians are, even if we're from two very different parts of that hemisphere. I'm Indian. One of the few million Indians who is also Muslim in a nation of over a billion people. Matty's family is from Thailand. The two places aren't that far apart. But to people born in America, like 99 percent of our class-mates, we might as well be from another planet. We get each other. The whole family structure, which, by itself, is foreign to most of my classmates. Their families are all about stuffing unwanted family members into nursing homes, out of sight. Not us.

My dad's parents are still together back in India. My grandmother lived with us until she passed away a few years ago. My grandfather still lives with us. In our language, we call him "Nana," which is funny because a lot of my white friends call their grandmothers "Nana." The pronunciation is completely different. Ours is more like, "Na, na I don't want pickles with my sandwich," where as theirs is more "Nan" and then an "Ah" at the end. Grandmother is "Nani." I know, right? Languages are so bizarre to me. Nothing makes sense, not really.

The silence is getting awkward. Well, as awkward as it's going to get for me and Matty. One of us has to end the stalemate.

Thankfully Matty steps in. "Fine. Do you want to swing by later?"

I have stuff to do, family stuff that I will be drawn and quartered for if I don't do, but I can make time for this. I have to. "I'll be by in a couple hours," I tell him.

I close the video chat and sigh. If I had told my brother, everything would be confiscated. Even though my family isn't overly technically competent, the cameras, the laptop, the external hard drives, everything would be taken. I try to be discreet, but I never knew what Mom or Dad might have discovered while I was at school. At least now, over summer break, I have a better idea of where everything is and if it has been moved or touched.

My parents have a strict regimen for me: get good grades, get into a great school, get married, have kids. Only the first two are really high on my priority list. I've got a year left of high school. The place is a zoo. Most kids don't take anything seriously. My advanced placement classes are a mix of rich kids not paying attention and 2 percent of the "others" in the school. The others make up what few minorities we have.

I take a quick glance at the summer reading pile, mine and the one the school issued. I can cram like no one's business. I lean backward, feeling my back tightening again. I am way too young to be in this much pain. I manage my way to the bathroom. My sister, the princess, has left the room a mess. Just what I wanted.

THREE

THE CLEANUP IN THE BATHROOM TOOK
way too long. The heat outside is unbearable. The humidity
has got to be 2,000 percent. My hair is frizzed out, again.
What I wouldn't give for calm, straight hair. My sister con-
veniently took the car and told me I could ride my bike if
I wanted to. As if there were some other option—oh wait,
there was. She could have given me a ride. That's ridiculous.
I'm not even sure why I brought that up. The jeans and
T-shirt I'm wearing over a pair of worn high-tops feel like a
winter coat on a warm spring day. I'm burning up and probably smell awful. If I dared to wear shorts, the ones that are
popular, that potentially show off your underwear, my parents would never let me out of the house again. Showing off
too much skin is inappropriate, they say. It's okay for other
people, but not for me.

The final turn into Matty's neighborhood comes as a
relief. The long driveway leads to a perfectly manicured
garden. The summer heat wave has killed most of the
flowers, but the bushes are lush and the grass is actually
green. I hurry to the front door of Matty's house. Both of
his parents are at work. His kid brother has been playing
video games nonstop since school ended a month ago. Must
be a nice life. Truth be told, I could be doing that too. But
there is something far more pressing going on. I knock on
the door once. A quiet moment passes before the sound of
dozens of hooved creatures pounding the hardwood floor

can be heard through the door. It swings open and Matty's little brother, Mikey, stares up at me.

"Oh, it's you." His eyes are on the floor, his body deflated, as if he'd been expecting someone more interesting.

This is some common thing with Matty's entire family. Like making eye contact with a woman is forbidden. I know it's sort of frowned upon to be forward, but making eye contact? That's silly.

I push past Mikey. "Matty upstairs?" I ask.

"Yep."

The kid is gone in ten seconds flat. I can hear the game playing from the foyer. I push the door closed and lock the deadbolt. I stare at my reflection in the window. My hair is even frizzier than it was before, and my dark skin only got darker in the sun. I should have put sunscreen on. I stop at the bathroom, hoping to dry the sweat off, at least a little.

The walk upstairs is quiet, the plush white carpet silencing my footfalls. The house is pretty big. There are pictures of the family on the walls. There are also awards everywhere. The walls of the home office are adorned with certificates and diplomas. Both Matty's parents are highly educated. If Matty doesn't get into an elite school, his father will probably have a heart attack. I stare at a picture taken at one of our field trips from elementary school. The bully, Blaine, is in the background. If only we could be held as unaccountable as he is. Must be nice to have parents who just want you to pass. Oh to be white and privileged. That isn't in the cards for either me or Matty.

I trek up the stairs; my right leg is starting to feel like it's on fire. I don't realize I'm limping until I get about halfway up the stairs. My fingers shake as I try to massage the pains away. Maybe it'll go away after a good night's rest. The moment I let the thought sit, I realize it has already been one night and the pains have only gotten worse, not better.

I'm trying to calm the tension that's growing in my mind. I need to focus on the task at hand. I'll be fine. I drag myself a bit farther and stop at Matty's room, knocking once on the door, even though it isn't shut. Like my family, we aren't really permitted to shut our doors all the way. My mother is convinced I'm hiding boys in my room. That's the last thing on my mind. I don't have time for boys. Besides, they seem to be big babies anyway. I stare across the room, spotting Matty.

"Hey."

I've been in Matty's room a few times. The desk takes up the majority of the space. Matty leads a bit of a Spartan lifestyle, possessing as little as possible, aside from his computer and the burgeoning bookcase. There's a poster of a movie that came out ten years ago on the wall. There are quite a few pieces of devices. Matty does his best to create what we can't afford to buy. I'm curious about the new equipment he's working on now. There's music playing somewhere in the background. A year or so back, when Matty had time, he was in the marching band. He has an affinity for small groups, and this was one he knew before they graduated. I can barely hear the lyrics over a drum that's louder than thunder.

Matty doesn't look up, but hands me a stack of pictures. I orient the first one. This is inside the house. The lighting is terrible. The flash obscured everything. I need to get the right setting for taking pictures in the dark. I can see the outline of what once was the dining room. The one I so unceremoniously fell out of. The thought begins and the memory replays. A cold sweat begins once again. I didn't fall, I realize now. I was thrown through that window with great force. I still my shaking hands as I stare at the image. What could have that much force to throw me, a moderately sized human, out a window? I swear I didn't see anything.

I need to get home and review that footage myself. What have I found? Or what has found me?

I flip to the next picture, but Matty grabs the stack. "Just jump to the end."

He thrusts a different picture into my hand. I stare down at it. I can feel my breath catch in my throat. This is one of the still images taken when I set the camera on a stand behind me. I was trying to catch a voice (electronic voice phenomena is catching voices through recordings that human ears can't hear). I was standing stock still. I can just see myself in the image: loose shirt, jeans, and high-tops as usual. In the picture, between me and the camera, is an unmistakable blur. More than that, it is in human form. The flash washes the background white, but the form is dark.

I stare up at Matty. "Whoa."

"I know." He's beaming. "We have to go back."

I can feel the grimace creeping across my face. After riding over here, I can also feel the aches throbbing throughout my body. "Matty, I'm not in great shape."

His demeanor changes, but only a little. "So you said. What happened?"

It wouldn't be prudent to show him, so I have to just describe. "I got thrown through a window."

"What?" Matty's gesturing to the chair at his desk as he shifts to the bed, the leather armband on his forearm sliding down to his wrist.

"I'm still not sure what happened," I confess. "I was upstairs, about ten minutes before that picture." I hold it up. "Then something—and I wish I could describe it better—knocked me down." I hold up both arms as proof, only pushing the sleeves up to my elbows, the scrapes apparent on my bare forearms. I wouldn't dare show him my knees or back, like where the bite marks are. That would be too much.

"Then," I continue, "I'm trying to see in the dark, and something grabs me by the shoulders. The next thing I know, I'm through the window, then outside, and then there are sirens."

His eyes narrow as he flips the desk light on to get a better look at the cuts on my exposed arms. "We have to go back."

"I have a family thing tonight," I groan. "I hate it, but Mom has to have parties every ten seconds. If we're not hosting something, it's like she ceases existing."

Matty shrugs. "I know. We're having a big get together before school starts, thankfully still a couple months away."

"Tomorrow?" I'm hoping he says no. "I'll be free to do whatever after this stupid graduation party."

"I might swing by the haunted house tonight." Matty glances at the computer. "You caught some audio, but I can't make anything out."

"Please don't go alone." It's hard to tell if he's ever really listening.

"I've got homework I have to do." Matty never doesn't have homework. His parents have his first year of college already planned. There is no end to study in his house, not at any point during the year.

"Me too." I get up, feeling my knee ache again. "See you."

I'm not looking forward to the blistering heat outside, but I still feel relief. I hate keeping something all to myself, especially something terrifying like this. Matty walks me to the door. I leave the pictures with him. Having proof I was trespassing is probably not a good idea. The last thing I need, as I trudge through the oppressive heat, is to go back to that house right now. I need to get my head on straight—figure out whether I want to interact with something that wants to kill me, or worse.

Four

BY THE TIME I GET HOME, PREPARA-
tions are beginning—even though the party doesn't start
for at least four hours. Everything has to be perfect, for
the perfect child, of course.

I'm trying to be quiet, not to be noticed, but I fail, as
per usual.

"And where have you been?" My mother speaks in a
heavy Indian accent, but don't tell her that. Now that she's
spotted me, there is no escape. "Why do you look so terrible? It is too sunny for you to be outside. You are as black
as the asphalt."

I shut my eyes and start counting to ten in my head.
The key is not to respond in kind. It won't end well. It
never does, but still. My perfect sister saves me (not by
choice, I expect) as she floats into the room.

"Mama," her voice sings through the space, "I don't
know about this outfit."

Any attention my mother had for me is long gone and
she's now focused on my sister. I breathe a sigh of relief. At
least this is a short reprieve. Or so I had hoped.

"Roni," she says, using her extra stern voice, "clean up
and iron your clothes. I put your outfit on your bed."

I nod, knowing not to respond otherwise. I do wonder
when the right time would be to either shower or get ready,
but I know better than to ask. My clothes stick to me as
my body cools off, sweat pouring through everything. The

shower is the first thing I need, but the space is mostly occupied. My sister has turned our mutual bathroom into her own. There isn't a millimeter of space available. There is one bathroom that is always free. I grab some clean clothes, my towel, and toiletries and head downstairs.

Nana used to be an imposing figure. Several bouts of serious illnesses later and he's a bit of a ghost. As a kid, I always looked up to him. Now, he's doubled over and can barely move. Most days he sits in front of the TV in his room, the volume loud enough for the neighbors two houses over to hear. I creep towards his room, careful not to be spotted by my mother a second time.

The room is dark, the bathroom across. I could just sneak in, but that wouldn't stop him from barging in or banging on the door to throw me out. I stop at the doorway, noting the sandals outside. Even in the dark I can make out the closet door ajar, a smattering of dark-colored garments sticking out. The room has carpeting, but Nana has a block rug in the middle, under his easy chair, that is facing the TV. The bed is against the wall, leaving little room for much else, save for a writing table that is piled high with papers, letters, and books, pens, and scraps of paper littering the surface. I take a quick glance. Since I can't hear the TV from the doorway and my hearing is still intact, I know it isn't on. It must be time for one of his midday naps. I take my time and spot him. He's sitting in his reclining armchair, just sitting there. Curiosity always gets the better of me and I take a step in. At least I took my shoes off upstairs, but the linoleum floor outside the room is making my feet loud as I move, the sweat sticking to the ground, making a slapping sort of sound. His hearing isn't great, but I take a few more steps in, just to check if he's breathing. He may not like me very much, but I don't want him to die.

A minute passes, and I'm pretty sure he's breathing. I back up, pulling the door partially shut. Hopefully this will warn him that someone is using his shower. I turn and enter the spotless bathroom. Normally, I'd never use this room. I don't think I'll have the luxury to bathe again in my own bathroom until after the party. I know I need to ignore everything here. The case, the house, the science behind it all—that's something I need to remember. In a few years, maybe I won't be in this dead-end house. I doubt my parents would even notice if I were gone.

Time is not on my side, and I'm feeling super gross. Just getting my clothes off is a chore. I throw everything into a pile and jump into the shower. Almost as soon as I have a good lather going, I can hear the banging on the door. I try to ignore it at first, but this is yet another battle I can't win.

"Just one second," I say as I try to hurry. The last thing I need is my grandfather barging in on me while I'm naked.

The banging on the door persists. There is no peace to be found in this house. I go faster still, being careful not to lose my balance as I towel off. The mirror hasn't even steamed up and I'm dressed. Now my clothes are sticking to me because my skin is wet, not because I'm sweaty.

I give Nana an apologetic look. "Sara was using our bathroom," I tell him. "I didn't mean to use your shower without permission."

When I bring my eyes up, his face is puckered, like he's sucking on a lemon rind. I am expecting him to shout at me, but he shrugs, saying something under his breath, and shuffles back to his bedroom. I glance at him once more before hurrying down the hallway. I don't want to rehash an awkward conversation with him today. It's always the same, as it is with all my family. "Why don't I find a nice boy and get married?" This is like a refrain in a song—it just keeps repeating and the song never changes.

The main floor of the house is being decorated. My mom's closest friends are already here. That means there are at least ten people running around our house. Streamers are being taped up to the ceiling, tapering down to the floor. There's a multicolored lettered sign congratulating my sister on her graduation from high school being hung behind the dining room table. All of the chairs have been pulled away from the table. There also seems to be an influx of folding chairs that we don't own.

The transformation doesn't hide the fact that this is still a small house that's about to host no less than one hundred people. Two of the ladies are staring at me disapprovingly, like my Metallica T-shirt and gray sweatpants aren't appropriate in my own home. There is no metal band that will ever surpass Metallica, as my older brother Jamaal taught me a few years ago. I push my mass of sopping wet hair out of my face, continuing upstairs. The music is blaring. My sister has her best friend here. I try not to make eye contact.

"Bushra is here." My sister's voice is echoing through the hallway, through my brain.

I try to control the immediate and visceral response, forcing a smile across my face. "Hey," I say to her.

Bushra is fair skinned with light brown hair. Her parents describe her as if she were a show dog, how much they spent on her teeth, her posture. They hope she catches a good doctor once she goes off to school. Silly me, I thought school was for learning, for bettering yourself. I guess bettering yourself doesn't get better than marrying a doctor.

The girl gives me the once-over. Despite all the praise her parents bestow on her, she's not all that attractive. She stares at me with her lips curled into a snarl before shutting the door to my sister's room. Good riddance. I don't need to be forced through that conversation. I push the door to my room shut, feeling like this is the quiet escape I needed. The lights are dimmed and I toss my dirty clothes into the hamper and stare at the conglomeration of colors that compose the outfit I'm required to wear. It looks like a unicorn pooped and someone took that and smooshed it into one piece of fabric.

There are certain advantages to being Indian. People often perceive that you're good at math or computers or even medicine. If you have to call one of those tech numbers, the person on the other end might be one of your third cousins. Getting to wear elaborate outfits is one advantage, but that they don't breathe and aren't made for humans is not.

In most cases, the clothes are a little loose. I'm not going to say I'm fat. Let's just say . . . I don't skip desserts. You only live once, right? Most of the loose-fitting outfit is fine. My calves are another story, as well as my upper arms. If toning were the issue, I'd be lucky. I'm staring at my reflection in the mirror, the mop of hair finally drying, looking almost like I've replaced my hair with an animal. My parents would never let me have a pet. I had a plant once. I honestly don't remember what it was. After a week, it was dead.

I have to put makeup on, but I might be able to put that off until later. Maybe no one will notice if I don't apply any. Once the party gets going, I'm usually relegated to the kitchen, where I won't be seen. Who would replenish the food trays if not the hired help? And that would be me.

The important thing on party days is to be extra alert. I open the door a smidge, letting a small line of light peak in. My sister's door is shut. There is a lot of noise coming from downstairs. One deep breath—that's all I have time for. I can't hide in my room. That's the first place they'll look for me.

The walk down the stairs reveals that the party is getting into the post-preparation/pre-party status. More people will be coming over, but the appetizers will be the only thing out until everyone gets here. I can see my mom wearing a deep blue sari with silver embellishments adorning the border. There is no way I would put on eight yards of fabric, wrap it around, and still be able to move. I've tried it. It didn't end well. It looks like Mom emptied the entire safe deposit box of all her valuable jewelry. I feel even more undressed now. Apparently when she got married, every relation, on both sides of the family gifted her a set. A set consists of a necklace, rings, and earrings. She could literally wear a different set every day of the month and not repeat.

The moment my foot hits the bottom stair, my mother's eyes find me. "You are going to put makeup on."

It isn't a question. It isn't a request. It is an understanding. I need to understand that this will be done and without any attitude. I doubt the makeup will really help, or make me into a Bollywood beauty. Bollywood is India's version of Hollywood, based out of Bombay, now called Mumbai, India. I give her a slight nod, but it looks more like a grimace.

"Don't make that face," she chides as she turns back to her friends. "No man will ever marry you with that attitude."

Another retort pops into my head. Later . . . that's for later, not now. The activity in the house has tripled by now. Every event is attended, it seems, by everyone we've ever met. My mother tries to drag me to events, but thankfully I can use the excuse that I need to study as a valid reason not to go. That is the only thing that potentially could get me out of the consistently onerous social engagements. The last thing I need is one more of my parents' friends to start up a conversation about how school is or what I'm going to study.

My grandfather is sitting with the men. All of them act like he has something impossibly great to say. I've never had a full conversation with the man, but I guess old people can talk amongst themselves and find something interesting to say.

Everywhere I look I can see people dressed in all shades of the rainbow. It could almost be a gay pride parade, except that being gay is pretty much not allowed. The men are dressed in more subdued colors, mostly grey, blue or beige. I envy the simplicity of their choices. It really is just pants, shirt, and preferably matching, un-holed socks. The men always take their shoes off. The ladies, on the other hand, have shoes that complete their outfits. Since we're Indian, there are generally more saris than anything else. There are a few Pakistani friends we have who always wear *shalwar kameez*, which is what I'm wearing, just a long shirt with embroidered work on it and annoyingly baggy pants.

I turn and head towards the kitchen. There's never a shortage of food. We have a sunroom in the back of the house, behind the kitchen. During parties, this space is reserved for the overflow of pretty much everything. Knowing my mom, there's enough food to feed the entire school here. I glance around before dipping a carrot in the ranch dressing. Just what I needed. I skipped lunch, and dinner won't be for a good long while.

My mother is hustling around with her friends close in tow like a gaggle of hens, speaking quickly, partially in English, partially in Hindi. I'm picking up bits and pieces, but nothing that I need to know. The conversation is almost always about clothes or gossip about what someone shouldn't be doing. There was quite the intrigue a few years ago when a woman got a divorce. I still haven't seen anyone from that family at any functions. Divorce is like wearing a huge letter D on all your clothes. I hope that doesn't happen in our family.

Things are getting a little congested in the kitchen. There's another tray of veggies in the sunroom. I avoid eye contact as I move in that direction. Something catches my eye, that feeling like someone is watching me again. I look up and see Matty with a flashlight pointed at my face. What part of "I couldn't go out" did he not understand?

FIVE

IT'S BAD ENOUGH I HAVE TO DRESS IN
these uncomfortable clothes, but to be seen by someone
who doesn't see this sort of shiny, showy stuff is another
embarrassing moment. He must think I'm totally insane.
I've never seen one of their parties; I wonder if they dress
as crazy as we do?

My eyes dart around the kitchen. My mother and her
crew are busy adjusting the direction of the serving dishes.
This obviously requires six people to accomplish. I skitter
towards the back door. My *dupatta*, which is basically a thin
scarf that's to be wrapped around my neck, is somehow
catching on the carpet. Matty is staring at me with those
insistent, doleful eyes as I open the door and step outside
into the wall of heat.

"Was I unclear earlier?" No use in being outright rude.
It is better to build up to that.

Matty gives a noncommittal shrug. "I think I cleaned
up the audio."

"And this couldn't wait until later tonight?" My eyes are
practically looking in two directions at once. If my mother
sees me outside, I'll never hear the end of it.

"No," Matty replies, pulling the audio player out of his
pocket. "Nice outfit."

"Shut up." I can feel the ends of my lips curl upward.

The moment he presses play, I can see the whole scene
again. Every few moments you can hear what would

have been me asking questions: "Is anyone here? Is there someone who wants to say something?" This is standard fare in ghost hunting. Never once have we gotten a coherent response. It's long after I've stopped talking that some sort of noise begins. I'm wondering if it's just some ambient sort of sound, but there is a tone, low at first, then growing louder, stronger. The words are unmistakable.

"Get out."

Matty hits the stop button, his dark eyes set, a smile on his face.

"We have to go back," he says.

"Are you insane?" I'm sweating through my clothes. There will be no hiding these stains. God, I hate this satiny fabric sometimes.

"They won't even notice you're not there," Matty points out.

This is a valid argument, except for the fact that I won't be around to refill the troughs. How can people eat so much? Or, more accurately, take so much food, but then throw so much of it away? I don't fast for the entire month of Ramadan for this. Well, at least that's what we're taught. People wasting food makes me sick.

I still haven't responded, but Matty hasn't noticed. The earbuds have been put in and he's nodding. "I swear, when you're asking questions, I can hear something else."

My eyes dart back to the party, then to my feet. I'm not wearing shoes. I'm wearing flip-flops. Those are not great for quick escapes, not to mention the fact that my clothes are not at all suited for any sort of ghost hunt.

"I can't go." I'm wishing I could just disappear. The family photo won't be for another three hours. Between now and then, will anyone really notice my absence?

Matty cocks an eyebrow. "Just a quick check."

I'm torn between what I should do: stay at the boring party for my sister or not let my only real friend go to someplace super dangerous all alone. With all the heat, my mother has resorted to hanging clothes out to dry. I see a pair of jeans and a T-shirt that are mine and I sigh, knowing I'd already decided long before this point.

Matty courteously averts his eyes as I make a quick costume change. I peek through the condensation that is creating a haze on the windows of the sunroom, folding my clothes before pulling the door open and slipping them under the table. The crowd has grown larger still. I doubt anyone will miss one more kid at this party. It isn't like I have a lot of friends who will be here.

There's a garish grin on Matty's face as he leads the way through the next two neighbors' yards. The size of the party has taken over most of the street and we duck around all the vehicles to the side road, making our way to the decrepit old house. That uneasy feeling is returning, and I feel the dampness on my skin all over again. Did these clothes even fully dry? Nope. This could be the punishment for skipping out on our own party. Who am I kidding? That punishment might bleed into my college years.

The walk is long and humid. The closer we get, the quieter it gets. Matty's removed the earbuds. Now he's got the camera up, pointed in the direction we're going. His voice startles me.

"That's a super long walk." Matty mops his brow. "I'm wearing flip-flops next time too."

I miss funny Matty. He doesn't make enough appearances. The nerves I was feeling earlier are calmed by his humor. "Well, the next thing you know, they'll be all the rage for the track team," I joke.

"I read once that flip-flops are the absolute worst for runners, no arch support for when you're not running." And there's normal Matty, almost. "Not that you'd ever catch me running. I'm better at watching and cheering on."

"I try not to listen to all those experts." I stare at my feet. The nails aren't manicured. I don't even bother painting them. My mother would be mortified. That is one plus to Indian clothes—they fall over your feet in a lot of cases. No one can see your legs (no need to shave all the time) or your feet (toe care is optional).

The old house is looming over us. The moon casts a sickly shadow across the front through a sea of clouds. The light doesn't penetrate the interior of the house at all. I can see the massive opening in the window, the one I crashed through. The glass is still littered across the ground. All the doors are boarded shut. The wood has rotted at places, but the window is still the easiest way to get in and out. There is a tree growing over the front door, not allowing any access to get in through it. An owl hoots off in the distance. And just like that, the eerie feeling returns. We shouldn't be here. I shouldn't be here.

Six

THE DARKNESS IS LOCKED INTO PLACE
above the old house. It's almost like the clouds don't move.
That is, of course, ridiculous. That isn't even possible, right? I
don't think there's a meteorology class at school, but if there
was one, I'm sure my parents would have signed me up for it.
As it is, I look forward to getting lost in advanced biology and
calculus. I use the phrase "look forward to" in a nonserious
way. It isn't that I don't find some enjoyment from figuring
stuff out, but getting perfect grades is beyond stressful.

My little internal monologue has allowed Matty to get
closer to the house than me. From where I'm standing, it
almost looks like the house could suck anyone in. Just like
last night, it feels like the darkness is coming from the house,
like light can't exist around it. Physically speaking, that isn't
possible. Well, not unless there was a black hole that was consuming the light. No. This defies all logic.

Matty takes a few more exterior pictures before he turns
to me, a headlamp on his ball cap. "Ready?"

"Nice," I reply, laughing. "Ladies first?"

"Maybe I should go first?" Matty looks nervous. He tosses
me a flashlight and starts forward.

I've always wanted to be cool—be the illusion of cool—
but I can never quite manage. There is a reflection of me in
the one non-broken window of the house. My hair has grown
in size and my dark skin is ashy. The heat is making the not-
so-dry clothes chafe against my skin. The flip-flops could not

31

be more uncomfortable. As I look down, I can't tell if these are even mine. Oops.

Matty looks to be entering from the gaping hole in the window I used last night. The glass crackles under his feet. I try to be extra careful. The soles of my flip-flops are unlikely to withstand any piercing of sharp glass. I gingerly walk around, using the flashlight to illuminate the ground. Something moves beyond us, inside the house. I'm standing still. Matty, not so much.

Fear is one of those emotions I hate to acknowledge. It starts with just a sort of queasy feeling in my stomach, like I'm going to be sick. A slight chill begins. I shiver. Considering how hot it is outside, I shouldn't be cold at all. This is completely idiotic. Even if we do catch something, I'm going to be fileted once Mom finds out I was missing in action. To her, parties are the only thing that matters. Appearances are everything. The worry is betraying me. I shouldn't even care. So what? I get in trouble and then what? I don't have much for them to take away.

The heat is mounting. Matty climbs through the window. The light on his head is moving back and forth. I flash the light through the window, climbing through the hole, making sure that my clothes aren't catching on anything. The second my foot touches the ground, I get that feeling. I'm going to be sick. The sweat is dripping off of my back. It isn't even hot inside. It is actually much, much cooler. This is another warning. In most cases, when there is a cold spot, that means a spirit might be passing through or leaching energy from anything around. The next warning comes faster than expected. The flashlight goes out. Matty turns, though I can barely see him; his headlamp is out too.

"Let me check the batteries," he says as he takes the cap off.

I already know this won't help. It isn't the batteries. I hope our cameras will still work. Matty fumbles in his pocket.

Another light comes on. This one has a crank. Talk about old-school. My grandfather has something like that in his room for when the power goes out. This doesn't happen nearly as often as it does in India, unless you have a generator. Best to be prepared, I suppose.

Matty keeps turning the crank. Both of our lights jump to life again. I'm too startled to react. Matty grins.

"This is great," he says.

"Should we set the cameras up?" I try to control the shakiness in my voice.

The stand is already out, produced from Matty's backpack. With a quick snap of his wrist, it is fully extended. The stand is about a foot high with four legs. It's tough to knock over. With it upright, Matty points it upwards, then sets an oscillate function. Back and forth the camera moves. It takes about thirty seconds for it to move from one edge of the room to the other. The red light is blinking. The memory card in it is massive. It should last at least a few hours, if not the whole night, depending on the quality of video it's capturing.

Though parts of the house are decayed, the stairs are still usable. Matty turns towards them, a camera in hand. "Can you hold the audio recorder?"

I nod and take it from him. With the recorder in one hand and the flashlight in the other, I take a deep breath and ascend the stairs.

"Is anyone here with us?" I ask hesitantly.

There is no response. Matty continues across the landing. The rooms upstairs are carpeted, but with the leaky roof, the smell of mold suffuses everything. I wrinkle my nose, trying to breathe through my mouth. That isn't helping. Matty edges into each room.

After the gangs came through the neighborhood, this house was somehow left untouched. The walls and flooring

33

are only marred by the environment. Other than me, I don't know who else would have ventured inside.

"Can you give us a sign that you're here?" I ask. "I know someone was here yesterday and didn't like me being here."

I wait a few seconds. Matty shrugs, continuing to the next room. I shut my eyes, trying to calm my nerves. I feel something move past me as my unkempt hair flies across my face. I turn around, illuminating everything around me. There's nothing. Matty is in the next room, just scanning with the camera. Something is there with us. Even if we can't see it. There is something here. Something is watching us.

"I'm not getting anything," Matty says as he holds up his EMF.

That little device detects electromagnetic fields. The idea is if there were a spirit or ghost or even demon around, the readings on it would fluctuate. Sort of like detecting the things the human eye can't see. Kind of like the thermometer we use. If something leaches all the energy out or if there is a cold spot, then either of the devices will detect it. This isn't foolproof science per se, but it is supposed to work. It occurs to me that we've never really had an investigation that had proven results. This would be the first. Not counting that time that inspired me to do this in the first place. It was just a spooky place at night and I am sure I saw something, I just don't know what. But that wasn't in this country anyway, and since I was such a young kid, who's to say I really saw what I thought I saw?

Matty stops in front of me, the light on his head just above my line of sight. "What's up?"

"I thought I felt something rush past me." I gesture towards the stairs.

He gives me the EMF meter and uses both hands with the camera, zooming. "Down the stairs?"

"I'm not sure," I admit. "I just shut my eyes, you know, to see if I felt anything, and then a breeze just blasted past me."

Matty cocks an eyebrow. "The window is open down there."

I try not to glare. "What direction would it have to go to get to me from here? We were in geometry together. The angle isn't right."

"Yeah," he concedes. "Come on, let's check the rooms up here."

There's no furniture, so we sit on the floor of the smallest bedroom in the house. One twin bed and a small desk probably would fit in here, but that would be it. There's no door on the closet and the window has been partially boarded up, a sliver of light coming into the room. A cloud of dust bursts up from the ground. I try not to cough, or inhale. The stench is pretty overpowering. All the equipment is out now. The audio recorder, EMF, and thermometer are there, as well as a new device Matty built, a REM-POD. It is an egg-shaped box with a series of lights around a larger central light. The ones I've seen online were a couple hundred bucks. With Matty's ingenuity, he was able to follow a guide, and after a few tests, we're pretty sure it works. Kind of like the thermometer and the EMF, the REM-POD will detect any fluctuations in temperature or magnetic fields. You might think we have too many toys, but you can never have too many

I set my camera off to one side. Matty does the same. This way, there will be two feeds of the same scene, but from different angles. All the dials are at neutral, ambient settings, and we start the questions all over again.

"I know there is someone here." It might be time to start antagonizing a bit. "Are you afraid of two kids? Show us something."

Nothing happens. Matty's got yet another camera. This one is not a video camera. He's snapping away. I wonder if we should get a Polaroid camera, round out the selection.

"I know you threw me through that window." I feel an ache in my neck from nowhere. "Did I do something to upset you?"

The temperature gauge begins to drop. The room was an almost pleasant sixty-five degrees and has now dropped to sixty. That was all in the time it took me to speak.

I keep my eyes on the digital numbers, turning my flashlight off. "Come a little closer. We don't bite."

Matty smirks at this, shutting the light off on his head. Now we're sitting in almost complete darkness, save for the digital display on the EMF and the marginal light from the window. The devices are giving off a very slight sort of electrical noise—whirring or humming maybe. The temperature gauge is now down to fifty-seven. My damp skin is cooling, like it did after I got home earlier this afternoon.

"Tell us what you want."

Speaking in utter silence, I feel like I'm shouting. The air is heavy, hazy, like a fog is there in the room. My breath is coming out hotter than the air around me. The digital numbers read fifty. How on earth did we drop fifteen degrees in a minute or two? My teeth are beginning to chatter, and not from the obvious cold. What have I gotten myself into? I want to rationalize; I want to believe that there is a logical explanation for this. I can't find one.

All the devices are silent. We sit there for some time. I can feel my heart pounding in my chest. I'm surprised Matty isn't scared, or at least he doesn't look scared. There is nothing there. Matty gives a sigh and starts to pick up the devices, shoving them into his bag. He reaches for the REM-POD as the outer circle of lights go yellow then the inner circle go red. Something or someone is there, sitting right next to me.

SEVEN

BOTH OUR EYES ARE TRAINED ON THE device that sits less than a foot away from me. The lights haven't stopped. Instead of adjusting, one side of the outer ring of yellow lights and the entire circle of red lights are illuminated. There is a slight humming sound. The real REM-PODs have a soft siren that goes off. Matty was nice enough not to include such an annoying feature. His eyes are on me. Even in the dark I can feel his gaze.

The thermometer is sliding between fifty-two and forty-eight degrees. I can feel the chill on my skin, but just the left side. It is sitting right next to me.

I don't want to make any sudden moves. Whatever is there is not for sure either good or bad. A moment passes as I collect my thoughts, slow my racing heart.

"Are you sitting here?"

What a stupid question. Of course something is there. It has got to be over ninety degrees outside, but I can see my breath in here. Small bursts of air as I breathe through my mouth to avoid inhaling the putrid smell of . . . something. This is new. Where once there was just a scent of mustiness, now it's replaced by that same sort of rotten eggs smell I detected last night. Once again, I shut my eyes, letting the darkness become pervasive.

This time there is no rush of air. Instead, there is a short burst of warm air on the back of my neck. It is synchronized to something. Whatever is next to me, behind me, is breathing. Matty is busy taking pictures.

"What do you want?" My voice seems small now.

There is no answer at first. The chill vanishes, the lights go out on the REM-POD, and the stairs begin to creak. The unknown something is going down the stairs. Matty is on his feet in seconds, the camera pointed forward. I stare at all the devices for a moment. The room is warming already. I stumble to my feet as I follow. The camera on the ground floor should have caught something.

"Where are you going?" This is the best thing I can think of to say. "You're that scared?"

Whatever possessed me to say this is far braver than I feel right now. I'm at the base of the stairs, the flashlight shining on the open space in the dining room. Nothing is moving. Matty turns to me, grinning once again. A great gust of wind blows through the room. The stationary cameras we'd set up topple over. A loud creak emanates from the kitchen. Matty moves before I can speak, and the second he moves into the kitchen, there's an ominous growl, and then the floor around the sink gives in, everything crashing into the basement, sending an echo across the structure. Matty jumps back, falling backwards, the hat sliding off of his head. I can feel my hands shaking as I edge closer. Matty scrambles on both hands and feet, getting up and hurrying to the base of the stairs.

"Maybe we should—" Matty stops the sentence short.

I don't need to say anything as I follow him back upstairs, collecting the equipment, my hands shaking all the while. Matty's eyes are downcast. I'm too scared to speak now. Where did the brave version of me go? That confined feeling is coming back. Something is still there. It is just concealing who it is, *what* it is.

It's been an hour, based on my watch. I pick up the pace as we head home. Matty collects all the devices from me as we part ways, promising to have something for me by tomorrow afternoon at the latest. I nod, feeling numb. Whatever was there, it was right next to me, breathing on me. The hair on the back of my neck feels like it is standing on end, but it's too humid out. I do my best to stay hidden as I get closer to our house, my heart hammering loudly in my chest. The party is really hitting the next level. And when I say that, I mean, there's more food consumed than left. The overflow room has more empty bowls than full. It doesn't look like dinner is done. I keep a close eye at the window. People are milling around everywhere. I need to be quick. I turn the knob on the door. It won't budge. This can't be good. The door's locked. I've been locked out, wearing American clothes at an Indian party, a party that's being held at my house.

There is always the option of going through the window upstairs. But my clothes are four feet away, under the table in the sunroom. I can't get dressed if my clothes are downstairs. My eyes scan the locks on the windows. A few of them aren't set. People are filtering in and out of the kitchen. I do my best to remove the screen on a window without breaking it. Once the screen is off, I coax the window open. Dear God, please don't let me get caught. Several aunties (this is what we call all my mother's friends) come bustling into the kitchen, laughing and joking. No. They're settling in. Two have their back to me. One is facing the food area.

My hand is now in the window. It isn't quite sticking out, but the window is open. It won't be long before someone notices the warm air. Do I risk tumbling through the window? Do I try to pull the window shut? Are there any other viable options? My God, I have a 4.0 GPA (weighted). I can figure this out. The real question is: How quiet can I be? The party has a lot of noise. If I stay low to the ground, I should be able to get in. I can't stay out here. At least I haven't spotted my mom yet.

I slide the window open a little more, my eyes trained on the aunties in front of me. They're all telling some hilarious joke about some white neighbor of ours. I'm trying not to get distracted by listening, but the guy they're talking about is a bit of a curiosity. The old guy has lived here for as long as we have, maybe a couple years longer. I call him "Mr. Get Off My Lawn," but I think his name is Mr. Steed or Steer or Steeple or Stewart. I don't know, white names all sound the same to me at some point.

No one has noticed me thus far. I can't quite reach the clothes from here. This was a poorly thought-out plan. That goes without saying. If I can just . . . Nope. I need to get inside that room and then get back out. I'm about to climb through the window when my mother barrels in. She's telling her crew, in Hindi, that she's serving dessert in twenty minutes. That's like a timer that is set in my head. If I'm not dressed (with fresh makeup), by then, I'm toast. The group disbands, everyone going in different directions. Most of the dessert items are in the kitchen in the garage. We're Indian—of course we have an extra fridge and freezer. Mom is the connoisseur of freezing foods, of resuscitating them after long spells in the frozen tundra.

I have maybe a minute before they see me. In quick fashion, I push the window up, slide through, and grab the clothes. Someone is coming. I scurry under the wide table. It is a huge circle, about eight feet across. If I sit right near the base, no one should be able to see me. One of the aunties is commenting on the window being open. There goes my escape route. There really are no other options here. I start to undress and get dressed again under the table. Please, please, please let no one see me. There's no worry about the clothes I wore outside. I can leave them under here and no one will notice them. The commotion around the sunroom dies down. I try to get a look, to see if any legs or feet are nearby. Nothing. Now or never, right?

I slide out from under the table, the far side, the one farthest from the doors. A few of my friends have spotted me.

Pooja, a dark-skinned girl, comes bounding forward. "We haven't seen you all night."

I love her energy. Never gets down on anyone. "I was trying to help and/or stay out of the way. You know how that goes."

My mother comes through, glaring at me. "Wash the dishes," she commands.

I give Pooja a half-hearted smile. "Back to the salt mines."

She laughs. "Is it hot outside?"

Does she know? Play it off. "I imagine so."

"Isn't that where you were hiding?" Her voice sounds low, hurt.

"I was," I admit. I don't need to tell her I was miles away wearing other clothes or that a ghost or something touched me. "I'm just a little overwhelmed. You know how parents get about parties of this size."

Pooja nods. "If you have time, you better touch up your makeup before the big picture."

"Right." I offer another small smile and keep my eyes down as I head towards the stairs.

EIGHT

NO WAY. THERE IS NO POSSIBLE WAY ON God's good earth that I just got away with escaping from this boring party. I'm surprised my mother doesn't have a tracking device implanted on me somewhere. Is it possible that the best time to do something is when the house is in chaos? Party chaos is like no other chaos. There's always one person who has a special need. There's one uncle (all Dad's friends are called uncle) who has to have a tablespoon. He cannot eat with a teaspoon or a plastic spoon. It must be a tablespoon. He does talk a lot, so the big mouth needs a big spoon. Some men just like to hear themselves think aloud. And this isn't sexist; men in general, as a species, they just love to hear themselves talk. My dad may not say much, but when he does, it just goes on and on.

My other favorite assorted chaos is the kids. The men don't want to watch the kids. The women don't want to watch the kids. Some other kids end up watching the kids. I use the term "kids" loosely. The younger kids are watched by kids my age, or a little younger. I did wonder why Pooja was upstairs. Who was watching those hellions downstairs? Have they destroyed the basement entirely? God only knows.

I'm doing my best to put makeup on. Each step is more laborious than the last. So many steps. Foundation, eye shadow, eyeliner, concealer, lipstick, bronze or blush, the list just goes on and on. My sister hasn't put her makeup away, so I help myself to her plentiful assortment. With this many colors on my clothes, I can match to anything. I could hide up here, but what's the point now?

The desserts are almost ready once I get downstairs. My mother is ushering everyone around the cake. Why are there candles on a graduation cake? It isn't like this is her birthday. Why do I even ask these questions? My mother is waving at me furiously, like she's holding a plate and the food was tongue-burning hot (a term my father uses regularly). I get to the requested position.

"Where have you been?" my mother is interrogating me while we all smile for a picture.

"I've been here the whole time." I'm lying, but what else can I say? *Oh, Mom, I had this haunted house I had to go to.* Yeah, that'd go over well.

"You didn't help." The accusations begin.

"I thought you had enough help." I'm wishing whoever is taking the picture could figure it out faster. It can't be this complicated.

"Wash the dishes when we're done." She's glaring now. She knows something.

I smile, a waifish sort of smile. "Yes, sir."

Her scowl grows, but now the pictures are over. I slink into the crowd. The rest of my so-called friends are there: Pooja's little sister, Chandhini (they look like twins, but are actually a few years apart), and their two overweight friends, whose names are escaping me right now. I smile at them, pulling the apron on over my clothes, getting to it.

They don't stop their conversation as they congregate around me. The fattest of the group has a hefty slice of cake. Her outfit is blue and she looks like a massive blueberry. It is not a complimentary look. Her sister is in red. Together they represent a nice fruit basket. Pooja and Chandhini are both wearing some combination of purple and turquoise.

Their outfits are far more fashionable than any of ours. Their mother is always going to Mumbai to see the newest Bollywood trends. Instead of loose, baggy pants, theirs are more like capris, shorter, more fitted. They don't look very comfortable.

I'm through one stack of dishes before the ache in my neck is kicking in again. My mother is still scowling, but she doesn't dare say anything in front of my friends. She can't know who might repeat her words to their parents later. Who has the time for all these intrigues?

Mita, the one dressed like a blueberry, keeps offering to dry the dishes. I am worried about her hand-eye coordination, but I do need the help. Now we're a team. Great. The chatter is background noise. I can see my reflection in the windows of the sunroom. I'm nodding, smiling, looking like I'm part of the conversation, but I'm so not present. Did I really just have my first substantiated paranormal experience? Could I have possibly worded that any more nerdily? The image of cool me is fading fast. There really aren't any cool ghost hunters out there. Most of them are mocked for believing in a science that is not easy to track.

"Roni?" Mita is nudging me with the chub on her elbow.

Crap. Was she talking to me? "I'm sorry. I was so focused on these dishes."

"You've been washing the same pan." Mita laughs a nervous sort of laugh. "I think it's clean."

"Right." I smile, passing the very clean pan to her. "You're a great help."

Mita can get super chatty. It looks like the rest of the trio are moving on, not wanting any part of menial labor. Of the four, Mita is the one who gets me the most. I feel like I'm ignoring her. At these functions, sometimes you only have a few people you know and you need to treat them well or you have to fly solo at the next event. If that's a wedding,

45

then it can be brutal. I don't want to get stuck sitting at a table with my parents and have no one to talk to for three or four hours, not counting the required dancing time. People think Indian weddings are so fun. After you've been to a few hundred of them, it is a lot less fun than it looks.

"How's the summer going?" I'm trying to start a conversation, find a way to keep myself rooted in this moment. I can obsess over the ghost hunt later.

"Boring." Mita moves around the room to set the pan in the sunroom.

The process is to wash, dry, set to one side, and repeat until everything is clean. This is actually the best job to have. Tedious? Absolutely. But then you don't have to smile or posture, pretending you're so excited to be at yet another function.

"What have you been doing?" Mita takes the next few plates, wiping them down and moving them to the other room.

"Me?" I try to sound nonchalant. "Sort of doing my own nonschool projects."

Mita's interest is piqued. "Oh? Is there a boy involved?"

Not this again. "Sort of. But he's my friend, so it isn't, like, a thing. He's just good at science and stuff. Not even the slightest bit of attraction there."

It's too late. Mita has found something far more interesting than plates and dishes. "Is he cute?"

I can cut this off at the pass. Sorry, Matty. "I'm talking about my science partner."

"Oh." Her mouth is fixed in this mold for a few seconds, realizing who I'm talking about. It is common knowledge that I have a friend who's "different," as we like to say so our parents won't freak out. "Yeah, that won't be a thing, like, ever. Your parents would eviscerate you if you dated a non-Indian boy."

"Non-Indian, non-Muslim." I'd never be permitted to even look at someone who wasn't from the Asian subcontinent.

"Yeah, I have nothing either." Mita shrugs. "Boys are impossible to talk to anyway."

"Why bother?" I ask. "I mean, aren't our parents supposed to be pulling names from hats or something?"

Mita laughs. "I can't remember the last person I know, or my parents know, who had an arranged marriage. I think they're just suggestions now."

She's not wrong. My parents and all their siblings had arranged marriages, back in India. Nowadays, parents suggest girls to boys (never the other way around, that would be imprudent), and the two are permitted to chat, while supervised or over the phone. I'm amazed more inappropriate things haven't occurred, like sexting and sexual assault. From what I can tell, most "good" Indian boys marry white. White is paramount to all in our culture—in every culture, it seems. That's why my sister is such a prize. She could pass as a white American if not for her name. Having a common-ish first name certainly helps.

"I'm sure my parents would be thrilled if I could not repulse all boys I meet," I say as I laugh.

Mita gets quiet for a moment. "Me too."

Oh boy. Do I comment? Do I tell her it's okay to be fat? Do I give her some tired advice about how the perfect person is out there? Somewhere? I wish my mouth didn't move faster than my brain. "Who cares? I mean, what's so great about boys anyway, right? They all think they're God's gift to the world. They do more harm than good. We're better off without them."

"Maybe." Mita moves to the other room, setting the latest item down. "It would be nice, you know, just to be—I don't know—wanted?"

47

Shut up, Roni. Shut up, I tell myself before opening my mouth. "Don't even, Mita. You're talking about approval, like the approval we'll never get from our parents," I hiss this last part so as not to be overheard. "Dating or getting married isn't a goal for life. If you find someone, great. If you don't, be happy with you. I am."

"Easy for you to say," Mita counters.

I set the dish I'm washing down. The inner witch is awoken. "It isn't easy, not even a little." I take a few quick steps into the other room. "My parents worship my brother and sister. I'm just an accident, an afterthought. If you think one second that anyone in this house cares if I live or die, other than the shame it might bring to the family, you're wrong. I have learned that I need to be okay with me, because everyone else might not ever, in my lifetime, be okay with me."

Mita is stunned. Her mouth agape. She nervously rubs her arm. "Maybe," she says.

I check the window. No one's there. I take a deep breath, letting it out slowly. "Sorry."

I turn and get back to the task. There's no chance to put those words back in my mouth. It's the truth. At least the way I see life. What is the point of waiting for others to realize I'm not a waste of space, that I'm not a failure just because I haven't done things that others intended for me? I'm still fuming. I'm sweating again. This happens when I get super angry. Yep, I'm super angry. Downright furious. Given I got away with a huge coup earlier, I should be quiet and triumphant.

Mita takes up her position near me again. Well, that ended that conversation, didn't it? I have always had a way with words, and zero ability to filter or gauge audience reaction. This should really come as no surprise. It isn't like I'd ever win a popularity contest. Why would I want to anyway? Well, I guess I would like to be the popular kid, be the one everyone looks up to. But that's not something my parents have instilled in me. That shouldn't matter. And if I'm reading all those religious texts correctly, God doesn't care if I'm popular. Being a good person is what's supposed to matter, or something. Then again, looking at the world—the big, grand picture—no matter how "good" you are, someone else is always cheating their way to the top. Or is that the problem? I shouldn't be looking at all. Gah, my head hurts.

Mita nudges me again with the elbow chub. "I don't think I could be as brave as you. You seem to have it together better than I do."

I try not to balk as she speaks. I didn't expect anything other than stony silence. "I'm not brave, not really. I'm just trying to be, you know, less worried about everyone else's opinions."

This is a better response than my earlier rant. A more controlled comment, one that she might take to heart instead of repeating to her little sister—or worse, her parents. She just nods. The party shows no signs of ending, but Mita's family is leaving, and with it, the companionship I didn't realize I'd miss.

NINE

IT IS HARD TO BELIEVE THAT ALL OF those pans, serving dishes, and whatnot were all ours. The sunroom looks like a yard sale. I'm cleaning the counter, wiping it down, and drying it as Mom comes in. It requires most of the members of the family to say goodbye to all of the guests as they leave. The exhaustion is clear on everyone's faces. My sister is, once again, floating. Does she have hover shoes I'm unaware of? I know Dad's an engineer (a typically Indian sort of job), but could he design something that cool?

Everyone is settling around the shell of the cake. My brother Jamaal is eating an Indian dessert, these little balls of honeyed goodness called *gulab jamen*, quite a few of them. They could melt your teeth on contact. He's a big guy, but even one is toxically sweet. Four, that's a degree of overkill even I don't want to experience. I can't even imagine the crash after the sugar high wears off. Like the rest of the men, he's just wearing a dress shirt and dress pants. I can't help noticing the sandals he's wearing, probably made it easier to come and go from the garage. He must have been helping move the extra food around for Mom, though I don't see one stain on his clothes, which is just rookie luck. My sister is sitting at the head of the table, looking quite pleased with herself. Somehow she's got a tiara. Who brings a tiara to a graduation party? How pretentious.

My grandfather is sitting in an armchair—not quite in the dining room, but close. It looks like he's asleep. All of the guests are gone. Mom's gang has left. Most of the leftovers were also distributed, so the fridges (one and two, plus the freezer) are not overstuffed. Too bad. I really liked the butter chicken. There were also some veg dishes I really liked. With American food, if there's no meat, it isn't great, but I'll give Mom all the credit. She can turn vegetable dishes not only edible, but desirable. I've actually gone an entire twenty-four hours without eating meat.

I hover in the doorway. Should I stay or bolt up the stairs? I know my phone must have at least a few dozen messages from Matty. I wonder if he's had time to go through all the material. The summer does afford a lot of time. Unlike me with my parents, he isn't hampered by overly watchful eyes. My feet are inching towards the stairs, but my mother is staring at me, the fury thinly veiled behind a forced smile.

"Did you hide in the backyard all night?" Her eyes are staring right through me now.

"I washed the dishes." This is the first thing that comes to mind.

"That is the only thing you did tonight." My mother lifts the box full of greeting cards and slides it across the table towards my sister. "Your round friend was being of more help than you were."

Silence, my unwavering cohort in crime, how I've missed you. Say nothing. Emote nothing. Stare at your feet. No. Don't stare at your feet. I'm still wearing the flip-flops from earlier. I shift my hips, allowing my flowing pants to fall over my feet.

"Go clean up." My mother is dismissing me.

I almost wait, but I feel like a cartoon character, bolting out of the room as fast as possible, a shadow of me vanishing in a waft of smoke to catch up with the real me. I pull the flip-flops off as I ascend the stairs. I pull my party clothes off, halfheartedly folding them and setting them on a stack of boxes in the corner that is already chock-full of clothes. My worn pajamas are at the foot of my bed, and I throw them on as I rush into the bathroom, excavating for my real face under all the paint and chemicals. It's a relief to feel my skin breathe again. When I stare at my reflection, I still feel unattractive, unfamiliar. The dark, dark eyes are mine, but the face and expression feel foreign. I shake the worry off and rush back to my room.

The phone isn't blinking, much to my surprise. I shut my door and turn the laptop on, watching as it whirls to life. My heart is once again hammering in my chest. Did I leave the curtains open all day? I stare at my reflection once again. My eyes must be tired. I turn suddenly, knocking some papers over. Was someone just behind me? When I turn back to the window, there's nothing there. I pull the curtains closed. I need to get some rest. Matty's online, the raccoon icon blinking in the video chat window.

"Did you get anything interesting?" I utter. There's no time for pleasantries. Matty isn't one to worry about that sort of thing.

"You have no idea," he says in a hushed voice. "What did you feel while you were there?"

"When?" I shut my eyes. I felt a lot of things.

"When we sat down to do the EVP upstairs."

Of course. I sigh. "It felt like someone was sitting next to me, touching me."

"Still have your necklace?" he asks.

I reach up and feel it under my shirt. "Yes."

"Pictures don't lie." He grins. "I was just wondering if it tried to take something from you."

The screen fills with a very clear image of me. Between the darkness of the room and my skin, it should be hard to make me out. There is a white mist to my left. It is creating all the contrast I need to make virtually everything out in the room. The REM-POD is all lit up and something—a white mist—is hovering over it, in the shape of a hand, all the fingers clearly discernable. I'm too stunned to make any sort of coherent response.

"The voice is a lot clearer this time." Matty fumbles with something and then taps the camera, his image shaking. "You should put your headphones on so it won't be too loud."

I'm staring at the still image in the top right-hand corner of the screen. It takes a moment for me to comprehend what he says. I sift through my desk before finding a pair of headphones, the left side broken, so I have to hold it up to my ear. For some reason there's a rock in one of the drawers. I wonder how it got there? Once everything is in place, he gives me a smirk and hits play.

At first I just hear us. There's a lot of background noise, a lot of feet shuffling, and then something else. When we're standing still, there is something. I lean in and turn the volume up. I'm not sure what it is. I shake my head, and Matty is still smiling, which is starting to get a little unusual.

In my mind, I'm trying to remember where we are. I hear myself say something about feeling something push me, and then I can see it in my mind. The tape gets closer to the EVP, but before we even sit down in the room, as Matty passes me, something speaks.

"Don't go in there."

It isn't muffled. It isn't low or grainy. The voice is as clear as if I had spoken, with maybe a touch of worry. Matty is entering the room now; I can hear him beckon me to follow. As I get closer, the voice returns.

"Get out of here."

I'm staring at Matty with wide eyes. The voice isn't threatening, not like you'd think from all the horror movies

I've seen. It's calm and controlled. In most cases, the real ghost hunters make it sound like it's hard for spirits to speak. It doesn't seem difficult at all.

I start asking questions. The voice isn't responding to this. I'm trying hard to picture the scene in my head. And then it happens—the REM-POD goes off. The volume jumps and I almost fall out of my seat. Matty's sort of laughing now, snickering maybe. The moment the REM-POD went off, a different voice spoke. This one was threatening.

"You're next."

I stare up at Matty, my whole body feeling ice cold. Was it talking about me? Am I next? Why would it be coming after me? I look up and see Matty's expression still hasn't changed. How is he not frightened? I try to replay the audio in my mind. The first statement sounded soft, almost feminine. The second was guttural, nearer to a growl than actual words. Were there two voices? Two distinct entities? My mind is racing.

Matty pulls the earbuds out and points to the monitor.

"Lower the volume," he says in a whisper.

"What was that?" I ask, feeling my raw nerves, my hands shaking as I adjust the audio.

"I have no idea." Matty pauses, and then a grin spreads across his lips. "Proof. This is proof."

"Yeah, but it also said one of us was next." I wonder if there were any more precautions we could have taken?

Matty's faces grows serious, his eyebrows lowering, his expression slackening. "I think we need to find out more about the place. I wouldn't worry."

I try to laugh, but a gasp of air is all that comes out. I look up at the window, the one I had just covered with the curtain. Someone, or something, is standing behind me.

TEN

MY EYES ARE FIXED ON THE FIGURE behind me. In the reflection, there isn't a face, just emptiness where there would be a face—like a void of light, a void of features, a void of any semblance of humanity. The figure is not fully defined. The outline of a human is the most I can make out, sort of. It towers over me, the top of the head nearly brushing the ceiling, passing through the unmoving fan above. It isn't solid, but concentrated black smoke. There are eyes—cold, dark, somehow darker than the mass that stands behind me. I'm too shocked, too unnerved to even move or react. I don't know if I'm even breathing. The lights flicker above and everything snaps off and then on again. The connection to Matty is gone, but my phone is buzzing. I can't remember the last time we spoke over the phone. I leap to my feet, knocking the chair over. I turn and see nothing. I check the window. The figure is gone. I answer the call as I turn, feeling a rush of cold around me.

"Are you okay?" Matty sounds downright terrified.

"Could you see it?" My heart is hammering in my chest as I finally take a breath.

"Of course," he says. "I recorded what I could before the power went out. Did it touch you?"

I'm feeling cold all over, like I'm standing inside a freezer. My heart is racing as I turn in circles around my room. Everything is where I left it. I pull the closet door

57

open, finding nothing out of place. I shift a stack of boxes away from the bed, kneeling to look under it. Nothing. My hands are shaking as I respond, "I don't know."

"You should check."

Of all the things to say, he says that? I have too many things going on to worry about checking anything right now. Or is that exactly what I should be doing? "I'm fine."

"Roni, it looked like it touched you." Now I know why he was being weird.

I set the phone down and turn the speaker on. The curtains are open and I pull them shut again. It still feels like something is watching me. I pull my T-shirt up over my head and turn towards the full-length mirror on the back of my closet door. Looking over my shoulder, I can see three light scratches on my shoulder, right where I thought I saw something. I feel another chill in the room and pull my shirt back on. According to what I've read, marks in threes are supposed to be a defiance to the holy trinity (the father, the son and the holy ghost), according to Christianity. In Islam, we also have a lot of threes (like reciting certain *surahs*, or psalm for those who aren't Muslim, in threes during prayers), so it might be a thing with all religions.

"Something touched me." I can hear my voice quivering.

"Are you okay?" Matty's voice is insistent and scared. "Where is everyone?"

"Party's over," I say, taking deep, slow breaths. "My sister is opening all of her presents."

"Do you have a cross or something?" The response is quick.

"I'm Muslim, remember?" I laugh. "If I had one, that would be weird."

"Your necklace is religious or something, right?" Matty is grasping for the right words.

"Yes." My fingers fly up, glancing at the inscription of a *surah*. It's supposed to keep bad things away, but it can't do that if I go right up to those bad things.

"My parents are home and think I'm asleep," Matty says in a quiet voice. "Are you going to be okay?"

"Of course." I nod. "Good night."

We both hit the end button. The whole room is just cold. I look at my clothes, look at my hands, still shaking. In some cases, ghosts can attach themselves to you, but what I saw, that wasn't a ghost. Ghosts usually appear as apparitions, see-through. Things that are black as night, those are something far scarier. I hate to use the word, but I can hear it echo in my head. *Demon.* Someone else is saying it, not me. That isn't my voice.

I try to busy myself. Every attempt to put something away, to organize the bookshelf, hang my clothes up, is quickly met with said object clattering out of my grip, slipping from my sweaty hands. The room feels too close, smaller, tighter than usual. I feel like something is watching me. It was in my room. It was in the haunted house. How long has it been here? If it is a demon, what does it want?

In some cases, a demon attaches itself to a person so it can use that person to live in this world, fully. I can't let that happen. But have I already done something irreversible?

Even if it was the last thing I wanted to do, I know I'm too scared to sleep and decide I need to join the festivities. I pull a track jacket on over my pajamas and go downstairs. My sister is gleefully opening her presents. No one notices me. I stare at the streamers that are hanging on for dear life. The heat of that many people in the house has rendered the adhesive useless, dislodging almost everything that was so painstakingly put up hours before.

Once all the presents have been opened and logged, because my sister has to mail out thank you cards, everyone heads to bed. I can't linger downstairs, even if I want to. My grandfather has fallen asleep in the armchair, and instead of waking him, we leave him there, throwing a blanket over him. He will probably wake up for the morning prayer without any help.

My feet are leaden as I make my way upstairs, dread growing in my mind with each step. Sara has been gushing nonstop about how perfect everything was. I haven't heard a word she's said, but I'm nodding and smiling in perfect rhythm to her comments. She bounds into the bathroom and I turn to my room, which looks blazingly bright. Didn't I leave everything off except the desk light?

The room is ice cold when I enter. I zip the pullover all the way up and glance around for my socks. When I reach down, I feel a pull in my back. A burning sensation begins right where the scratches are. I'm shaking. I want to run, to find someplace to hide. There's nowhere to go. I can't tell my parents. They'd think I'm crazy. Am I crazy? Have I lost my mind? Did I really experience anything?

The proof is there. I turn the laptop back on. It needs to boot up in safe mode after the abrupt cut of power. The pictures are all there. Matty had sent them to me in bulk. I scroll through the images. In each and every one, there is the white mist, but also something else. The audio is attached and I shudder as I put it on, playing it from the beginning. There are two distinct voices. One is calm, not threatening. The other is filled with malice. The low, guttural tones sounded inhuman. It sounded like one entity was trying to warn me, while the other was threatening me. It makes me wonder if one is good and one is evil. Based on the scratches on my back, one is certainly evil.

And I think the evil one is here, with me, making good on the threat.

I've stared at the monitor for so long that the words are jumbled, not making any sense. There is a haze hovering in the room, like I burned something while cooking. I blink a few times. Everything seems out of focus.

When I get up, I see myself sitting at the desk, head slumped over the laptop. I reach to grab myself, finding nothing but air. A moment passes as I feel my heart hammering once again. Am I asleep? The me sitting in the chair is asleep. But then, what am I? I glance at the window, seeing me in the reflection. I take another slow breath, trying to steady my nerves. This wouldn't be the first time I had a lucid dream. When I was little, sometimes I would sleepwalk into different rooms. This really isn't any different, is it?

I turn, seeing the haze move around me. It reminds me of how, when I walk outside, after being inside all day, and my glasses fog up, making everything look like big moving smudges. I shut my eyes for a second and the day feels like it's replaying itself. The latter part of the party moves quickly and things slow down, in reverse, as I stumble through the house with Matty and back to the party. Time slows for a second, and I follow me as I come out of the house. Am I controlling this dream?

Can I stop the movement? Backtracking through the old house is confusing. This time around, I see the movement, the things I couldn't have seen before. This has to be my imagination. Though, I did just sift through all of those images. Maybe I saw something that planted this in my head? The movement is obvious with me and Matty upstairs. If this was real, how did we not notice? I take a couple slow steps around the lower level of the house, feeling my shoe catch on something. In the floorboards

I see something is etched in, like with a pocket knife. It looks like a rising sun or something. I've never been good at recognizing symbols. I hear our footsteps backtrack, and now I can see me, how completely mismatched all my clothes are. I am such a mess.

I amble behind myself and Matty as they begin to walk back home. I hear something in the house and I'm surprised I'm able to stay while they leave. I move around the first floor, watching as the light grows brighter. The house is stitching itself back together, the walls losing the mold, the floors losing the gaping holes. The house looks perfect, fitted with appliances and furniture. The door slams open, and as I turn to look, everything vanishes.

I wake up with all the lights still on, and my neck is as tight as ever. I fell asleep at the desk. The computer screen has gone black, and the sun is beginning to spill in. After the late night, I hope the rest of the house will still be asleep. My childhood blanket, Fat Face, is wrapped around my shoulders. I do a double take. He's been in the bureau for a few years. I don't take him out ever. How did he get out here? When I was a kid, I wished he'd move, talk back; as an almost adult, I now know he can't.

Whatever tiredness I was feeling is gone. Something is here. I can feel the cool presence. Almost every supernatural entity would make me feel cold, as they need to find energy from somewhere to manifest, to show itself. Is it using me as a battery? Is it just trying to confuse me? How do I retell this story to Matty without including the part about Fat Face? It's bad enough he had to see me in funny clothes, but to be caught with the blanket I had since I was born is too embarrassing for words.

All these ideas are running through my head as I fold Fat Face up, squishing him once before putting him back in the bureau. I look around the room. Nothing else seems to be out of place. I can hear some sort of commotion going on from downstairs. Sara is looking half-awake in the doorway of her room as we both edge towards the stairs. Mom and Dad are shouting, but not at each other. Sara is trying to push past me, but I'm not moving, and I'm a tad bigger, so she isn't moving me. When I peak around the corner, I see all of the cupboards are open and everything has been strewn across the floor. All the serving dishes are still sitting where I left them, but anything that had been put away was littered across the floor. The entity is escalating activity faster than I've ever seen or heard of before, and now I'm terrified. The scratches on my back are beginning to burn again and my body is shaking, though I'm not cold.

Eleven

It TAKES MOST OF THE MORNING TO clean the kitchen. My mom is losing her normal composure, muttering a variety of prayers as she sweeps the mess up with a grass broom. Instead of having a long pole with the broom part at the bottom, a grass broom has a shorter handle, maybe a foot or so, with longer bristles matching the length of the pole. I used to play with the broom— my grandmother called it a *jharoo*—when it would flood during the monsoons in India.

All of our good teacups are in pieces, shattered across the kitchen floor, including the bone china set we got from England a few years back. Those had the most beautiful inlaid gold designs of the London cityscape. Even if I never drank tea, I really wanted those for when I grew up.

I don't want to get any more involved than I am, so I just listen, hearing my parents confirm that all the doors to the house were locked. My dad did mention that the screen had been pulled off of one of the windows, but the window was secured inside. The level of chaos in the house isn't quite matching party chaos, but it is getting close. The kitchen is not big. Mom often has to use the sunroom to spread out while preparing dishes. With both of them running around cleaning, collecting everything in garbage bag after garbage bag, it is a sight that I haven't seen before. It is rare that my father, on a Sunday morning, isn't at the mosque for the early morning prayer. If I weren't already frightened, I would be after seeing their panic. My parents don't get panicked, unless I get bad grades. There is a rushed phone call I can barely hear. I wonder who my mom would be calling.

I don't dare leave the house amid all this bedlam, so Matty rides his bike over pretty early. My mother gives him a disapproving look, but lets him in. We head towards the sunroom, now devoid of the serving dishes or any signs of what happened before. Matty is wearing an oversized pullover, despite the heat.

He was polite enough to take his sneakers off at the door, but his socked feet look tiny outside of those massive shoes. I've finally dressed, wearing jeans and a long-sleeve T-shirt (to cover up the cuts on my arms) with the logo of some fast food place on it that went out of business years ago. Matty keeps his head down as he enters. Out of the corner of my eye, I can see a device in his hand. He's measuring something. I rub my eyes as we sit in the sunroom.

"Are you okay?" Matty asks this after my parents are no longer within earshot.

My eyes dart around. "I think it's here."

I didn't answer his question, but his expression tightens. "What happened?" he asks.

I go through all the details from after we got off the phone, doing my best to not look like some terrified little kid, which I basically am right now. When I finish, Matty gives me a sad look (perhaps hoping to be reassuring), opens his bag, and pulls out his laptop and some cameras. Each one is pretty small, the size of a wallet, just thicker.

"I think you need to set these up … discreetly." He slides the cameras over, forcing a smile. "I can set up a network for us to use. If we record everything, we might be able to figure out what's going on."

I push my hands through my mop of hair. "Maybe I never should have gone there."

"Maybe," Matty admits. "Too late to worry about that now."

I nod, trying to force a smile to my face. It isn't working. I want to cry. I can feel it coming, but something cool passes me and I sit up straight. Matty feels it too, his eyes growing wide as he jumps in his seat.

"Whatever it is, it's drawn to you." Matty opens the laptop, his eyes darting around the room. "I don't know what else to do. I did message some local groups, but they think we're just pranking them."

"Did you give them the video?" I ask, feeling calm again as the room warms from the morning sun.

Matty nods. "Yes. I was a little worried at first, but this is outside of our expertise."

My father gives us a guarded look as he enters the room, offering some reheated samosas from last night's party. Matty takes one, his eyes growing wider at the spice. I laugh and start to uncover the cameras I stowed under one of the towels I used to dry the dishes. They're still a little damp. A minute later, my father is back with glasses of water.

I sigh, picking one of the towels up. "I'm going to hang these up."

I slide the cameras back to Matty, who shoves them into his pockets. We step outside, the blistering heat a relief compared to any signs of cold inside the house. We work in silence, Matty helping me reaffix the screen while we're outside. As I glance back into the house, I can see the clothes I wore yesterday are still under the table. Could that be what had the attachment on it?

Matty stops at the door. "If the activity is around you, set the cameras up in your room and maybe in a couple other places where you spend a lot of time."

I nod as we head inside. The plate of samosas now has a couple friends, cut-up apples and mangoes. I can see my father trying to find some cake to serve.

"Dad, please stop," I say as we sit down. "I don't think Matty is that hungry."

"Thank you, though, Mr. Khan," Matty says.

I can always count on Matty to be the picture of politeness. My dad is okay with him, as long as nothing other than studying happens. I've never told my parents about Matty. I wouldn't even know how to explain it to them. Their heads might come off. I know Sara has accepted it, but Mom and Dad would probably not be okay with it. Though, in India, there are people, always around weddings, who are men dressed as women, *Hijra*, soliciting money after singing and dancing for the celebration. I never understood what was happening, but my grandmother would always give them money. My dad sets the cake on the table, clearly having ignored my request, and heads out of the room.

"Sorry." I shake my head. "You know how the constant hospitality goes."

"Yeah." Matty laughs. "All too well. Give me a few minutes and I can get the network going. Do you want to set those up so I can add them into the network? If there's a power source nearby, we can stream the video constantly."

The cameras will be an invasion of my privacy, but I need something else to help me figure out what's going on. The laptop is out, a black box filling the screen, setting up the framework for our network. Matty is quite the computer whiz. I head up the stairs, feeling the heat as I climb. The entity must not be anywhere near me.

My eyes pass across my room. Now I feel jittery being in here alone. Last night the entity appeared in the window behind me, at the desk where I do my homework, the room I live in. This is supposed to be my safe haven. I shudder, trying to remember my task. The bookshelf in the corner still hasn't been filled, and I set the camera on the top shelf, putting books on either side of it. That might secure it a little. I don't want to give anyone a view of the closet or me sleeping, but I think I have to. The camera captures the doorway, so I set another one pointing towards the bed and closet, sharing a plug that isn't being used behind the bookshelf.

That leaves me with two cameras. If I were a really mean sister, I could place one in my sister's room. That'd be a waste. The other activity was in the kitchen. Something nags at me, and I take both cameras back downstairs. Matty gives me a slight nod and I continue, moving around the kitchen towards Nana's room.

With the kitchen shelves and cupboards newly cleaned, this might not be a great idea since there's so little clutter for me to hide things behind, but I set both cameras up above the highest shelf in the kitchen, each pointing in a different direction. The cords to the outlet can run behind the refrigerator. Now we get two views in my room and two views in the kitchen area. This will cover my grandfather's room and hallway towards the garage, as well as the kitchen and backyard.

When I sit back down, I see Matty has all four feeds displaying. "I'll send you the details and you can watch this all live—well, mostly live. There might be a slight delay, ten seconds at most," he explains.

"Might be weird watching myself live." I try to laugh, but I'm still scared.

"You should get some rest." Matty shuts the laptop, his eyes on the plates before him. "Is your dad trying to fatten me up?"

"Maybe." I laugh, feeling a little lighter. "I don't think I took anything with me when I left."

Matty leans in. "Something touched you last night—there, not here. Are you sure there isn't anything that was put on you?"

The clothes under the table are still there. I glance towards the kitchen before grabbing them. The pockets in my jeans are empty. The shirt smells like I ran a race in it. With nothing to find, at least nothing physical, I'm not sure what else to look for.

I shrug. "Doesn't seem that way."

Matty reaches a hand out, stopping short. "I'll get someone to help us—help you—okay?"

I nod, but I just feel alone. Nothing is following Matty. Why did it attach itself to me? I have regrets about a lot of things, usually about eating one too many slices of cakes. This is one regret I hope to live through.

Twelve

AFTER SPENDING HALF THE AFTERNOON searching on the internet, and glancing at the different feeds from the camera from time to time, I told my parents I was going for a walk. How did I end up back at the old house? Was I drawn here? Or am I just so upset with myself about attracting the entity in the first place that I want to return it from where I got it? Ghost hunting is supposed to answer the question about where all my loved ones went after they died. It isn't supposed to be about me trying to fight something I can't see.

I stare straight forward, my vision blurring, remembering the first time I saw my dad really cry, after his brother died in car accident when I was barely five. There was some talk about cause, as my uncle wasn't even in the car at the time. After that, my family was not touched by death, not directly. Every time death comes near, it feels distant, surreal. I keep expecting to see my uncle come bounding through the door, lifting me on his shoulders and feeding me sweets. Well, maybe not those last two. He would probably buckle under my weight and then opt not to make me heavier.

A slight laugh escapes as I picture the scene. I didn't tell Matty I was coming, but I probably should have. The heat isn't abating. I walk to the house, thankful for the constant cloud cover as I get closer. The air is heavy and sticky.

In the light of day, the place doesn't look nearly as terrifying. Something about it seems almost serene now. I don't feel scared, but I do feel like eyes are on me. The feeling isn't nearly as unwelcome as it was last night. I guess I might be a little afraid of the dark. I glance around, but the neighborhood is empty, as per usual. I step through the window. It feels cool inside, much, much cooler than it did outside. Does that mean the entire house is haunted?

A slow burn begins in my chest and I stomp towards the kitchen. The appliances were never installed. The fixtures, sink, and faucets, are long gone. I can still see the shadow of them from my dream last night. The hole around the sink doesn't seem nearly as scary now. I look for any signs of life. The room looks undisturbed, as do all the others. There's that rotted smell everywhere. The pantry has dead bugs littering the floor. I turn away in disgust. I stalk across the room, what would have been a dining room, and into a living room. Unlike the floor upstairs, underneath the gaping hole in the ceiling, this carpet isn't quite as grotesque.

The scent of battery acid fills my nose. The pungent odor hangs in the air. Everything is rotten in this place. I had expected to be assaulted again. I wanted someplace to direct my anger, my indignation. I have nothing but an empty house to get furious with. The rest of the bottom floor is silent. I trek up the stairs, bursts of dust exploding off of the carpet as I stop at the top. The sunlight is gleaming through the opening above. The fresh air wafts in. The last two nights, it felt stagnant and still. Today, it feels like a brand new day. I would sit down, but the carpet looks even grimier in the light.

I head into the room where we performed our EVP session. There isn't anything that indicated we were even there the previous night. Other than the broken glass outside, it really does look untouched. I step to the window, staring out across the overgrown lawn. The heat is keeping all animals away. I can see some insects crawling up out of a hole in the ground. A trail of ants is making its way from one bush to the next towards this hole.

My anger is fading, at least enough for me to not notice the creaking noise coming up the stairs. I jump, but the alarm fades as, much to my surprise, there's a person—real and in full color and not an apparition. I'm at a loss for words, not to see another living soul, but because the girl is pretty, prettier than you see in a town like this. Her light brown hair offsets the dark button-down shirt she's wearing over a white T-shirt and a denim skirt. Her sandals make a distinct noise as she comes up the stairs—like a knocking, but muffled. I'm too taken aback to come up with words, but she smiles like we know one another.

"What are you doing here?" she asks.

My mind is faltering, but I mumble. "Nothing."

She cocks an eyebrow. "Strange place to come do nothing in."

"It's quiet, and cool." Phew, that was a better response. Why am I so tongue-tied?

"It is." She nods. "I come here just to get away from the chaos in my house."

"I know that feeling." I laugh, trying to keep myself from staring at this girl. What is wrong with me?

Her hair almost shimmers in the sun from the hole above. "I doubt we could ever afford a sunroof."

"For your house?" Stupid, Roni. Really, really stupid.

She just laughs, a light, airy laugh. "I'm Marissa."

"Roni." I smile, thankful for an easy answer.

"Come here often?" she asks, a slight drawl and something else in her accent.

"Lately, yes," I admit, my eyes darting away from her insistent gaze. "It's part of a hobby."

"You have a hobby that involves old houses?" she laughs.

I feel silly for having said this and the defensiveness kicks in. "Better than studying over the summer vacation." Where are these ridiculous responses coming from?

"If you say so." Marissa grins, flashing a perfect smile. "There's a rumor this place is haunted."

I blink. "Really?"

She continues laughing. "I'm just kidding. Don't be so serious. You're not old enough to be that serious."

My nerves are feeling a little frazzled. "Do you go to school around here?"

She shakes her head. "Nope, just passing through."

"You look like you're my age." I try to assess her without leering.

"I guess," she answers, her voice growing flinty as she passes me, continuing to the window. "You looked very contemplative."

"Bugs." God, I am such an embarrassing nerd. How could I ever talk to boys if I can't even maintain coherence with a pretty girl? At least most boys are pretty ugly, so no distraction there.

"Oh, now I see them." She's up on her tiptoes, pointing. "Gross."

"I know, right?" I try to force a laugh, thankful I'm not sweating through my clothes. It is still pretty cool inside, but not as cold as it had been with the ghost present. "Not that I'm into bugs, but they're just being weird."

Marissa shrugs. "I guess." She checks her wrist, though I don't see a watch, just a bracelet; I think it's antique by the quick glance I get. "I better go. See you around."

I wave dumbly as she hurries down the stairs, disappearing through the opening in the window. I can't quite see her anymore, but I turn back to the window. "Dumb, Roni. You sounded like a lunatic."

And now I'm talking aloud to myself. The oppressive feeling is starting to return. That's just what I need. I've been kind of out of it since that morning. I really need to get focused. Something keeps distracting me. The earlier coolness is being quickly replaced with a wave of hot air. The cloud cover has hidden how late it's gotten. I didn't bring my phone with me, and I'm again wondering why I came here as I hurry after Marissa, but she's long gone.

Thirteen

NONE OF MY PARENTS' CARS ARE HOME
when I get there. After all that heat, my shirt is sticking to
me once again. I open the door, thankful for the rush of
cool air. I've been afraid to come home, to be home, but
going to that house probably wasn't smart. A slow, deep
breath relaxes me before I push the door shut, feeling sort
of safe inside. That feeling doesn't last too long. An eerie
silence fills the space. No TV in the background. No music
playing. No chatter. No thrum of appliances. Nothing. I
start for the stairs, but stop and head to the kitchen for a
glass of water.

The stale taste throws me off a little. Water usually
doesn't have a taste at all. Sometimes my mom will put
cucumber or lemon in it, but this is like old water, like it's
been out all day, uncovered and touched by every air par-
ticle in the house. I pour the water down the drain, shaking
my head. When I turn towards the stairs, I swear I see something out of the corner of my eye.

Nana's room is around the corner. I'm staring straight
at the hallway and I see the light in his room shift. The
camera is stationed right above me, pointing in that direction. I glance up, see the lenses staring back at me. I wonder
if Matty's watching. My hands are sweating and I wipe them
on my shirt as I take a couple steps closer.

"Nana?" I know he can't hear me, but it's worth a shot.

If this were a horror movie, I'd be in a sealed building with no possible escape. One of the first mistakes is not having an exit strategy. I should run towards the front door and not the garage or sunroom. The front door is currently unlocked; the other two will confound me as I'm overcome with fear as to how to unlock them. A few more steps are taken. Nothing is moving. After last night and this morning, I'm not sure what to expect. Once I get to the door, I realize there is nothing there. The room is dark. I can't tell if Nana is inside, but there's just enough light for me to see nothing is moving.

My heart is slowing again as I turn, and that's when I see it. I turn back around, staring into the growing darkness. Yes, it was dark before, but now it is somehow darker. Usually my eyes adjust to the darkness, making it seem not quite as dark. In this case, either my eyes aren't adjusting or they are, but it's getting too dark too fast. I feel my pulse quicken, heat rising up my back, a small bead of sweat at my forehead. There is movement, but I can't make it out. A voice begins in my head, telling me to bolt. There's a quiet counter to this, telling me to face my fears. My fists are clenched at my sides as I glare at whatever is there.

"What do you want?" Did I just shout that?

The answer chills me, and not from the wave of cold air that pushes past me towards the room. The familiar chair Nana sits in is slowly turning, by itself. It lurches to one side, weighted by something I can't quite see. The slow revolution reveals a person in the chair. I can't help the curiosity as I take a slight step forward, freezing when I recognize who it is. In the chair is my grandfather, but he's not moving. His face is frozen in a grotesque way, his jaw off center, mouth agape, his eyes open and glassy. Both of his arms appears stuck to his sides, his fingers wrapped around the armrests. I don't need to touch him to know he's not breathing. What happened? The tears are threatening and I stumble backwards, onto my backside.

The chair has turned all the way around. The darkness is now moving, forming into the shape of a person—but not a person, a shadow. Darkness can't move. Logic and reality are competing for space in my mind. Is this the same thing I saw last night? The room is dark, the sole light coming from a clock on the nightstand on the opposite wall. The shadow moves, melting through the darkness. It lets go of the chair, rocking Nana precariously, before pounding to the ground. I can feel the vibration as it slams one limb, then the other, on the ground before advancing. My necklace is jumping on my chest as it advances. It falls forward onto all fours. The human form has morphed into a mass of smoke, of darkness, leeching the light around it. The thing is crawling across the floor towards me, and I'm using my hands and feet to crab-walk backwards.

Is this happening? Did I let this thing in?

The black mass is inching towards me, as if it's having a hard time coordinating all of its limbs. I'm too scared to move again when I bump into the wall, at most fifteen feet away from Nana's room, the fridge right next to me. I squeeze my eyes shut, praying that this thing will just go away, repeating over and over again the things I learned at Sunday school. Even though my eyes are shut, I can still hear it. The cold crackle sound of ice hitting the linoleum floor. A piercing sound each time a finger, elbow, or knee of this thing touches the ground. I pry my eyes open and see it only a few feet away.

The door bangs open and suddenly I'm staring at nothing. Sara bounds into the kitchen, a bag of groceries in her arms, and looks at me half-confused, half-annoyed. "What are you doing?"

I'm shaking from head to toe, unable to make a response. Did it stop because she came home? Is it still here? Is Nana okay?

I push myself up and sprint to Nana's room. That wasn't something I imagined. He's still sitting there, staring at me with these glassy eyes.

Sara is right behind me. When she sees what I see, her voice flounders and she calls out to Mom, the sound turning into a muffled cry. All I can keep thinking is that this is my fault. I did this. I let this thing in. It could have been me. It should have been me.

I don't have any tears to cry. I'm too shocked, too scared, to register anything. The next few hours are a blur. I remember the ambulance, emergency personnel, dozens of people we saw just last night, now dressed in normal everyday clothes instead of party clothes. The house has once again fallen into chaos, but a different sort, one with far less fanfare but just as much food.

The sun is somehow fading from the sky, like I've been gone most of the day. My feet head upstairs without my really thinking it. No one notices me, notices my disappearance. I sink into the chair at my desk, feeling a rush of cool air pass me, hover behind me. I shake my head. I'm imagining all of this. My phone is blinking and I pop the laptop open, seeing the familiar raccoon icon.

"I went back." This is the first thing I say. I don't want to talk about my grandfather.

"I'm so sorry, Roni." Matty's face is fully in the screen, for once. The worried expression is hiding a faint smile.

"What?" I say, trying to sound nonchalant.

"I caught it all," he says.

I blink. Should I even feel this rush of excitement? "What did we bring into the house? What killed him?"

"I don't know, Roni," Matty's voice softens. "But it was very real. To have that sort of manifestation. It was making sound, wasn't it?"

I nod. "I could hear it clicking across the floor."

"Roni, I'm really sorry about your grandfather." Matty gives me a sad look. "This might not be related to that. We just don't know enough. He was old."

I know he's right. "I can't think about this right now."

"I know," Matty says. "But it's still there. It vanished when your sister opened the door. It was weird . . . when you first spotted it, right before you fell over, it came towards you. But then it stopped for a good second before pushing through something." He clears his throat. "When you're feeling better, we can watch it. You need to put salt or something across your door."

"What about everyone else in the house?" I ask, knowing that salt is a tactic used in ghost hunting to stop entities from coming in. An earthy substance known to repel them, though I've never tried it. This might be just as good a time as any to see if it is true or just make-believe.

"It isn't affecting anyone else except you and your grandfather, as far as we know." Matty is looking less certain than he sounds. "If you tell your parents, they'll think you're crazy."

I nod. He's right again. "I should go."

"Roni . . ." Matty looks almost like his eyes are brimming. "It isn't your fault."

Again I nod, uncertain I can muster any other words. I close the laptop, staring at the uncovered window, the night creeping closer. The house is abuzz, but I'm lost, staring at a reflection of nothing, wondering if this will be the beginning or end of this horrible saga.

Fourteen

Just like the night before, I find the room filled with a haze. This time I'm pretty sure I'm sleeping. I don't want to rewind the day's events. I can't go through that again. I shut my eyes, seeing the sun stay in place. Am I in control of this dream? I try to shake my head, clear my vision, but the haze is locked in place no matter where I look. This time, as I get up, I notice how fast I can move. In an instant I'm across the room, standing in my sister's bedroom doorway.

I really just want to sleep, to get some rest, but I can't seem to quiet my mind. There is a lot of noise coming from downstairs and I seem to nearly leap from the top of the stairs to the first floor. A group of people are congregated in one room, sitting on the floor on some white sheets, reading from the Quran. This is customary after someone passes away. Praying for the loved one who has passed on. I expect this to be going on indefinitely.

I want to know more about that thing, but when I venture towards Nana's room, there's nothing there. Is the thing still here? As I get closer, the house—*my* house—vanishes, being replaced by my old house. When I turn around, I can't hide the surprise when the current house is totally gone. I'm standing in the front of our old house. It is bigger than our current house, by a lot. I never understood why we moved.

Everything feels somehow smaller. I also feel a lot less scared, knowing that I'm dreaming. I vault up to the top floor. The rooms are empty now. I wonder if this is what the house looks like now. I wander through the empty rooms. I used to take baths when I was little in my parent's bathroom. It was much bigger than all the others. I meander back towards my room, looking out the window that overlooks the garden. My mother loves to garden. But she left all of this behind. The summer heat hasn't done the plants any favors. In another month, this whole place will be dried and cracked. Even now I can see the dirt under the topsoil Mom put under the hydrangeas. Those flowers would always bloom this beautiful purple-blue color. I always wanted to steal a few and put them in my room, but that wasn't sanctioned by Mom. Once I needed permission, it didn't seem worthwhile doing.

When I turn back to the house, I've somehow made it downstairs. Where the family room used to be, there's a solitary desk with an old-school typewriter on it. I've seen one in storage once. My mom collects antiques. This doesn't look like that one though. It seems smaller. Though everything has shrunk from where I stand. I move around the table. There's a stack of paper to one side, a sheet inserted. Each letter is on a separate key, shaped like buttons for a coat. My fingers glance across the keyboard, and I can feel each letter on each key. This must be one of those really old antiques. They don't make things like this now. The keys aren't in order. I remember reading once that if you try to read while dreaming, nothing will make sense. Dreams are controlled entirely by the left side of the brain, whereas reading is conducted from the right side. Good to know I'm a complete nerd even in my subconscious.

There is text typed out, but nothing makes sense. I look closer and realize the letters have shifted from English to Arabic. Well, that's going to end that exploration. I learned classical Arabic, in the sense that I can read it. But understand it? Nope. I turn away, but the room is growing darker by the second. I take a step back, bumping into the table. This jolt throws the typewriter from the table. The keys tumble across the carpeted floor. Somehow I can hear it, as if it were in the kitchen on the linoleum floors. I feel scared, like I broke something, and the walls begin to melt, like that thing did as it moved around Nana's chair. I jolt and start running, bobbing and weaving, but no matter how fast I move, the feeling that something is following me doesn't fade.

Once again, I wake up with my head on my laptop, the last light of day fading from the room. Once again, Fat Face is wrapped around my shoulders. This time, the bureau isn't totally shut. My head hurts. My entire body feels empty. I don't think I've cried once. No one has come up here. The last time someone died in our family, my mother's mother, I was too young to remember. We, thankfully, haven't had too many deaths in our family. There's an old wives' tale that says everything happens in threes. I hope that's not true.

All the food from the day before is gone, but as I make my way into the kitchen, I see the room is once again full. There isn't an inch of free counter space. The crowds have dissipated, but the religious contingent is there, all dressed in a somber color or, dare I say it, American clothes. Some sort of prayer is being done. I should have paid more attention during Sunday school, but I only know just enough to finish reading the Quran, do my daily prayers, fast during Ramadan, the basics. My mother is crazy religious, praying at all hours of the day and night. Dad was not quite as dedicated as he's been recently. Even my sister has been more religious. I swear I catch her reading or sitting in prayer for a lot longer than we used to when we were younger. I often wonder if I missed some sort of religious revolution that happened in our house.

I pick at a fruit tray. The food is at room temperature. I peek into the fridge. It's brimming with trays of food. I ignore the people in the sitting room, at first. It is hard to miss the massive white bedsheet they're sitting on, just like the one from my dream. I give the obligatory nod of recognition, coupled with the proper greeting spoken in an undertone so as not to disrupt those praying, before turning back to the sunroom.

I have no appetite, but I see Jamaal scarfing down some rice mixed with *chana masala*, a chickpea dish. "Hey," I say to him.

"Hey, dude," he says, his tone softening as he wraps an arm around me. "Heard you found Nana first."

I nod. "I did."

"I got home after you passed out." He stuffs his hands into his pockets, a very Jamaal thing to do. "You okay?"

"No," I say meekly. "It's my fault."

I can't tell him why I think that, or why I even said it aloud. Talking about things almost always ends up with me sticking my foot in my mouth. This is already going great.

Jamaal pulls away, stuffing another spoonful of food into his mouth. "We all feel awful. That doesn't make it anyone's fault. He was in his eighties. He had a good life."

"I guess." My eyes pan the room. The rice does smell good. "Where'd you get that?" I shift, looking around the room.

"Second kitchen." He sets his plate down. "I'll get it."

The second kitchen is in the garage. I'd have to pass Nana's room to get there, so I'm thankful for Jamaal's offer. My eyes find the floor for a moment, before I glance up at the cameras. What all did we catch? That can't be a ghost. A ghost wouldn't suck the life from someone. A demon could, among other things. I could spend hours speculating as to what it was doing and I might never get an answer.

Was it something else? The grief is clouding my ability to think straight.

A few minutes have passed and I don't even realize Jamaal is microwaving a plate for me. "Hope you're hungry. Mom said you didn't eat at all yesterday."

I'm shocked anyone noticed. "Yeah. I haven't been hungry."

"Did you eat last night?" Jamaal nods at the beeping device.

I open the microwave and grab the overflowing plate. "Jeez, did you leave any for anyone else?"

"You're losing weight."

"Finally."

Jamaal rolls his eyes. "You're not fat."

"I'm not thin either," I counter. "You work out for your job. I can barely get moving these days."

"Go running then." Jamaal turns back to his food as I hear my sister prance into the room.

"Are you okay, Roni?" She places a hand on my back, forcing me to turn.

I try to hide the surprise at her concern. "I'm okay."

"Did you just come home and—" She stops, her eyes swimming. "I just couldn't form anything coherent to talk to you before."

I nod, not wanting to provide more information. "Are you okay?" I ask her.

"He was fine last night. I talked to him just an hour before, when we left to go grocery shopping." Sara is losing the battle against composure. Despite that, she still looks picture perfect, jeans and a nice shirt.

Jamaal sighs and sets his plate down, patting Sara on the back. There isn't a whole lot of touching in our family. I don't know if it's an Indian thing or a Muslim thing or an "us" thing. We just don't touch. Much to my chagrin, my mother bursts into the kitchen. She's been crying... it looks like nonstop. It's been a few hours, maybe, since I fell asleep. She doesn't spare me too much of a glance, consoling my sister, who's a mess.

The two end up in the room where everyone's praying. I turn back to my plate, not feeling hungry, yet still wanting to eat. I have to keep reminding myself that food isn't going to fill the emptiness. I stuff a spoonful of food in my mouth, but I don't taste anything. It takes an effort to swallow. My appetite is gone.

"I need to head to the mosque soon." Jamaal sets his empty plate in the sink. "Get some rest."

"Hey." I stop him before he goes. "What are all these people doing here?"

Jamaal gives me a wary look. "You know, the usual prayers, reading of the Quran."

I shrug, turning to the sunroom, pulling on the sleeves of my plaid flannel shirt. Everything still feels so chaotic. What are those people doing in our house? Is there some special prayer they're doing? The list of different reasons to get groups together to read the Quran is quite extensive. I basically know the ones around starting and finishing the Quran and the ones for people who have passed. I vaguely recall a small one being done when we moved into the new house. At the time, I joked with Jamaal about doing one in my car, when I get one. I want to get a closer look, but I don't want to be asked to participate. I might embarrass myself. I finish what I'm eating after a few minutes, staring at nothing.

The room is growing darker as the sun has vanished from the sky. The light from the kitchen is creating a nice buffer. I don't quite feel alone. It feels like I'm sitting with someone. Is it possible my grandfather could haunt our house? But that wouldn't explain all of the activity. If we did bring the entity in, did it just go after the weakest person? That's what all the experts say, especially for demonic entities. There are countless studies of animals being attacked or possessed before humans. In our house, Nana would have been the weakest, the least likely to defend himself.

The anger is once again building in me. If I had confronted it sooner, would it have left him alone? But why did it attack me last night if it meant to hurt him? Or was the entity here before and I only just noticed it after going to the haunted house? There are way too many variables. I can't think straight. I can't think at all with all these people in our house. I need to clear my head, but I can't do that; I won't be able to do that for a while. The funeral activities will go on for another couple days. Mom was really close to her dad, so she will probably act pretty weird. Sara was his favorite, so I am sure she'll feel awful and need constant attention. That sort of chaos might give me time to get away without being seen.

FIFTEEN

THE FUNERAL PRAYER IS TAKING PLACE the next day. Somehow, a few of my cousins, and their families, are flying in for the religious gathering, for a lack of a better term. Basically, it's just more people coming over bringing food, but since Mom is the matriarch, everyone should come pay their respects here. I could stay up to wait for them, but I'm running on negative sleep right now. Once the prayer (*Janāzah*) at the mosque is done, everyone will come over and read from the Quran. I'm not sure how long that'll go on. My Hindu friends will come by to pay their respects, but they won't be praying. I don't really understand their religion that well. One time Mita and I went to their temple. There were Gods on every wall. She knew the names of about three.

I rise early the next morning. It's freezing in my room. But I'm relieved I didn't wander in my dreams, for once. Just as Matty instructed, I had a line of salt at the door to my room, on top of a towel that's folded over so the salt won't spill. It just looks like I'm being messy. As I sit up, I can see the towel's been moved. Well, that didn't work. Anger is simmering just under the surface. I'm not sure who I should be angrier at: myself or the entity. Entities, I correct myself. At this point, I think Matty and I both agree there are at least two. Are they both trying to take over? If there is a demonic entity, it can terrorize us, but it can't possess a person until they give up. Then it can be a part of this world. Ghosts can't possess humans, as far as I know.

My neck hurts. I rub my tired eyes, once again finding Fat Face around me, this time mixed in with a heavy blanket. Did I put him away last night? God, I don't even remember. I trudge to the bathroom, hoping to wake up a little. The girl looking back at me looks dead tired. The humidity is wreaking havoc on my hair and I just tie it back, not bothering to put anything in it to calm the frizz. My sister's door is shut, as are the rest of the doors on the top floor of our tiny house. The whole area seems extra dark. I keep expecting to see that thing crawling across the floor again, but it's only haunting my dreams.

Back in my room, with the door shut, I pop the laptop open. There are a few files from Matty. I don't think I can watch the one from last night. Then curiosity gets the better of me. I start to feel sick. The first time, I look away once I hear the scrabbling sound, the ice to the floor, almost like getting my teeth cleaned at the dentist. I can feel it more than see it.

There won't be any answers if I don't force myself to watch. I start the video again, this time watching as, before I even venture to the room, there is a wisp of white, a wreath of something all around me. I lean closer. In the video, I fall to the floor, but just as Matty said, the white smoke creates a buffer. It only lasts a moment before the figure crawls through it. I rewind and watch it again. The smoke is almost human, the form of a body, legs, arms, a head, sort of. I leave that window open on my laptop, hurrying to find the video from the EVP session in the house. The figures are too distorted. But did the ghost from the haunted house follow me home? Can ghosts leave places? Can ghosts haunt people? Did it protect me from the dark entity? Am I just grasping at straws to make sense of nothing? For all I know, all ghosts look that way. That could be Nana's ghost in the house.

This is stupid. I'm being slow-witted from the lack of sleep. There's a distinct pressure behind my eyes. I press my fingers against my forehead as I hear footsteps approach. My father is already dressed for the mosque, wearing a dark blue *sherwani*. The outfit is different from American clothes in that the top is longer and the pants are looser. We shouldn't be leaving for hours.

"Your aunt is here, from California. You should come say hello." He gives me a nod as he shuts the door.

My cousins from California are younger than me. They never knew Nana like we did. When he started to get really old, we would have him stay with us or them. Here in Illinois, the pace of life is a little more exciting than San Jose. Nana knew way more people in our community than he did in theirs. This aunt is my mom's sister. They have one other sibling, my uncle, who lives in Michigan. They probably got here sometime yesterday. His kids are pretty young. Nana didn't really notice them much.

I don't bother getting dressed. This is as good as its going to get. I barely make it down the stairs before I see the signs of lots of people being in my house. There are suitcases everywhere. Some are open; some are leaning up against different pieces of furniture. With all the boxes around the house, the place looks like we're housing twelve families. I edge down the stairs, finding my cousins passed out in the sitting room. My aunt and mother are in the kitchen with Sara and my uncle.

My mom always wants to feed everyone. The moment her eyes catch movement, she points to the fridge. "Make yourself something to eat."

That's the welcome I was hoping for. If it were Sara, my mom would have laid down a red carpet for her to prance across. There are muffins on the table in the dining room. I glance over, seeing my two cousins asleep, and grab one, cutting it in half and buttering both sides generously. I still feel like I haven't eaten in days. The hunger and lack of sleep are making the days hard to track. If the party was Saturday and yesterday was Sunday, then it has to be Monday. Mom and Dad must not be going to work.

My eyes dart towards Nana's room. I keep seeing it. The thing. The dark entity. Was it the same one I saw the night before? Our house was never haunted before. Maybe I should have asked Matty to do research on our house. I think he was looking into the haunted house. Nothing started until we came back from that EVP session. Something nags at me as I think this. I shake it off.

I could keep eating muffins, but I glance up at the camera, giving my aunt a nod. She gets up and hugs me, asks if I'm okay. This is going to be a nonstop question. I don't really respond, deciding that I could use some air. I head back upstairs, not bothering to tell anyone my plans as I begin to get dressed. When I come back downstairs, my cousins still aren't up.

Sara gives me a wary look. "Where are you going?"

"I need to go and just not be here." I don't make eye contact.

"We're leaving at eleven," she says. "Don't be late."

The heat is already setting in as I open the door. I don't dare go back to the haunted house now. I feel lighter as I walk in the early morning sun. The darkness can't close in. I feel relaxed, free. The town we live in, far outside Chicago, is quiet. Everything is close by. I walk to the local coffee spot. The last thing I need is coffee. I'm Indian. We mostly just drink tea. I have a few bucks in my pocket. I stop outside, pulling my cell phone out. At this point, talking about our case is the only thing that interests me. I message Matty, not expecting a response. He tells me he can be there in fifteen minutes. The place is half full. There are kids my age, as well as older ones, college age. I find an empty table towards the back and settle in. There's a paper nearby, and I flip through the comics while I wait.

SIXTEEN

THE COFFEE SHOP CONTINUES TO FILL up. When this place was first established, it was billed as being trendy. After a few changes of ownership, it has turned into a hangout for teenagers. The black-covered tables haven't aged well and some artist came through and painted them with splashes of color or scenes from nearby Chicago. The walls are lined with posters on top of posters of indie bands that have played on the patio outside, with a smattering of missing persons. There are autographed pictures of the bands bordering the top of the room. The tiled floor used to be black and white, but is now just a grime-covered mix of colors.

I end up ordering a mocha. The jolt of caffeine is more than I expected. I'm jittery in about three minutes. This might help mask the overall malaise I'm feeling. The recirculated air is making me see things. I'm watching a speck of dust float around the room as Matty comes in.

The laptop is on the table in seconds. "How are you?"

"Crappy," I respond. "The whole family has moved in. It's like a bus terminal."

Matty cocks an eyebrow. "That bad? You do live in a smaller house now."

"It doesn't help when two other segments of the family fly in." I drain the cup, the warm liquid soothing me. "My cousins from Cali and the ones from Michigan are already here. My brother went to the mosque. I think Dad's going later."

"Is there anything I can do?" Matty asks, his normally downcast eyes set on me.

I shake my head. "Help me figure out what's going on."

The video and still images are scattered across the screen. Matty pulls up an archive site. There are several news stories, none of them referencing anything disturbing happening in my house.

"There's nothing, Roni," Matty says. "The haunted house has a more sordid past. During construction of the current house, two people died when equipment malfunctioned, all in the basement. That's when they found all those tunnels. The property company just cemented everything up, so we'll never know what was down there. Before that, well, we still need to do that research. But whatever is there, it isn't a demon."

"How do you know?" I'm still jittery. "Yeah, I know we never found anything. Nothing strange—nothing supernatural—according to the reports."

"Right." Matty takes a deep breath. "I studied the footage from yesterday all night. I compared that to the footage we got at the EVP. I also called in a favor, so to speak."

"Who do we even know that can help?" I ask.

My eyes catch the senior quarterback of my daydreams, Blaine, walking in with his little sister. Even though I know he was a bit of a bully when we were kids, I think he's grown out of that. Like my sister, there is an air of coolness all around Blaine. He's a year older than me, a junior starting on the school's football and baseball teams. I don't believe I've ever had the guts to speak to him directly. I stare down at my somewhat clean shirt and hand-me-down jeans and realize he'd never have anything to say to me. He is literally the dream guy—tall, dark hair, blue eyes—wearing the quintessential summer teen outfit: jeans, polo shirt, big boots, all despite the heat.

My eyes settle on his sister. I know I know her, but I'm not sure from where. Unlike her cooler brother, she's dressed in a cotton T-shirt and jeans, wearing running shoes that could rival my own. Neither of us will be winning any beauty contests. I try to avert my eyes, not staring. The girl has Down Syndrome. I can tell the moment my eyes land on her. I never know if I should act differently or what. I'm so awkward sometimes. A lot of the time, really.

"Oh, there she is." Matty's expression brightens as the girl I've been trying not to stare at comes towards us. Matty pushes his chair in her direction and grabs another. "Roni, you might remember Abigail from my physics class."

I nod and smile. I'm not sure I've ever spoken to her. "Hi."

"Hi." She smiles, pulling the seat a little closer. "I'm Abigail." There is a slight lisp in her voice.

"Roni," I say, my eyes darting to the table and back up.

"Since I graduated last year and started college, I have been working with a team of—" She stops, lowering her voice before she continues, the rubber bracelets in yellow and red jumping on her arm as she gestures to move closer. "Of ghost hunters. They're all science kids, though I'm there for the math."

I nod. "Okay."

"We have a few programs that filter the videos, trying to find wires or other contraptions that might assist in manufacturing something like this." She gestures towards Matty's laptop. A smile breaks across her face. "We couldn't find anything. This could be bona fide, real, not-at-all-doctored, paranormal footage."

I'm not sure what to say to this. "Right."

Her enthusiasm doesn't falter. "It's better than that." She turns to Matty. "They want to come and see what's going on."

A moment passes before I realize what she means. "Come? As in come to my house?"

She nods. "We'd have to. Whatever it is, it's focused on you."

I'm still trying to sort through the notion that the girl I've never talked to is actually super knowledgeable about something I seem to know very little about, despite all the research I've done. What software did she use to determine this wasn't doctored? We know it's real, but that doesn't mean anyone else would believe it. The flutter I felt in my stomach returns as Blaine, the football star, walks towards us, his boots echoing off of the grimy floor.

"Hey, nerds, how long is this going to take?" His voice is laced with disdain and mockery.

I'm too shocked to respond, but Abigail isn't daunted by her brother. "You're getting paid, so go talk to your loser friends, Blaine."

Blaine stops behind her chair. I feel scared for her, but Abigail isn't troubled. She consults her notebook as if he wasn't there at all.

"Watch it, loser." Blaine flicks her ear. "This stuff is all fake and you're all just weirdo losers. Math and science losers who won't amount to anything. Go back to where you came from."

I had never spoken to Blaine. I'd always watched him from afar, so easygoing and energetic. It never once occurred to me that he'd be this mean. It deflates the impression I had of him, but not entirely. It isn't unreasonable for me to see perfect people like Blaine, like my sister maybe, not to be the nicest. I mean, if I were that attractive or successful, I wouldn't need to be nice, right?

A huge roar of laughter erupts across the room as Blaine sits down, jerking a thumb in our general direction.

Abigail lets out a loud sigh. "He is such an ass."

Matty chuckles. "We know."

I start to say something, but stop, dragging my eyes away from the cool kids. "You're paying him?"

Abigail laughs. "I'm not." Her smile grows, revealing dimples. "Mom wants him to spend time with me, encourage my hobbies, maybe learn how to study better."

"I wish my parents understood my hobbies," I admit ruefully.

"This isn't a hobby. Not for you. Not for me." Her expression darkens.

"Not for you?" I ask.

"We had a babysitter who didn't much like me," Abigail continues. "She didn't like that I was always reading, drawing, something. She would stuff me in this crawlspace. There was no light, no sound that wasn't muffled. It was terrifying. I kept hearing this scraping or knocking sound. I would shut my eyes, will it to go away, but it never did. After a while, your eyes adjust. What I saw I won't say, but it left an impression."

"That, that sounds awful," I admit. I'm not a fan of tight spaces, so I can't imagine how she handled this.

"Thanks." Abigail glares. "This was at our first house, and it was spooky. I swear I saw things, things that weren't living. I would have nightmares for months, years, afterward. Mom finally asked me what was going on, but I didn't want to say. Blaine fessed up for me, but more a bit of a humble brag than anything, to show that he was the preferred kid. After that I just needed to know. Turns out, our house was a site of a murder. Some old lady killed her husband, poisoned him. Then she hid his body in the crawlspace."

I feel the blood drain from my space. "Someone died in your old house?"

Despite the statement, Abigail just nods as if this is normal. "Happens all the time, I mean it would have to, right?"

I arch an eyebrow. "I guess."

Abigail turns the laptop to face me, getting back to business. "It looks like something touched you. Did it?"

I nod. "Yeah. Left scratch marks too. Three of them."

"You know what that means, right?" she asks.

I lower my eyes, feeling the pit in my stomach growing, the anxiety and caffeine making me feel sick. "Yeah, I think so."

"Based on what I've seen, I feel like there are at least two, maybe more, distinct entities in the video." Her tone is businesslike. "The team wants to be able to move freely about your house, and have access to whatever Matty's set up. There's a disclosure form we need so we can get started."

"Would an adult need to sign it?" I ask, feeling my breath catch, dreading having to ask for approval.

Abigail nods. "At this point, we're assuming you're okay with it, but we'd still need, for legal reasons, a disclosure citing that we're there because you've allowed us on the premises to investigate a disturbance."

I try to hide the panic racing across my face, but I'm sure my eyebrows are at least an inch higher than they were a second ago. "A real adult?" I could have tricked my sister, but she's seventeen. "We have to have it?"

"For liability reasons," Abigail explains. "Just covering all our bases. Nothing will happen. Although, I've never been on an actual investigation yet."

"But you know what to do." Matty is speaking fast again. "I mean, you've done all the homework."

Abigail nods. "All the theory is down, I just have to get the classroom lessons, so to speak."

I try to laugh, to be calm, but I'm freaking out, my hands clasped under the table to keep anyone from seeing them shake. "I'm sure you'll be great at it."

"Matty said this stuff, the recent attacks, were prompted by a solo ghost investigation by you." She flips through her notebook. "A couple days ago? Is that the first time any of this started? Do you have previous paranormal experience?"

I shrug. "I don't think so."

Matty clears his throat. "I told you everything over the phone."

Abigail nods. "Just wanted to hear it myself." She scribbles something in her notebook, which, from the side, looks like "unaware of previous occurrences" in tight print. "Why did you go that night? By yourself?"

I shrug, my mind feeling muddled. Something specific drew me there. I have been going there for weeks, but usually during the day. This time I went at night. Why? "I knew there was something there," I say finally.

"You knew something was there?" Abigail says the words slowly, pausing after each.

I nod. I feel so stupid. No matter what I do, I embarrass myself. My mind jumps to meeting Marissa, right before finding Nana dead. I sounded so childish and unfocused then too. Why would I ever think anyone would believe me?

Abigail jots this down. "Anything else?"

"I got thrown through a window." I try to force a smile, but it fades as Blaine lopes towards us.

"Nerdland." He slams both hands on the table, nearly knocking Matty's laptop to the floor. "I have to go get a haircut."

I know I shouldn't stare, but my eyes slide up his articulate body and perfect, chiseled features. Everything we've been taught to love, and I couldn't get even a kind word out of him, let alone a passing smile.

Abigail shuts her notebook. "I'll call you, Matty. Be careful, Roni."

SEVENTEEN

I GET HOME JUST IN TIME TO GET READY
for the funeral gathering. My uncle has two small kids. They
are rambunctious, and I would just as soon avoid them.
Based on the mess in the TV room, it seems they aren't even
remotely aware of what's happened, and at their age, I'm not
sure I'd be any different. The room was never tidy in the first
place, but now the cushions for the sofa are scattered across
the room. The TV is blaring some kids show. There are empty
bowls, cups, and plates all over the place. Two of my cousins,
Robia and Rana, are in the kitchen. Rana is closer to me in age.
Robia is a year older than my sister, engaged to be engaged to
some arrogant doctor I've met twice.

Rana gives me a quick hug. "How you doin', buddy?"

When we were younger, our parents tried to ingrain the
notion of using respectful terms for the elder siblings. My
brother was Jamaal Bhai, the *bhai* indicating that he was the
oldest. Robia is *apa*, eldest sister, leaving me and Sara as both
baji. Rana was about four and couldn't quite say baji, so she
just kept calling me buddy. It stuck. She calls my sister Sara
Baji, but I'm just buddy, and I'm actually okay with this, even
if my mom thinks it's disrespectful.

Though, the world according to my mom would be a far
different place. Deer would be extinct, for instance. She has
a real vendetta against them for eating all her pretty flowers.
And her views are surprisingly liberal, given that she was

brought up in a pretty conservative house. If I ever dared to vote with the red states, all hell would break loose.

All this floats through my head as I survey the house. Rana is dressed with some makeup on. Robia looks like she could be going to an engagement party. For weddings, she'd be wearing quite a bit more makeup. In this case, you just can't see any blemishes, but the eye shadow is like a portal to another world. That isn't meant to be a compliment.

"How was the flight?" I ask.

"Long. We got in right before the late, late prayer" Rana nudges me towards the stairs. "You'd better get dressed. Where'd you go anyway?"

"Coffee." I hurry up the stairs, knowing she's right behind me. If they got home that late, she must be just as tired as I feel. The latest prayer is a bonus sort of prayer, done between the last prayer of the day, but before the morning prayer the next day. There's a whole chart for times online. I never manage to be awake to worry about it.

I didn't make my bed earlier. Someone must have come through. The bed is still a mess, but Fat Face isn't there. I do a quick check in the bureau and find him right where he's supposed to be. My mind is kind of hazy. I can't remember whether I put him back, but I feel the hairs on the back of my neck standing on end, sort of. After the heat outside, my hair is pretty unmanageable. Rana pulls my outfit from the hanger that's hanging on the outside of my closet, shaking her head.

"I know it's a funeral, but God, you in more black isn't a good look." She chances a smile.

I laugh. "I know."

Thanks to my father, who is from South India, we all trend darker than the rest of our family. My mother's side of the family is from the north of India, closer to Kashmir, which is known for the fair-skinned tones of its people. Because of our skin color, my cousins get to see how we're treated like African

Americans, and we get to see how they're treated like Hispanic Americans. It's the same everywhere I go. Stand in line, watch someone of a lighter shade get treated nicer, more politely, with more respect. In some places, they don't even make eye contact with me. For my cousins, there is always an assertion that they can't speak English. People tend to talk real slow to gauge whether English is their first language. On a dare, I had Rana try to speak Spanish. We ended up running for it, but it was funnier to us than the white guy behind the counter. Either way, to the white supposed majority, it isn't good.

"I stupidly went outside the other day." I hold my hand up. "I think I'm getting close to pure African over here."

"A few more hours and we'd release you to the next continent over." She's laughing, but I can see the tears in her eyes.

"You okay?" I lean in, smelling a brief, errant whiff of cinnamon.

She nods. "I just thought he'd never die, you know?"

My attention is torn between Rana and my ghost. "He was old. I mean, remember Nani?"

"Yeah." She cracks a slight smile. "Remember how she used to steal all your chocolates at Halloween and you never knew where they were going?"

I laugh. "God yes. I was convinced it was J. She was so sneaky."

Rana's smile fades. "I don't want to grow old anytime soon."

"Me either." I'm turning in a circle, following the scent, and notice the coolness in the room. Is the ghost here? Is it watching me?

"He never really liked any of us, I know." She sits on my bed. "God, Roni, have you heard of making your bed?"

"Uh-huh." My room isn't big, yet I'm stopped in front of the bookshelf, staring at the camera. One of the books is teetering. Was it like that before?

"Mom just couldn't sleep." Rana is continuing as if I'm fully engaged in this conversation. "Dad, he was quiet, not that there's anything new there."

"Uh, yeah." I pull the book out and a picture falls from it. I pick it up, blinking. It's the old house, the sun rising behind it. Why do I have a picture, vintage, yellowed from age, of a house that's haunted?

"Robia is acting like this is about her." Rana falls back on the bed. "Jeez, your room is like ten degrees colder than the rest of the house."

My eyes widen as I turn. I see the wisp on my bed, near, but not touching, Rana. The entity that scratched my back was all black. Is this the other entity? I certainly don't feel scared, and so far my instincts have been pretty on point. I take a deep breath, feeling perfect calm—more than that, safe. I stare at the picture, shutting my eyes, trusting that the ghost won't hurt Rana. And I'm right. The wisp dissipates, but I feel the rush of coolness all around me. It feels comforting, familiar now.

I can't help the smile that crosses my face. The picture is brushed by the unseen wind. I turn it over. A date is on it: 1952. How did I get my hands on a picture that's over fifty years old? And why don't I remember it? The book it fell from is an old yearbook. I did work on the yearbook last year. Maybe it somehow got mixed in?

"Roni," Rana began, staring at me, "what is going on with you?"

"You wouldn't believe me if I told you." I turn, setting the book and picture back. I can't get distracted with this right now. The book is nudged forward again. I can't help the eye roll, and the book is pushed farther forward. Jeez, am I fighting with a ghost now?

"Oh, tell me." Rana is on her feet.

In a second, she's in my space, the ghost's space. I'm nervous for a second, but the coolness backs away. I miss it once it's just out of reach. Am I crazy to miss something I don't fully understand?

"It's been crazy, even before Nana died." I lean in, holding the book to my chest.

"Right." Rana screws up her face. "I remember."

I wonder what she means. But I push on without asking. "Matty and I were doing a ghost hunt," I tell her.

"Is that a good idea?" Rana crosses her arms. "That's especially dangerous for you."

"Wait, what?"

We're both staring at each other with confusion when Sara bangs the door open. "Get dressed. We leave in ten minutes."

Rana smirks at me, moving towards the door. "See you downstairs."

What did she mean it's especially dangerous for me?

What is she talking about?

I can feel a timer set in my head after years of being screamed at for being the last one ready to leave for every event. While we're Indian, a chronically late people, I am positive we can't be even a second late to a funeral prayer being held for a member of our family. I take a moment to wait for the door to close before opening the book. The yearbook is heavy in my hands. I flip through a few pages, but nothing stands out, except the lack of signatures, the customary way to gauge whether you're popular or not. Without a doubt, I am not.

I snap a pic of the aged picture, back and front, and send it to Matty. I hope he can figure something out about it. I look around the room, almost expecting to see my friendly ghost. There's no one here. This doesn't stop me from talking aloud.

"You better not be watching while I'm changing." I leave the closet doors open, affording privacy from Matty's camera as I change.

The outfit isn't quite fitting right. Have I lost or gained weight? Why are Indian clothes so strangely disproportionate? Did anyone iron this? The leg crease needs to face forward, but I'd be wearing the pants backwards if that were right. Wouldn't be the first time. This makes no sense. I'm too tired to care at this point. I grab my dupatta, a dark-colored scarf, and turn to the mirror on the back of my closet door.

If my hair could do something other than frizz, I'd be thrilled. I press my hands to my head, trying to flatten everything out. This isn't working. I've still got a few minutes. I check my phone. Matty's given a noncommittal response.

I shut my eyes, feeling a weight on my shoulders. If I invited all of this into our house, then I caused Nana's death. "I'm sorry," I say aloud.

The words echo quietly through my head. Something cool brushes a piece of hair off my face. I turn, looking for the wisp of smoke. There's nothing there that I can see.

"Are you here?" I venture. "Did you stop that thing?"

The room chills before me. It's close, right in front of me. The hair on my arms stand on end. The scarf around my neck is given a gentle tug. I didn't imagine that.

"Thank you." I say the words, trying to will the entity to appear.

Nothing happens. I glance up at the camera, wondering if Matty caught this latest action. It was anything but threatening, flirty even. I felt safe. If the ghost is from the house, since we saw it there first, why is it protecting me? I don't have any answers and move towards the door, walking through a wall of cold that chills me to the bone. The family is congregated around the door below. I glance into my room for a second before heading down the stairs.

Eighteen

THE SERVICE WAS DONE ENTIRELY IN Arabic. I didn't understand any of it. I spent most of the ceremony staring at the wooden casket sitting before us, Nana's body hidden within. In Muslim tradition, the women and men pray in separate parts of the mosque. There are usually more men at prayers than women, so they set the men up downstairs and the women upstairs. I can see the casket from a vantage above. Quite a few people have turned out. A Janāzah prayer is done at the midday prayer and is open to all. For a Monday, the place is pretty well packed. There are a lot more kids here than I had expected. It is a well-known fact that attending this sort of prayer gets you extra "points" with God, or at least that's how I see it. If I turn religion into a point-based system, it makes a little more sense.

When we get home, even more well-wishers are there. It's like a twenty-four-hour open house. I'm now glad Mom got rid of all of the extra food. People are bringing dishes, baskets, anything, and everything. All the competing smells are coalescing into one pungent scent, the one that emanates from the second kitchen when Mom's cooking a vegetable and meat dish. It is somewhat appetizing. All functions revolve around food. Eating is a primary activity, even during Ramadan, where we can spend up to seventeen hours a day not eating or drinking a thing. My friends from the party are also here. I wish I had more energy, but I'm pretty exhausted. Rana gets me upstairs and in bed. This time, I find myself rummaging through the bureau for Fat Face. Ever since I was born, that blanket has been my best friend, even if he's really just an imaginary friend. It didn't matter that he was folded up safely, I still imagined him there. I feel like I could use a friend right now. Matty is the closest real friend I have, and he's just not what I need. I could talk science or school stuff with him, but how I feel—how guilty I feel—that isn't something Matty will understand. Or maybe I just feel weird talking to him about it.

I curl up on the bed, feeling the tiredness begin to take over. I start to dream, or at least I think I'm dreaming. The white smoke, the ghostly wisp, has returned. The features aren't in focus, but I can tell it is a person. I roll over onto my back, staring at the ceiling, seeing the room grow darker. It isn't two o'clock. How is it getting so dark? My eyes stretch towards the windows and I see the curtains pulled all the way back. Sunlight should be pouring in, but there is no light. It looks pitch black. My eyes adjust to the lack of light, making out the contrast between black and everything else.

My breath hitches as I look up at the ceiling, unable, initially, to process what's happening. I blink a few times, but the shadow isn't moving. It is fixed in place above me. My shirt is beginning to chafe, the collar stuck at an odd angle. Panic is setting in. Above me, clinging to the ceiling like Spider-Man, is the dark entity.

The features are coming more and more into focus as the seconds tick away. My gaze won't budge. The eyes are burning coals, making the pit in my stomach grow deeper and deeper. The features of the rest of the face are still out of focus, blurred, like the face is moving super-fast, but the eyes are locked onto me, staring through me. The hands and feet have tapered into lances, piercing the ceiling, cracking the drywall. Dust falls all around it, on it, suspending in midair. Is this real? I keep repeating a prayer in my head, but

I'm not waking up. I'm not moving at all. A burst of hot air blasts at me as it opens what I assume is its mouth, roaring, shaking me in bed. How is no one else hearing this? I must be dreaming. Please let this be a dream.

I try to move, to call out for help, but nothing seems to be working. I'm frozen in place. My hands and arms are stuck to my sides. My knee is bent under me, my other leg stretched out long. In my other dreams I was able to move freely. My muscles are beginning to ache from the force I'm exerting trying to move. The pain in my neck is doubling. The cuts on my back are burning anew. It feels cool in the room, like the comforter I was sleeping under has thinned in a matter of seconds.

The ghostly wisp is floating closer, between me and the entity. I can't make out any features. It is a mass, a moving block of gas. It moves, shifting, throwing its weight forward. It's acting like a rubber band, throwing the entity back, through the ceiling. Gone. The covers go flying as I sit up, free of the control. I look around the room. The white wisp is gone.

The top half of my shirt is drenched in sweat. The feeling of the wet fabric against my skin is gross. A quick glance at the clock. It's been twenty minutes since I came up here to take a nap. Did I sleep at all? Was that real or did I imagine it? It felt real. I look up at the ceiling, seeing no marks where the thing was fixed in place.

Once again the room is chilly. The windows are covered in condensation. I hope Matty recorded all of that . . . if it wasn't a dream. The idea starts and I grab for my laptop, my clammy hands having a hard time holding on. I access the stream, rewinding for about an hour. Before I got home, the room was unmoving. I step in, lie down, and then the room grows dark. There is no sign of my ghostly protector. Nothing happens. Besides the room growing darker, I did imagine everything else. Did I? Is that normal? That isn't possible. Maybe I'm hallucinating. I haven't slept, really slept, in days. I stare at the screen on my laptop for several seconds, then open another browser window, searching for an answer. My hands are shaking and I keep hitting the wrong keys. After a few tries, I come across too many sites to sift through. I can't think straight. I can't concentrate on one thing, one idea. It could be anything. I'm not crazy. I know I'm not crazy. I can't be crazy, can I? There's no response, so at least I'm not talking to myself.

What had started as a dull, distant ache has now turned into a driving pain reverberating through my head. With each exhale I can feel the pain worsen. I need to get some rest. I've had so little sleep in the last few days. The very tips of my fingers are creating waves of an undulating pain as I try to massage the headache back.

I can't hide in my room all day. Though, given everything that has happened, I should be using this rare opportunity to act like a brat—might be the only time I get the chance. I ease up, feeling the tightness in my neck. The stiff chair is making my back begin to throb. Pretty much everything hurts.

I check my phone. Matty's still looking into the picture. He seems as confused as I feel. Rana has sent me about a dozen messages, the last of which is telling me to get up to have something to eat. Apparently my friends have come and gone, though Mita tried to stay a little longer, according to Rana.

The hallway is quiet when I come out. For whatever reason, all of the doors are shut, making the hallway very oppressive, like the ceiling might come down, that the walls might narrow inwards. I head to the bathroom first. My eyes look sunken in. I definitely did not sleep. The cold water on my face reminds me that I'm indeed awake. Only slightly more awake than I was before. I probably should put the funeral clothes back on, but I don't bother and head down the stairs in my pajamas. Robia gives me a scandalized look, but says nothing. Rana's in the kitchen, doing her best to corral our youngest cousins.

"Thank God." She laughs as she spots me. "These two are giving me a run for my money."

"No TV distraction?" I ask, pouring a glass of water.

Out of the corner of my eye, I see a whole group of people praying on the white sheets. There are always sheets spread out on the floor, even though there's carpet. My grandfather would always sit in a chair, but if you're physically able, it's customary to sit on the floor. Many a time I've been unable to stand up without falling over because my foot or leg has fallen asleep. But I've never seen these sheets. Are they new? Did Mom buy them just for this?

It looks like the same group is here from before. The one guy who teaches the Sunday school is here. I involuntarily shiver as his eyes land on me. My skin crawls when he's around. His eyes follow me, see right through me. There's a much older guy here, too, one I've never seen before. He gives me a warm smile, and I try to return it as I head into the sunroom with Rana.

"Your mom said no to the TV." Rana sighs. "God, you look like hell."

"I had a bad dream." I lower my eyes. How much can I say about it? "How long are you all staying?"

"Well, the word is your parents and my parents are going to head towards Michigan, and then take your sister to college for early orientation on the way back." Rana smiles. "I had hoped that since they're doing a circle because our flight goes out of Midway, you wouldn't mind if I just stayed."

"Oh my God, no!" I exclaim, quickly realizing that I was saying one thing, meaning the other. "I mean I don't mind at all. . . . I would love it if you stayed. Remember our sibling exchange program?"

Rana laughs. "I do. Though we could never get the paperwork through."

"So, it'll just be us?" I'm more hopeful than anything.

"No way." Rana rolls her eyes. "J will be watching us."

I breathe a sigh of relief. "That's good."

Rana raises both eyebrows. "I guess."

"I have to tell you something." I lean in. "I have some friends coming over."

"A party?" Rana gives me a questioning look. "I don't think that's a good idea."

"Do I look like the party type?" I ask.

"No." There's no hesitation in her response.

"It isn't a party." I give her a cold stare. She knows I've never been the party type. I'd rather go to the dentist and get my teeth cleaned twice, with that awful water tool that feels like a high-powered laser, than attend a party. "We can talk about it once they leave."

Her interest is piqued. I can see it. The group of people praying has hardly moved. Dad keeps coming by, doing his best to get people to eat the abundance of food in our house. I try to stay out of sight. This might work out. Maybe.

NINETEEN

AFTER THE NIGHTMARE DURING THE
day, I barely sleep that night. I end up sitting up, imagining
that I'm sleeping, knowing that I'm not. I keep seeing the
dark entity in my mind. I am never one to sleep with the
lights on, but I haven't felt brave enough to turn them off.
The short nap I took this afternoon reminded me that I'm
not safe in my own home. At some point I must have dozed
off. I try to force myself to wake up, but I'm outside of my
body, watching. For once there isn't blind panic and dread
in me. I'm almost relieved. At least this isn't beginning like
the last dream began.

The house is quiet, empty, as I move through the rooms
effortlessly. I guess, in a dream state, I don't have to worry
about doors and stuff. I wonder if this is how the ghost
moves, how the other thing moves. The idea settles and suddenly I'm outside. The sun is blazing, but I don't feel hot. I
feel comfortable. I take a slow pace, letting my feet move
me, and I know where I'm going to end up long before I get
there. Sitting on what would be the stoop of the old house
is Marissa.

My face begins to burn as I realize that I'm dreaming
and I've dreamt a girl, and not a guy, into my dream. Since
it's my dream, I'm glad she can't hear my heart pounding in
my chest. Once again, she looks pretty. The sun is catching
her dark hair, giving it a golden sheen. The moment her eyes

land on me, I feel warm all over. For once, I'm dreaming, asleep even, and I don't feel scared.

Dream me might be cooler than real me. I smile, mustering the courage, certain I won't get tongue-tied.

"Hey."

"Hey yourself." She gets up, winking at me. "It's nice out. Up for a walk?"

I don't hesitate, nodding and following as she reaches a hand out, which I take without thinking. Her grip is firm and gentle. I stare at our joined hands for several seconds before I realize we're not in front of the old house—or we are, but it looks different, not broken down.

"I used to hang out here." She glances upward. "But you already knew that."

"You mean before?" I ask. "Like before this summer."

She nods. "Uh-huh." Her expression darkens. "You need to be more careful."

The dream me is apparently way more confident than I normally would be. I take a step closer; we're barely a foot apart. There is a soft scent around her, I can't quite place it in my dream, but it makes me think of baking.

"I'm being careful," I say. "I don't know how much more careful I can be."

Her eyes narrow. She's glaring at me. "There are dangers around every corner."

Something draws my gaze, and when I look back, she's gone. The old house looms over me and I take a step closer, being thrown backwards. I feel the gravel bite into my hands and forearms, surprised to see blood. Can I bleed in a dream?

My attention is divided enough that I don't notice that the scenery has switched once again. The cavernous room looks familiar, but I can't quite place it. There are rows and rows of wooden bookshelves. Each row is brimming with musty, hardcover books, boxes with papers attempting to escape. On the walls are documents, framed and hung. I don't bother trying to read them—the letters are mixed with numbers and symbols.

The scent I'd noticed earlier is there and I turn, stalking across the room. For some reason I'm wearing sneakers and I don't make a sound as I turn the corner. I stop short, jumping back. The ambient noise I'm used to is gone. In its place is a strange sort of elevator music. It doesn't fit with the surroundings. I edge closer to the corner. I'm still not sure what I saw, but my reaction was to hide. A firm hand grabs my shoulder, pulling me back. I don't worry, recognizing the grip.

"You disappeared earlier." Marissa is standing super close to me. I should feel uncomfortable. I should feel embarrassed. I don't feel either.

"I didn't go anywhere," I reply. "You seemed mad at me."

That winning smile nearly knocks me over. "I'm never mad at you, Roni, just worried."

I let out a soft sigh. There's a weird feeling bubbling up inside, something I can't say I've experienced before. I shouldn't be this distracted in a dream. I want to ask her more questions, but the thing I didn't see, it's beckoning for my attention.

"This is just a dream." I lean closer to her. "You don't have to worry."

"It isn't here I'm worried about you," she insists. "Out there, when you're awake, you're not safe." I move half an inch and she pulls me back with more force than I expect. I jostle against the bookshelf, hearing the books rattle against each other. "Listen to me." Her voice lowers to a whisper. "Stop trying to see what you shouldn't see. I will keep you safe. I promise."

I want to say something, to respond, but a long second passes as we stare at each other. I blink a few times, seeing the morning sunlight spill into my room. I watch it drift by before getting up for early morning prayer. I'm awake. It was a dream. This time I'm absolutely sure of it. The house is abuzz with activity. I drag myself upright, lumbering down the hallway, yawning, stretching, and going to the door. We have two cars. Dad drives a station wagon, and Mom has a sensible four-door sedan. The two cars are being packed. Of course they'd take both cars. My aunt's family is a few people and so is ours. All of them wouldn't fit into one car. I try not to stare.

My mother gives me a sad sort of look as she stops. "Are you sure you and Rana will be okay by yourselves?"

"Of course." I smile. "Besides, J is here."

"Jamaal Bhai." She always has to correct me. "We are a phone call away."

"And several hours," I add.

Relief is washing over me, mixed with a tingling sensation when I think about the pleasant parts of the dream I just woke from. It isn't that I don't love my family, but there is no way on earth I could get this investigation done with them here. As it is, Jamaal won't be easy to deal with either. Maybe I'll luck out and he'll have to work. Rana, on the other hand, will have to be told the truth.

I continue watching the packing process. Before they go, Mom prays something and blows on me, as if the lips that spoke the prayer and blowing on someone will somehow make everything stick. The sun is just over the horizon as the two cars head out. Rana and I are left alone. We head back inside, settling down in the nice sitting room. My cousin is falling asleep again, so I let her sleep, feeling someone watching me. Not the friendly ghost, or what I hope is a friendly ghost, but the darker, dirtier feeling. Whenever I turn, there's nothing there.

I snap the laptop open and send a video call to Matty from my room. "You up?"

The raccoon was not active, but I see a very tired Matty, with a beany on his head, looking at me. "Did you sleep?"

"I'm not sure," I admit. "I feel like there's something watching me."

"Your ghost friend or the other thing?" Matty asks.

"Both." I scrunch my eyes up, seeing Marissa bathed in sunlight, distracting me. "I'm sure they aren't the same, but both appeared at about the same time, you know?"

"I had considered that." Matty runs a hand through his short hair. "Roni, you need to get some sleep."

"I know." I feel like I have no energy. "My parents left this morning. They're visiting with my uncle then stopping on the way back for the college thing. We have three or four nights to work with. Want to tell Abigail?"

Matty nods. "Sure thing. Where are we on the disclosure?"

"Uh." The answer came way too fast. "I have to figure out whether my brother will be here or not."

"You need to tell him the truth." Matty is staring at me, the dark eyes unmoving. "I'm serious. If you don't, I will."

I wasn't expecting an ultimatum. I handle it as well as I can, given the circumstances. "Don't tell me what to do." Jeez, Roni, that was childish.

Matty's expression doesn't change. "I'll call Abigail. The team should be there before nightfall."

The video cuts out. I'm too tired to be really angry. I crawl back into bed, hoping to sleep a few hours. The room is cool when I feel someone shaking the bed. Thankfully, it is a real-life person and not something else.

"Roni," Rana says, rocking the bed, "can you please get up?"

I blink up at her. "What time is it?"

"Two." She pulls her sweater close. "Buddy, it is freezing in here."

I nod, almost seeing my breath. "AC must be cranked or something."

"Are you hoarding it for yourself?" she asks, grinning.

"Nope." I sigh, feeling a little more rested. "What have you been up to?"

"Wasting time watching pointless TV," she says as she plops down at the foot of my bed. "You know, I poked around Nana's room. No one has moved a thing."

"You went in there?" At this I sit up, unable to hide the alarm in my voice.

From her expression, I can tell she's taking my tone the wrong way. "I didn't take anything."

"No." I stop, taking a slow breath. "Didn't you hear I found him in there?"

She nods absently. "Yeah."

"Rana, I have something I have to tell you." I pull the comforter closer, Fat Face with it. "Something you can't tell anyone. And you might not believe me."

"Try me, buddy." She smiles.

"When I found Nana," I start, the whole scene replaying in my head. How do I distill this? Blast forward? "I was home alone, but I wasn't. Something was in the room with him."

"Someone killed him?" she asks the obvious question.

"No, not a person." I furrow my brow. "It was all dark."

At this she sits up straight. "Like a person, but dressed in black, like a thief?"

"Yes and no." Now I sound like a lunatic. "It didn't have a face, but it had, like, claws for fingers. It made this weird clacking sound as it crawled across the floor."

"Wait, what?" Rana is staring at me. "When did this happen?"

"When I saw Nana in his room, dead." The way his face was frozen is stuck in my mind. It won't replace all the other nightmarish images I deal with, but it will always be there, just under the surface.

"Are you sure you saw it?" Rana's expression is distant. "You're not taking anything, are you?"

"No, and for reasons I'll have to explain anyway, I recorded it." This conversation is going sideways.

"You were holding a camera?"

"No."

"Roni, you need to get up and try to speak a version of English that I can follow." Rana laughs.

I throw the covers off, feeling the coolness of the room. The laptop is on my desk and I turn it towards her, finding the video. Her skepticism fades as she watches the video. I can't quite listen, scrunching up my eyes, trying to somehow close my ears, hearing the same things. It hasn't made me any less scared.

I set my jaw. "I'm not making this up. It really happened."

Rana arches an eyebrow. "Buddy, I love you, but you and your friend are really good at making movies."

I get up, pacing the room. "Remember when we were kids, how we used to hear all those weird stories?"

"Maybe." She pushes my laptop farther across the bed, away from her, as if it were infected. "I mean, yeah, we have heard all kinds of things to keep us in check. Like when my dad said if I ate watermelon seeds I'd grow a watermelon in my stomach."

"Not like that." I shake my head. "How that one auntie couldn't see at night, when she was a kid? You know the one."

She's staring at me blankly. "No."

"Aargh." I'm losing my patience, not an uncommon thing.

123

She looks at me with worried eyes. "Did you tell your parents about any of this spooky stuff?"

"No." I throw my hands up in the air. "They'd never believe me."

Her eyes grow wider. "They don't know? They don't know this happened in their house?"

"I don't know what they know," I admit. "They don't tell me anything."

Rana gets up. "Let's eat something. We need to tell an adult."

I glare at her receding figure. After Matty's ultimatum, I know I'm stuck. I can't expect her to help me convince Jamaal of anything if she isn't on my side. The cool wave fades. I pull a sweatshirt on, grab my phone and computer, and head downstairs.

TWENTY

RANA AND I ARE STARING AT MY BROTHER. Jamaal has a distasteful look on his face, like something really smelly is in the room. It borders on disgust or revulsion. I'm imagining the traveler's ailment that I suffer from whenever we go to India. I never feel clean after I get better. The laptop is the only thing between us. I tried to queue the videos, but either way it looks like nothing at first that becomes more and more of something. It would be hard to argue what's on screen. I feel like everyone's acting like I have this wildly vivid imagination. Like I'd make something like this up just to get attention. Why would anyone want attention that's derived from blinding fear and panic?

"J, say something." It's been at least a couple minutes of awkward silence up to this point.

"Don't you and Matty have something better to do with your time than make really bad home movies?" His voice is laced with fury. "Did you find some friends to help you move things?"

I try to hide the surprise and hurt. "No. You know I don't have a lot of friends."

His expression softens. "I had it tough in school, too."

I laugh, feeling the anger bubbling up. "No you didn't. You were super popular. If not for Mom and Dad not letting you play on every single sport, you would have been the coolest kid in school."

"I see you, Ron," Jamaal says. "You don't have to draw attention to yourself. You're special."

I'm honestly not sure how to respond to this. My family doesn't treat me like anything but the mistake I've always been. The accidental extra that they didn't need to disrupt their perfect lives.

"If I were so special, maybe you'd show some faith in me." I pretend like he didn't just say something super nice. I know, I can be a jerk sometimes.

Jamaal sits up taller, the perfect posture checking in as I slouch farther across from him. "I just spent fifteen minutes looking at grainy videos of you and your friend playing pranks on each other in a house you're not supposed to be in and a really crude joke with Nana."

Rana clears her throat. "Bhai, it isn't made up. Don't you feel it?" She shifts in her chair. "Everywhere I go in this house, it feels like someone is watching me, like something is watching me."

"This is ridiculous." Jamaal tries to laugh, but I can hear the nervousness in his voice.

"I am not making this up." I start to stand up, feeling my heart rate quicken. "When ever have I made something up? Like really? I saw that creepy thing with my own two eyes!"

People say that each of us have parts of our parents. I can see my mother's no-nonsense glare staring back at me. In my head I can hear the chiding begin.

"Never," he relents. "But this isn't proof."

"And how would I create that proof?" I ask. "It isn't like a thing that I can't see is going to do what I ask just to prove itself to you? I mean, besides, evil things usually prey on the weak."

"You're not weak," he states.

I glance at Rana. Another compliment. Is this my brother? "You don't think anything was strange with Nana's death? I mean, come on—look at that chair. How do you think it moved by itself? Do you think I did that for fun? I was scared. I was terrified. Something I can't see stopped whatever that was from getting me."

His expression softens. "Are you okay?"

"Sleep is a distant memory," I admit. "Otherwise, I'm mostly unharmed. Better off than Nana."

"That isn't . . . this can't be real." He stops, his brow tightly knit. "This all happened in the last couple days? What were you doing at that old house? Don't tell me you were there the night we got a call for it."

I don't say anything. Silence is my friend in most cases. In this instance, it is an admission of guilt.

"Roni," Jamaal says, staring up at the ceiling, "what were you thinking? That place isn't safe. The floor could've fallen in. You know there's tunnels or something down there."

"Matty and I ghost hunt." This sounds even stupider than I thought it would. "It usually amounts to nothing."

"And you don't think you should be careful?" he asks me the question, but he's looking at Rana. "Mom and Dad told you and Sara not to go there, especially after the crazy stuff happened."

"I know." I glare. Besides the random death, when the gangs were there and supposedly performed devil worshiping rituals, some crazy stuff happened. Most kids wouldn't go near it, but things have died down since then. "We can't tell them. They won't believe me anyway."

"I'm not asking for your permission." Jamaal gestures to the laptop. "What is it? What is it that's moving all those things? If you're investigators, what have you found out?"

"We don't know." I feel like I'm five all over again and my brother is interrogating me over a missing cookie, the crumbs of which are still stuck to my face. "Matty and I know some people. They want to investigate."

"The old house?" He rubs the stubble on his face as he speaks.

"No." And here comes the next argument. A moment passes and neither of us say anything. I don't want to say it.

"Here?" His eyes are boring through me. "In our house? You think our house is haunted?"

"Yes," I answer. "This is where all the activity is. This is where Nana died."

"Are you crazy?" He stares daggers at me, his face falling. "I know you're not crazy."

"I would think I'm crazy too," I lower my voice. "I'm not sure what I got involved in." The guilt is compounding. "I should have never gone there."

Rana pats me on the arm. "It isn't your fault."

Much to my surprise, Jamaal looks remorseful. "You're not crazy, Roni. This stuff we learned in Sunday school, just not to this degree." A moment of awkward silence pervades the room. "Do they know what to do?"

"Yeah, I hope so." I admit. "Mom and Dad would just pray it away."

"That does work." He doesn't sound very certain, though. "It has worked in the past."

"Right." I roll my eyes. "Just be here to make sure nothing unsafe happens."

"Are you serious?" He barks at me. "Absolutely not. Am I being unclear?"

"Don't you want to be sure?" I argue. This might be a better tactic. "Whatever Mom and Dad might do, they'd still need to know what we're dealing with."

My brother isn't stupid by any means. It will take a millisecond to grab the phone and call our parents. Something is stopping him. I don't think it is any of the presences in the house. His eyes land on Rana, who seems nervous.

"Will they get rid of it?" Jamaal sets both hands on the table. "Those shows sometimes have people making it worse, you know? Not that I watch that sort of thing."

"I think they're just going to do an investigation." I shrug. I honestly don't know. "If we ask, they might, but I think we're still in the fact-finding portion of the investigation."

"How many people?" he asks.

"Four or five." I hope this is about right.

"Cameras and everything?" He taps the table.

"Yes." I can just imagine the cramped space getting more cramped. "And they need us to sign something saying that they are permitted to conduct the investigation."

Jamaal massages his forehead and rolls his eyes. "Is Matty the ringleader?"

I laugh, realizing that isn't helping my cause. "Oh my God, no. Matty and I are novices at this. Abigail is bringing a team with her. She's friends with Matty and is the one who knows the team that's coming."

Jamaal shakes his head. "When are they supposed to come?"

"Tonight, just to look around." I cringe.

He glares in response. "I have off of work for the rest of the weekend. I'll decide once I meet them."

His eyes land on Rana before he shakes his head at me, getting up. Neither of us say anything until he's gone.

"Wow, I thought he was going to go through the roof," Rana says, leaning back in her chair.

"Think he'll let them in the house?" I ask.

"Just to be polite, yeah." Rana smiles. "You aren't crazy, Roni. It's right there on tape. Proof . . . sort of. But what is it?"

I shrug, feeling my skin crawling. "I don't know that I want to know."

Once I tell Matty about Jamaal, he seems relieved. The crew are set to be at our house before dark. I try to tidy up.

Rana follows me around. Neither of us want to be alone for too long. I can tell she's scared. She's jumping at nothing. I'd like to say I'm calmer, but I'm just as scared as she is. The thing hasn't resurfaced for almost two days. Does that mean it's gone? It would have attacked me, a few times, if not for the white mist. I can only hope it's gone, but that's just wishful thinking. I wouldn't feel like someone's watching me all the time if it were gone.

For whatever reason, we start putting snacks together. This is such an Asian thing to do. When you know someone is coming over, you have to be a good host. If I've learned anything from my parents, this is it. There are tons of leftovers around the house. I pull together some chips and dip. It isn't a party, I keep telling myself. I find the backup teacups, since the regular ones were broken, and set those out. Tea is a staple for all functions.

Matty is the first to arrive. He's met Rana a few times, but they seem especially awkward this time. It occurs to me that Rana that doesn't know Matty is transgender. When would be a good time to bring that up? Now doesn't seem like a good time. Honestly, I think it would be fine if I just let her treat him like the guy friend that he is, there's nothing that needs to be said. I am starting to feel like I am at a party. I'm filling the pauses with nonsense. Jamaal gives Matty a sturdy handshake before pulling him onto the porch. I glance over, wondering if I should have told Jamaal. It isn't me I'm telling them about. Should I say nothing? I can't quite hear what is being said, but my brother would never yell at someone in a social setting. Well, not someone he isn't related to.

There's no visible change when they come back inside. Rana is busy munching away on the chips. Matty shoots me a tight smile as he starts pulling things out of his bag.

Jamaal is hovering. "When are these people going to be here?"

"Soon." Matty doesn't make eye contact.

"Is this safe?" Jamaal asks.

"Of course." Matty turns at this. "They're just looking. And like I said, they've been doing this for years."

"Are there schools for this sort of thing?" Jamaal leans against the wall in the hallway as we stand around the kitchen.

"Just what you can find on the internet." Matty glances up at the cameras in the kitchen, glancing over his shoulder towards Nana's room. "Have you been in there since?"

"No," I answer. "Rana has been, though."

She wipes her hands on a dishtowel, nodding. "I went in for a second. Didn't notice anything."

The EMF and REM-POD are out. Matty arches an eyebrow. "Wonder if they'll have their own toys."

"I'm sure." I laugh. "But if you want to take a quick check, no one is stopping you."

"Or going with you." Jamaal turns to the door. "Looks like they're here."

TWENTY-ONE

THE SUN IS JUST BEGINNING TO SET AS
the team arrives. The first car to come into view is a small,
four-door Honda. My father would love the sensible choice.
Two college-age women emerge from the car—one busily
using her phone, the other walking towards me. She isn't
carrying a bag, but has a light jacket on over a pair of jeans
and a T-shirt that says "Chicago" in a fancy print.

"You must be Roni." The woman offers a hand, revealing
an impressive number of rings. "I'm Sondra. That's Amanda.
She's giving the details to Eric. Abigail will be here shortly."

I smile. "This is my brother Jamaal and my cousin Rana.
I think you know Matty."

She nods, her eyes landing on my brother. "Are you the
resident adult?"

I've never quite seen my brother at work, but I imagine
that this is his official stance. His legs are hip-width apart
and his arms are crossed. If he were wearing his uniform, I
would mistake him for a cop. I can never see him as that,
he'll always by my goofy older brother.

"Yeah," he says.

From inside her jacket, Sondra produces a sheet of
paper. "I will need your signature. It's just a waiver of sorts
saying we are allowed on the premises, permitted to do this
investigation, and most importantly, that you won't sue us
if things get out of control."

"Is that likely to happen?" Jamaal asks. His body is rigid.

133

Sondra tilts her head, her hair falling away from her face. "Well, I can't tell you that, honestly. Whether you're a skeptic or a believer, this stuff is hard to predict. I can't guarantee that nothing will happen. And really, we want to witness this firsthand."

Jamaal sets his jaw, taking the paper, and much to my surprise, signing it. "Nothing better happen to them," he warns.

Sondra's dark eyes land on Rana and me. "It seems like Roni is the target of the activity, so that one might be tough. We can try to keep things in front of us, but that's the best I can give you."

I'm waiting for my brother to start yelling and screaming. But that doesn't happen. We stand in the growing darkness as Amanda saunters towards us. The trunk is popped and she pulls a laptop bag out, leaving the rest of the items where they are.

"I'll wait for the porter to get here," she quips. "I'm Amanda. You must be Roni."

The immediate recognition is starting to make me uncomfortable. "Hi," I say.

Sondra offers the sheet of paper to Amanda, who slides it into a file. I can see a Hello Kitty tattoo on the inside of her wrist and a small South Korean flag on her upper arm. My parents would never let me get a tattoo. Defacing your body, in Islam, is a major sin. Actually, I don't know that there are any minor sins, as per my mom. Pretty much anything that might be even a little fun is probably not allowed, but it seems like every religion is like that, until you start turning it into an à la carte experience, like my Hindu friends sometimes do. Mita only does some of the required things the rest of her family does, like when they're fasting, she just gives up a couple types of food.

A small van comes roaring up with salsa music blaring. Sondra rolls her eyes. "Here's the porter now."

I'm not sure what I expected, but the driver door pops open and a thin, Hispanic guy comes strolling forward. He's wearing oversized clothes, his underwear showing like a gangster or something. "Buenas noches, señoras."

"Do you have all the gear?" Amanda asks.

"Si." The man flashes a toothy grin. "Todo está aquí."

"Get the stuff out of the truck, Eric." Amanda laughs. "Speak English. They're going to think you're an illegal immigrant or something. Be careful, the five-o is here."

The last remark is tossed in Jamaal's direction. This isn't anything new. "I'm not a cop right now," he tells them.

"I thought cops were always wearing the badge," Sondra says in a teasing tone, pushing the braids in her hair away from her face. "Don't worry, big man, nothing we can find you can stop with your standard issue gun."

Eric is humming something under his breath as he unloads Amanda's trunk, moving everything to the door and pulling out tubs from his trunk. "I got the new high-def cameras. If the video is any indication, this should be amazing."

I try to hide my surprise at this one-hundred-eighty-degree switch. One second he did sound like he'd just moved to the States. The next he sounds like every other kid I know. "I'm Roni."

"I know, chica." Eric laughs, pushing his sleeves up. "Saw the footage. Who's the ghost?"

I shrug. "Don't know."

"Seems to know you." Eric narrows his eyes. "Matty, my man." In a second I'm forgotten as Eric grabs Matty, dragging him towards the van. "Fair warning, Abs is bringing that annoyance with her."

"Wait, what?" I stumble after them. "Blaine is coming?"

Eric makes a face. "I tried to give Abby a ride, but her mom wants Blaine to make sure she's okay." He nods at Sondra and Amanda. "Abby could not be in safer hands."

"Funny." I set my eyes on them. "Sondra just told my brother she couldn't be sure we'd be safe."

"We've had no fatalities or accidents in seven years." Eric stands up taller. "We investigators, well, that's another story. No one's dead, but I've got some wicked scars."

I try not to let this news alarm me. Rana has been hovering near me. I'm still shocked that my brother hasn't done anything embarrassing. I give Matty a slight nod as I head to the front door.

Rana is pulling on my sleeve. "Ron, buddy, this seems ten thousand times more serious than it did a few hours ago."

"I know." I'm not sure what to say. "I don't know what to do, so this might be the best option right now."

"What is it?" Rana asks.

"I have no idea," I admit. "I hope they can tell us something."

We continue to the door. Jamaal is laughing and joking. I try not to ever watch people flirt. I start to get embarrassed. If I didn't know better, he was chatting up both Sondra and Amanda. My brother does have the tall, dark, handsome thing going for him. I shudder even entertaining the notion that my brother might be attractive. I turn back to the group. Never in my wildest thoughts would I have imagined a more diverse group. Three entirely different continents are represented, Africa, Europe and Asia.

I stop at the door, pushing it open. "Come on in."

TWENTY-TWO

THERE IS MORE STUFF THAN I COULD have imagined, like Christmas in the middle of summer, if we celebrated. All of the things Matty has built is nothing compared to this treasure trove. There are at least two dozen different cameras. The group quickly takes over the sunroom. (Eric is apparently the brawn of the project. Sondra and Amanda are busy giving orders.) The sunroom is the one room that was added after the house was originally built. There's also been no activity reported there.

Rana and I are keeping out of the way. Matty is eyeing the network they're setting up. Sondra's proving to be quite adept at computer stuff. She's created a closed network, like Matty did, but the encryption is quite complex. They have a couple EMFs that are connected wirelessly to software on the laptop. If I didn't know better, it looked like there were about ten different filters that could be applied to the footage being streamed.

The chips are almost gone by the time they think they're ready. A sharp knock sounds from the front door as we're about to start the tour of the house.

Sondra smiles. "Abby's here."

I take a quick glance in the windows, hoping I look okay. Rana arches an eyebrow, but turns back to what little is left of the chips.

The door opens and Blaine is leaning against the door frame. "Got room for one more?"

137

The saucy, sultry look has me catch my breath. I can't help noticing the expensive watch, one you see in those magazines that retail for over a thousand dollars. Everything he has on looks brand new or freshly pressed. I wonder what it's like to be so lucky, to be so privileged. His family always looks like they're living in excess. While my family is barely seeming to get by. I wonder what his house looks like compared to ours. Something cool blasts past me and I jump. No one notices any of this.

Abigail rams into her brother with her bag. "Get out of the way. You're here because Mom made me bring you." Her eyes turn to Sondra. "I'm sorry. I couldn't get rid of him."

Blaine straightens his collar, smoothing out the front of his button-down shirt. "Anything, at all, that I can help with, you let Blaine know."

I roll my eyes. Watching my brother try to flirt is one thing, watching Blaine flirt is somehow worse. I can't hide the stab of jealousy that I feel, that Blaine finds Sondra more attractive than me. I look down at my black T-shirt and bargain jeans and realize that I probably don't have a lot to offer. With this dejected feeling in my head, I turn back to the window, seeing my reflection and a white wisp around me. It feels comforting.

Abigail sets her bag up on the table. Eric gives her a half hug. "I was worried you'd miss your first big investigation, bonita."

Abigail flushes slightly. "I am super excited. Have we set everything up?"

"No." Eric shrugs. "The cop wants to watch us super close."

Abigail flashes a smile at my brother, who returns it. "I've always loved seeing a tall, dark and handsome man."

He takes a step closer. "Why would you find this interesting?"

Abigail's expression sours. "You know, I bet you see all sorts of things as a cop."

Jamaal's interest is piqued. "Yeah, the best and worst of people."

Her smile doesn't waver. "When I was a lot younger, I went through something of a haunting." Blaine's eyes are glued to his phone, but I can see he's listening. "We lived in a haunted house and to make a long story super short, I wanted to know why it happened. I mean, I was being hunted, we both were." She gestures to Blaine. "But I was considered weaker, I guess, so the primary target. After that I didn't want to be a victim."

It had never occurred to me how different Abigail would have been treated growing up. Looking at her, the answer is obvious. It would be just as bad as, if not worse than, Sondra or Eric, whose nationalities are often seen as negatives.

"You're not still scared?" Jamaal presses.

Abigail let out a nervous laugh. "Not really. No reason to be. These things are dead. They can only hurt you if you let them."

"But you must watch all those horror movies?" Rana chimes in.

Abigail shakes her head. "That's all so fake. Even if there's an ounce of truth in there, once Hollywood gets its hands on something, it's made-up garbage."

"We all met through a seminar at a local book store." Sondra comes up behind Abigail. "She and Matty were sitting together. Of course, Abby was the one who kept asking questions, and I decided to introduce myself. We usually don't let anyone underage in, so having Matty, Roni, and Rana here is an exception, so to speak. It is Matty's case. So he has a right to be here."

Blaine coughs something under his breath. "You're all crazy. You know that, right?"

"You can sit outside, hombre," Eric tells him, standing up taller. "Don't want any accidents to happen."

Blaine stands up, a full foot taller than anyone else in the room, except my brother. "That wasn't an accident. You did something."

Eric's smile remains a straight line. "I can't help if you're clumsy."

"I'm not clumsy." Blaine is moving in, the boots echoing hard off of the floor. "You let that thing trip me up and I got soaked."

Before any further argument can erupt, Sondra cuts in. "Enough, both of you. Blaine, you are a guest in this house. Try not to interfere too much."

An exaggerated eye roll is his only response as he turns down the hallway, pulling his phone out. His heavy boots echo off of the floor as he steers himself into the nice sitting room.

The tension fades. Jamaal edges around me. "Is there some starting point here? You've got a lot of stuff in our sunroom."

Sondra smiles at him, almost relieved to hear him call her attention away from petty squabbling. "We do, but I promise we need all of it."

Amanda giggles, and I can't help moving towards her. "Is this not the first time Blaine has hit on Sondra?"

Her eyes are on her laptop, but she curls the edge of her mouth up. "He just needs to feel validated. Poor Abby. She deals with this daily, and he always has to make her feel ugly, which she isn't."

I nod. "How are we going to avoid any danger with him here?"

"No different than your brother being here, or your cousin," Amanda says, turning the laptop towards me. "And we are live, folks."

"Recording?" Sondra asks.

"The feed backs up on the cloud every fifteen minutes," Eric volunteers as he sets up a UPS, a super battery for PCs. I've seen them in the server rooms at school. "We are good to go, Mama."

"Don't call me that." Sondra sighs. "Let's get the hand-held cameras and see if this tall, dark, and handsome gentleman can give us a tour."

I can't help rolling my eyes, but I can see Jamaal's cheeks grow a little red. Rana elbows me. Her expression matches mine. Matty keeps his own camera rolling, as does Eric as Jamaal starts at the front of the house. Blaine doesn't look like he's even paying attention, flopped across the couch on his phone, his boots on the coffee table.

"So, here, to the right, the TV room, it's a little bit of a mess." Jamaal gestures. "To the left, the nice sitting room and the dining room. The kitchen and sunroom are straight back."

There are a few pictures being taken. I try to see through Matty's camera, see if I can see anything more, but there's nothing. I notice we're all ignoring Blaine's presence, as he's ignoring all of us.

"To the left, past the kitchen, towards the garage is our grandfather's room, where Roni found him dead a couple days ago, a bathroom, and the garage. I live above the garage." Jamaal stops. "Did you want to go inside his room?"

Sondra nudges Eric. "Let's get some footage. Where's the camera?"

Without skipping a beat, he offers her a camera. She hands it to Amanda. "Should I be taking shots of everything?"

Sondra pauses before nodding. "I think so."

"I feel it too." Amanda starts clicking. "There's this very oppressive feeling."

Rana pokes Amanda. "Oppressive how?"

Before Amanda can respond, Abigail lets out a sigh. "You know how it feels disgusting outside because of the humidity? Well, that's what it feels like. But it isn't heat, it's just pressure. Like someone's watching you or you feel uncomfortable."

"But that's—I mean, is that something you can judge, objectively?" Rana continues.

Sondra laughs. "How many skeptics can you keep in one house?"

"All of them." I laugh.

Sondra pushes Eric forward. "Keep shooting. Move around this whole area. I think there's something more we're not seeing." She turns back to Rana. "There are a lot of reasons people get into this sort of thing. Sometimes people are hurt by something they can't explain, like in the movies, but real, like *The Exorcist* or *Poltergeist*. Those things happened. People just don't believe."

"It isn't that I don't believe," Rana argues. "I just don't know how you can feel something."

"Everyone thinks there are only five senses, but some people are blessed with more." Sondra gives her a matter-of-fact smile. "I got into this because I could feel something was off—wrong, sometimes—but I could never explain it. It wasn't until I went on a school field trip where I felt so sick at this museum that I started to understand. It turned out someone had been killed there. The body was found a week later. I was feeling that person. Ghosts know when people are attuned to them, as do demons. Based on the video we all saw, demon's my best guess."

"What would a demon be doing here?" I ask, feeling my heart skip a beat.

"In most cases, a demon wants to break people, then destroy them or possess them. We can't be sure which." Sondra motions to Amanda. "Abby, you getting the scans?"

"Yes, ma'am." Abigail nods to the tablet before her. "We're mostly clear right now."

Sondra turns to Amanda. "We done down here?"

Amanda nods. "Jamaal, if you don't mind?"

"Not at all." He leads them up the stairs.

Eric is busy snapping pictures, and now I'm wondering if I at least made my bed. Abigail is hanging in the back with me, holding an EVP device mounted on her tablet with a thermometer built in. I can see it's not fluctuating at all. My ghostly friend mustn't be too close.

"In an investigation," Sondra continues explaining, "we're just trying to confirm or deny that there is something going on, supernatural or otherwise. We can do research on the property, on the people, but we may never get an answer as to why it's attracted to you, other than the demon saw someone whom it could take advantage of."

Am I someone who can easily be overcome? I'm mulling this over as I see the dial on Abigail's thermometer drop a couple degrees, then a few more. I grab her arm, my eyes widening. The rest of the group is getting farther ahead of us. The temperature is dropping. It was warm, but I can feel the hair on my arms standing on end. Whatever is in the house, it is right here. Abigail clears her throat, and the group before us stops.

The device is turned to face them and Sondra nudges Eric. Everyone stops talking. I'm not sure what I'm supposed to do. If it were just me and Matty, I'd start asking questions.

Sondra motions for us to keep moving. Abigail gives me a slight smile, and I feel a brush of cold air shoot past me, towards my room. I know she felt it too.

"You're not going to ask any questions?" I ask as we catch up.

"Not right now," Sondra says. "Though I really want to."

The photo session continues. Sara's room is impeccable. My room is an organized mess. I cringe, seeing my lucky orange underwear on top of my laundry basket. No one comments on it, so I'm trying to act like they're not there for everyone to see.

Sondra turns to me. "Where's the book? The one the picture fell out of?"

"Yearbook." I point. "The bookshelf, in the corner."

I start to move, but she puts a hand up. "Eric, get some shots. Abby, has the temperature dipped?"

Abigail scratches her head. "I can't get any baseline readings with Roni this close. Wherever she is, it's colder than anywhere else."

"Want me to go outside?" I joke.

"Not yet," Sondra says. "The entities, both of them, are connected to you somehow. If you leave, it might leave with you. So, stay put for now." She turns to Abigail. "Get in here and Roni, no offense, can you scoot back?"

I start to back away, feeling rejected. Matty materializes near me, handing me one of our toys. "Maybe you should get your own baseline."

I take the device, leaving the activity behind. I'm not sure how far I should go, so I head down the stairs, deciding to sit on the bottom stair. This is the most alone I've been inside the house in what feels like forever. It's chilly where I am. The baseline temperature is about fifty-five. So far during the investigation, the temperature dipped to below fifty. I didn't have a thermometer when I saw that thing. I wonder if there's a threshold. At what point is it the ghost versus the entity? Are they one and the same? I've read investigations where the entity appears as something kind to little kids to lull them in, then turns into something horrific. I don't know how I'd be fooled into something like that. I'm too old to believe just anything, or so I hope.

Footsteps approach. In most cases, I wouldn't be worried. With everything that's happened, I jump, seeing Amanda and Eric giving me amused looks.

"The book had some slight EMF readings on it," Amanda started. "We wanted to check you."

Eric leers at me, in a comical sort of way. "So what are you doing later?"

"Dude, my brother would flatten you in a millisecond." I laugh. He's cute, for sure.

"No doubt. Your brother is intense." He chuckles. "And I think he knows what this is."

"What makes you say that?" I ask.

"Because I do know." Jamaal is standing on the step above the one Amanda is standing on. "Think about it, Roni. They didn't want you to remember, but I think that you do."

I stare at him. "I'm drawing a blank. What? What is it?"

"A djinn."

TWENTY-THREE

THE WORD TRIGGERS SOMETHING. I FALL
back, bumping into the wall. Jamaal is staring through me.
All I hear is a slight laugh.

Blaine, from the sitting room, sits up, laughing. "What?
Like a genie? Come on, man. I thought you people were
for real."

How is it possible that someone like Blaine would
understand what a djinn is? He never struck me as the
reading type. Jamaal is not even responding. I'm not sure
why he keeps staring at me. It isn't quite a glare, but it is
making me uncomfortable. I turn away, feeling a cool presence flow past me. Eric's sensor goes off.

"Whoa." The temperature is dropping further. "I'm
freezing."

"Me too." I wrap my arms around my body. "A djinn?
Come on, J, that's something from a fairy tale."

"Didn't you ever pay attention during Sunday
school?" he asks.

"You're not Christian. Why would you go to Sunday
school?" Blaine saunters into the hallway, shaking his head.
"Sunday is *our* holy day."

"Do you even know what you're talking about, man?"
Eric asks, sighing.

"Your religion isn't even real," Blaine scoffs. "Just a
bunch of people killing people."

"Have you heard of the Crusades?" Eric leans back, shooting me an amused smile.

"Dude, that was so long ago." Blaine shrugs.

"Be quiet, Blaine, your ignorance is showing." Abigail gives him a severe look before shifting her attention to the rest of the room. "Sorry, guys."

"J," I persist, as if I didn't hear Blaine's grossly oblivious statements just now, "I paid attention. What are you talking about?"

"It's all there. You just have to think about it." He gives me a hard stare before turning away. "I shouldn't be telling you any of this. You've dealt with too much already."

I blink at him as I slowly get up. "Nothing interesting has ever happened to me."

Rana pats me on the arm. "It's gonna be okay, buddy."

There isn't much for me to go over. I have lived a pretty uneventful life. I shut my eyes, but I see nothing. Just a blank, dark nothing. No memories or images fill my mind. What is Jamaal talking about?

Footsteps echo above and Sondra is standing at the top of the stairs. "The shape of the entity, like a human shadow, matches a djinn."

At this Jamaal turns, breaking his stare. "How do you know?"

"I've been doing this a long time." Sondra smirks. "I had thought demon, but given your ethnicity, djinn is certainly a possibility."

The cool presence draws closer. I'm not feeling cold. It's almost like I'm getting used to the feeling. Without even realizing it, I'm smiling, not bothered by the revelation that not only is my older brother aware of the supernatural, he may have known, from the beginning, what was going on. The EMF flickers. Eric turns it over, shaking it, but I already know the batteries are dead. My ghostly friend drained them.

There are several conversations happening at once. Sondra and Jamaal are facing off in the TV room. The rest of the group is heading to the sunroom. I'm too distracted by how many people I've been crushing on in the last forty-eight hours. I'd be kicked out of my house if I admitted I thought Marissa, the girl from the haunted house, was pretty, downright gorgeous. Then, of course, there's Blaine, who has proven he is truly mostly brawn and little brain. And now my ghost, my friendly protector. I'm imagining the arms of my spirit wrapped around me, protecting me, and I have to shake myself from this far-too-pleasurable daydream.

Eric is already in the sunroom, Amanda looking over his shoulder. Matty and Abigail are consulting her notebook and an image on the tablet. Sondra has my brother's attention, or maybe it's the other way around. I make my way towards the sunroom, feeling the cool presence moving with me.

Rana is staring at me, her eyes narrowed. "Where'd you just go?"

"Nowhere." I can feel my face burning.

"Buddy, none of them are cute enough for you to get tongue-tied over," she chides.

"I know." I take a deep breath. The cool air around me isn't moving. "I'm okay."

Rana nods toward Jamaal. "He's so got a crush on her."

"She's his type." I stick my tongue out at Rana. "Come on, let's see if they found anything."

Once I draw closer, I see Blaine is standing in Nana's room with his phone up, as if he were recording something. Matty's makeshift REM-POD is in the hallway. It's blinking, which means it's active. Eric and Amanda both stare at me wide-eyed as I stop near the now-empty chip bowl.

"What?" I say, guessing that something scary is on the screen.

Amanda beckons me over, waving her hand. "You should probably see this."

Rana is a step behind me as we turn the corner around the table. The video is playing, with choppy audio. There are too many voices speaking at once. The group is moving towards my room, then I hear Abigail clear her throat. The video turns and right behind me, in full view of the camera, is the dark figure. It wasn't my ghostly friend. It was the dark entity. I feel my heart plummet. How do I know which is which? Maybe one is masking the other?

I let out a shaky breath. "That can't be good."

Rana wraps an arm around my shoulders, putting on her most convincing "everything's going to be okay" face. "Don't worry, buddy. This isn't permanent."

"How do you know?" I ask. I feel sick. I know she's trying to help, but she can't possibly know that this won't be permanent or that anything will ever be normal again.

The coolness returns. This time, Eric has the camera rolling and in it, there's nothing. What made the dark entity appear before?

Amanda turns back to the screen. "Can we keep a camera on her?"

Eric nods. "Let me rummage through the truck. Maybe I have something I can point at you. Are you up for wearing headgear?" I must be giving him a serious "no" look because he laughs. "Maybe something else."

"I'd rather have it be human pointing the camera, something that can follow the action," Amanda says. "Did you see this while it was happening?"

"Nope." Eric stops. "Should we ask Sondra?"

"Let's show her the footage." Amanda grabs my wrist, squeezing it. "I've seen worse."

Matty clears his throat. "Maybe we should wait for Sondra and Jamaal."

Amanda replays the video, despite Matty's warning. With the images slowed down, the features of the entity are more in focus. There are claws where there would be fingers, just like I remember. The body is a human shape, but the face—there's nothing there. It isn't exactly a void, but there are no features. No nose, no mouth, no ears. The eyes are hard to discern through all the darkness. One clawed hand is reaching for me. I check my arm, my wrist, but there's nothing. As the video continues, I see the white wisp fly by. The ghost was there. I glance down, seeing Abigail feverishly drawing the entity into her notebook. The detail she's adding at only seeing it once is disarming.

"Now I see our friend." Amanda points to the screen. "That your ghost?"

"Yes," I say with relief in my voice. I had hoped it was there.

"Doesn't look like it engaged with the dark entity." Amanda tries to zoom in. I'm looking over her shoulder, but the screen is too small, and at an angle where I can't quite make out what I hope are not dark figures or shadows roaming around.

Sondra stalks into the room. "What do we have?"

"We have so much." Eric gestures to the laptop. "The dark entity. I caught it on tape."

Sondra raises her eyebrows. "Really?"

A strange sort of gurgling noise comes from nowhere. I instinctively grab onto Rana, who's closest. Something cool reaches out and touches me. Everyone's on alert. Eric grabs the camera while Matty pulls out his EMF. I can see the readings are fluctuating. The lights flicker, and the blare of the REM-POD startles all of us. A loud thud shakes the house. The group begins to move towards the noise. I try to move, too, but there's a wall of coolness in front of me, slowing me down. Jamaal is the closest to the noise and his eyes get big.

"Stay there." He's using his cop voice, the one that even I don't mess around with.

Sondra snatches the camera from Eric's hand. Even though the action is happening right before me, both Rana and I lean into the sunroom, glancing at the laptop. The feed is live. I'm expecting something from my nightmare, or even the awful thing that I saw the day Nana died, but this is something new, something different. Rana is grabbing for my arm, but is repeatedly missing because her eyes are wide open, staring at the scene unfolding before us. I want someone to hold onto, but my hands are still at my sides. I feel frozen. Blaine is not quite walking, but his toes are touching the ground as he floats forward. In the screen, I can see the entity, carrying an unconscious Blaine. I feel like I can hear something. Abigail audibly gasps.

I shut my eyes and turn my head.

"Don't move."

It isn't the voice of the entity. It isn't coming from the laptop. I can feel the hair on my neck moving. Someone is speaking. The ghost? A moment passes before Blaine's body is thrown into the kitchen, making a sickening thump right where I sat when the creature came at me just days ago. I'm not sure where the screaming is coming from, but it won't stop.

TWENTY-FOUR

THE CHAOS THAT ENSUES SHOULD HAVE been unsurprising. It looks like a scene from a sketch comedy. The team (Sondra, Amanda, and Eric) are pretty under control. My brother goes into cop mode and immediately checks to see if Blaine's okay; Abigail stands right behind him. Matty is frozen in place. Rana is trying to get out of the locked door in the sunroom, with little success. I can feel my ghostly protector. It's like there's a wall in front of me, all around me. I know I'm safe.

That is the last thing I should be feeling. Blaine's not moving. Sondra is inching closer. Amanda is scared; her hands are shaking, but she takes the EMF from Eric, who is snapping pictures. The coolness begins to fade and I know the entity is done, for now. A moment passes and I can hear everything again.

Rana is already outside. God knows where she's run off to. Matty has snapped back to reality, turning to his laptop to see the video we have running. Blaine is blinking, sort of looking alert. His head hit the wall pretty hard. There's a dent in it. The entity threw him in the exact same place I was when I saw it last. I look down the hallway, moving a toe closer. Despite any sibling tension, Abigail looks downright terrified that her brother might not be okay.

"Stop." Jamaal is moving in a second, staring at me. "You need to leave."

"What?" His rebuke snaps me from my thoughts.

"It isn't safe." Jamaal puts his hands up. "I don't know what happened. I only know what I saw with my own two eyes. Whatever is here, whatever threw that kid ten feet, it isn't going to just stop. You all need to leave."

"Are you kidding?" Sondra turns, still holding the camera in the opposite direction. "No dice, sir. We are not leaving. Not yet."

"This isn't your house." Jamaal stands up a little taller. Being Indian, he isn't that tall to begin with, but he's trying to glower. "Please. I can't protect all of you."

"Blaine will be fine," Sondra swears and turns back to the room.

Eric lets out a soft laugh, seeing my stricken expression. He keeps his voice down so no one else can hear him and says, "Don't worry about the beefcake. He has a solid rock for a head."

I can't help cracking a smile at this. Blaine is sitting up, rubbing his neck. He's disoriented. Sondra is standing over him with a device of some sort. Eric has a camera trained on them; he shakes his head when Sondra gives him a quizzical look. I'm assuming they're checking for something supernatural. Not much is being said. Blaine goes through a methodical check of everything, slowly getting to his feet once everything seems to check out. There is a grimace on his face, contorting the usual handsomeness. It doesn't seem like he's surprised or scared in the least. More than anything, he looks bored.

The room is still tense. The rest of the team are taking all kinds of audio and video, except for Abigail, who is rubbing Blaine's arm, asking him if he's okay. I hear Matty clear his throat.

"If you have to leave," Matty whispers, "don't wander too far."

"Did you get all of that?" I ask.

Matty nods. "Oh yeah. I switched to high def. The quality is unreal. We could make our own horror movie out of this."

"I think we're living in a horror movie right now." I try to sound glib, but I know I'm scared.

"If that were true, we'd all be dead and Blaine would be the only one to survive." Matty laughs.

This is true in almost every horror movie I've ever seen. It is rare that any characters of color survive. I doubt demons or whatnot are really racist. I think Hollywood just doesn't care about any of us. We're not the desired product. Everyone has to be thin and pretty and white. I'm none of those things. No one here is, except maybe Amanda, and Marissa looked whitish.

Jamaal steps into the sunroom. "Where'd Rana go?" he asks.

I had been wondering this too. "She tried the locked door before making a break for it."

"How about you go find her?" Jamaal is trying to be nice.

I glare. If anything, he's the cop; he'd be better at finding her than me. I know the look he's giving me and I turn. "Fine," I say.

The moment I step outside, I don't feel like I'm being threatened. The heat is stifling. But there's no oppressive feeling, as Amanda described it earlier. I feel hot and my feet start moving. I realize I was tasked with finding Rana, but I know that isn't where I'm going. Why does the haunted house keep calling to me? I almost feel like I need to thank the ghost. The warning from Sondra still rings in my ears. She's right. I have no way of knowing if there is something good about this attachment or not. I know I heard the words. It was like the ghost was there—right there—standing next to me, telling me I'd be safe. That it would

155

protect me. I'm starting to sound like a crazy person. I know this is real, or at least I believe it's real.

I should be more scared. I should be wondering what my brother meant. He effortlessly labeled our attacker. How could he have known? None of this is really on my mind. Everything feels blank. I see the house in the distance. It's calling to me.

I don't even have a flashlight. I might have an audio recorder. After what happened, if the ghost is here, I'm sure it has the ability to talk to me directly. The first step into the old house makes me apprehensive. For some reason, I expect everything to transform, like something happened and all the secrets will be unlocked. Nothing happens. The gaping hole in the ceiling is providing some much needed moonlight through the cloud cover.

The quiet is soothing. After the craziness of the last hour, I should be relieved. I sit down on the bottom step of the stairs. My eyes are just scanning, seeing yet not seeing. I don't realize I'm crying until I feel my T-shirt dampen. At first I thought it was just sweat, but I wipe my hands across my face and feel the tears. Why am I crying? I take a few deep breaths, wondering what's come over me.

"And we meet again." A voice calls from behind me.

I turn, stumbling to my feet. "What are you doing here?"

Marissa smiles. "It was getting a little toxic where I was. Thought I'd take a walk. Didn't expect company."

She sits on a step halfway down the staircase. Just as before, her eyes are holding me in place. I'm stunned by how pretty she is, how much prettier she is than me. God, I need to stop. Women shouldn't be comparing themselves to each other. We're all attractive in our own right.

"Hello?" Marissa is laughing. "Why are you staring at me?"

Words are jumbled in my head. "I didn't expect to run into you again."

Marissa raises her eyebrows. "The bigger question I have is why are you crying?"

God, let the ground beneath me open. A vision of the underground tunnels pops into my head and I shudder. That's the last thing I need right now. A vision of all those dark things coming from those tunnels pops into my head. My mind falters a second time as I feel the warm sun from the dream, for a second, and see that me, that Marissa. It was a nice, safe dream. But it wasn't real. I wish it had been.

"I don't know." This is the only response I can provide. "It's been a long night."

"Family issues?" she ventures.

"Sort of." I don't know what to say. "I'm not sure you'd believe me."

"Sit down." She gestures to the space next to her. "Lay it on me. I'm not going anywhere. I won't judge. I don't know you."

This is so bizarre. I'm not sure what to do. The polite Indian in me says I should sit down. The agitated teenager is telling me to be cool. I take a step closer, settling on standing so I'm at eye level with her.

"What's your story?" I ask, forcing a smile to my face, hoping my tone is soft, like hers always feels as it comes across my ears.

Marissa laughs. "I don't have one, kid. Saw this creepy house. Thought it would be cool. Met a cool girl inside and didn't get to know her, so I kept coming back."

My face is burning. "Yeah, I know the feeling."

I've never flirted before. What am I even doing? I can't cheat on my ghost. Good Lord, I've really lost my mind. Shut up, Roni. Just be cool. Thankfully this takes all of a few seconds. "I don't want to sound completely crazy, so . . ." I cringe. "Do you believe in things that aren't real?"

Marissa laughs. "Like Santa Claus?"

"No." I feel a smile at the edges of my mouth. "I mean not of this world."

"Aliens?" Marissa leans forward. "Of course. I mean, it'd be crazy to think we're alone in the universe."

I put a hand up. "Okay, good to know, but no." I sigh. "Like ghosts and stuff."

Marissa leans back. "Sweetheart, there's no such thing."

My heart plummets. "How can you be sure?" I ask.

"My mother died a long time ago." Marissa's expression sours. "If she were a ghost, she'd have talked to me, don't you think?"

"Not necessarily." God, I am such a dork. "Usually spirits only hang around if they've got unfinished business."

Marissa runs a hand through her hair, saying with a drawl, "Sweetie, if that makes you feel better . . . But, I mean, come on, if there were ghosts, wouldn't they be here of all places?"

"They are." I say this with more certainty than I should.

"What?" Marissa sits up. "That's what you're doing here, isn't it? What you were doing here before?"

"Yes," I admit. "My friend Matty and I do this all the time. We were doing some EVPs—"

"Is that a drug?" Marissa narrows her eyes. "You didn't strike me as the type."

"No." I laugh despite the rush of energy to explain. "Electronic Voice Phenomenon. It's how ghosts can talk on a frequency that we humans can't hear."

"You're serious?" Marissa stares skyward. "I always find the crazy ones."

"I swear I'm not crazy." I want her to believe me. I *need* her to believe me.

"Of course not," Marissa says. I notice she has that skeptical look that I expected to see from Jamaal earlier.

While I didn't bring a flashlight, the audio recorder is still in my pocket, still recording. I stare at the dial. Will there be anything on it? I press stop and then rewind.

"This was recording while we were just at my house." I stop the tape after a few seconds.

"Wait—you were looking for ghosts in your house?" Marissa arches an eyebrow.

"It's a long, convoluted story." I rewind some more, seeing the timer go back, and wait for it to hit about thirty minutes ago. "There might be something on it."

Marissa isn't quite giving me the pathetic look I'd expected. I hurry up the stairs and sit next to her, smelling a soft cinnamon fragrance nearby. The tape is mostly nothing. It is recording, or it was. I hear distant conversation, but it's far away. I shut my eyes, feeling Marissa's eyes on me.

"Don't move."

There it is. Not only did I hear the voice in my head, but the words were spoken aloud right before Blaine got thrown through the kitchen.

Marissa sits up. "Who's that?"

"My friendly ghost." I smile.

"Your what?" Marissa inches away to get a better look at me.

"Bear with me, please." I turn to her. "We think there are two entities. A good one and an evil one."

"How can you be sure?" Marissa asks.

"I just . . . I don't know." I fumble for the right words. "I feel scared when one is around. I don't feel that way with the other."

"Okay." Marissa shakes her head.

"Anyway, some crazy stuff has been happening, and Matty, my friend, invited some professional ghost hunters over." I make this sound normal, somehow.

"People have entire jobs doing this?" Marissa asks.

159

"Not exactly." I laugh. "They have school, but in the summer they do this."

"They're kids?" Marissa asks.

"College kids." I can't believe I'm calling Sondra and Amanda kids. "They're going to school." This is pathetic. Get to the point, Roni. "But they do this sort of thing and are trying to help us figure it out. They don't think the ghost is dangerous, just the other thing."

"I'm sorry." Marissa eases closer. "You've lost me, kid. Though this sounds as exciting as ever."

I lower my eyes. "I'm not crazy."

"I didn't say you were crazy." Marissa nudges me with her shoulder. "I just don't think I can handle the idea that there are dead people, or worse, walking around ready to get me, you, everyone."

This was stupid. I shouldn't have said anything. "I guess."

It's quiet for a moment before I feel Marissa lean in. "You are allowed to believe whatever you want, Roni. I just don't think I have the capacity to believe it. I'm the one being a Luddite."

"I'm being crazy." I start to get up. "I'm sorry."

"Don't be." Marissa's dark eyes are on me. "You have nothing to apologize for."

"I should go." I'm on my feet in a second.

"I know how to clear a room." Marissa tries to force a laugh, but gets up as I do. "I'm sorry for being a jerk. It's been a long, well, everything, you know?"

"Right." I feel like such an idiot.

"Either way, Roni," Marissa says, following as my feet are moving towards the hole in the window, "please be careful. Sometimes, believing in something can make it that much scarier, powerful, I don't know."

Her warning seems familiar. Did she say that in my dream too? "Right," I say.

"Roni . . ." Marissa reaches out, her hand icy cold. "I'm sorry. I just don't want to see you get hurt."

"Why would I get hurt?" I ask, once again hoping the ground would open beneath me.

"I don't know." Marissa holds my gaze. "Please don't leave because I'm being a jerk."

Flashing lights in the distance are my easiest way out. "I bet that's my brother."

"Your brother is a police officer?" she asks, her voice lowering.

I nod. "I'll see you around."

The look on her face deflates me completely. I'm such a loser. I couldn't pretend to be cool for six minutes. It doesn't matter. I edge outside and see the patrol car stopping at the edge of the road. I trudge forward, noticing Rana and Matty in the back. Jamaal is just glaring. And the night isn't over yet.

TWENTY-FIVE

THE CAR IS SILENT. JAMAAL IS FUMING. To his credit, he hasn't said one word. This solace will surely be short-lived. It takes about five minutes to pull back up to the house. Blaine is sitting in the back of Eric's van, an ice pack on his neck. Abigail is shaking her head, on the phone, shooting us an apologetic smile. There is, surprisingly, no ambulance. I start to ask, but stop, knowing I'm in a whole heap of trouble for disappearing.

"In the house. All three of you. Now." Jamaal doesn't turn his gaze from the closed garage door.

Something in me bubbles up. "You told me to leave, so I did."

I can hear Rana pulling on the lever inside. This is a cop car. The back doors don't open from inside.

"I told you to find Rana." Jamaal turns to me. "I did not tell you to go back to a haunted house. To *break into* said haunted house. Trespassing is illegal."

I bite back the smart retort. Do I fight back? I can't think of anything coherent to say. I pop the door open, opening the back door for Matty. Rana hurries after him, giving me a worried look.

"I hid in Bhai's car," she admits. "Are you okay?"

"Yeah." I shrug.

"Is Blaine okay?" she asks.

"I have no idea." I don't care. I just want to curl up in a ball and go to sleep. Then it occurs to me that I haven't really slept in days. Maybe I'll dream about Marissa again. At least in my dreams I can be a lot less uncool.

Jamaal is having a quiet talk with Sondra. The two aren't noticing any of us. I pull on Rana's arm, hoping she'll follow me as I get closer to the van. Matty is just a step behind us. The closer we get, the more of Abigail's phone conversation we can hear. It sounds like she's alerting her mother there was an accident, a generous way of describing what happened.

"Eric," I say as I stop a few steps behind him, "what did you find? What happened?"

Eric grins. The guy has the most infectious smile. I was feeling like garbage just a moment ago, and now things don't seem quite so dire.

"What didn't we find?" he counters. "The house, I don't think, is haunted. But that thing is one pissed-off son of a gun. It threw Blaine clear across the room. After you guys all disappeared, we got a closer look. I can't wait to print these images. I've never, in the seven years I've been doing this hardcore, seen anything so clear. It is real, and it isn't alone."

"You mean the ghost?" I ask.

"No." He leans in, grinning further. "The ghost left with you. There was more than one dark entity. It's like a family or something, maybe. I don't know for sure yet."

Rana's grip on my arm is starting to hurt. "What?"

My mind is running in sixteen different directions. Why is there a family in our house? How do they know the ghost left with me? How many did they catch? Why did it throw Blaine out of Nana's room? How can he be so calm about this?

Eric must not realize how frightened we're getting. The tablet is out in seconds. The images are way too real for me to look at. Each image taken after Blaine was thrown is featuring not one, not two, but up to three dark figures. None are bigger or smaller than the other. How is this even possible?

Matty cuts between us and the tablet. "Man, I think they're freaking out."

"Oh?" Eric sounds genuinely surprised. "My bad, ladies. This is crazy stuff. I'm just being an oaf, again."

"Okay, okay." Abigail turns to us. "I might have to bolt, guys. The playboy is too fragile to stay." Despite her words, Abigail looks worried. "Don't worry, Casanova, you'll be breaking hearts again in no time."

"I don't think I can drive." Blaine winces.

"Clearly." Amanda comes around the corner. "We're going to have to get Blaine home soon. The entities waited for him to be alone."

"I was alone when it first attacked," I offered, shuddering at the memory. "Hey, how do you know the ghost went with me?"

Amanda's eyes slide to Matty. "He had a camera on you as you left. The white smoke left with you."

"When all of you moved," I start, still feeling foolish after talking to Marissa about this, "I felt like it stopped me."

"There was something between us and it," Rana chimed in. "I felt it."

"There are, for sure, more than two entities involved here," Amanda says. "The ghost doesn't appear to be evil, per se, but I think we can all agree that the dark entities are not good. Although, one could argue that the dark entities are trying to protect you from your ghost. And it's also very possible that your ghost could really be a demon in disguise. There are just too many variables right now."

My mind is spinning trying to process all of these options. I'm not sure I'd given it that much thought and Amanda distilled it all in seconds. Jamaal and Sondra came up behind us while Amanda was talking. Sondra gives me an unexpected hug. I can't remember the last time I really hugged someone. This could be an Indian thing, but I think my parents are just not huggers.

"Don't worry, Roni," Sondra says. "I called a few friends in the business. We're not leaving. I think Jamaal doesn't want us to stay, but is too polite to ask us to leave again. Beside, you know we're here to help. Amanda and I are going to camp out in your sister's room, taking turns watching the feed in your room. Eric will be downstairs with Jamaal after he and Jamaal get Blaine and Abigail home."

I want to be relieved, but now I'm more scared than I was before. "Thanks."

"Don't worry." Sondra's voice is soothing. She also hasn't let go of me. "I get that you're scared. Hell, I'd be terrified right now. It can't hurt you. We won't let it."

"Is that what you'll tell Blaine?" I ask.

Sondra laughs. "I have told that boy to be careful. We replayed a lot of the tape. He was baiting. The best way to get an entity upset is to call it names. He says he wants to learn about all of this stuff, but I wonder. I wish he were smarter, like his sister. How you doing over there, Abby?"

A forced smile crosses her face. "Worried. I have no idea what to tell my mom."

"He fell." Sondra winks. "Tell her the truth and they'll think we're all crazy."

Abby nods. "I hate lying."

"And you should. But in this case, the truth could be worse," Sondra warns.

"Ready whenever you are, chica." Eric smiles at Abby before turning to Roni. "Don't worry. We won't let anything happen, okay?"

I nod, uncertain what to do. Jamaal nudges me towards the house. "Don't forget, you've got a cop in the house."

Rana pulls me close as we head to the house. Matty isn't far behind. He and Abigail are talking about something as they separate. I can hear the camera taking pictures. I doubt my ghost friend will appreciate the accusations. At least twice tonight the ghost has saved me. But could it be saving me for itself? I turn to Matty, the question in my eyes.

"Don't worry, Roni," Matty says. "I've got the cameras rolling all the time. I would stay, but my parents aren't okay with that, you know?"

"Right." The words come naturally, but Matty is the one I trust the most. I don't want him to leave, but I hate to ask him to stay when I know he can't. "Did you see it all?"

Matty lowers his head, the beanie covering his features. "Yeah, Roni. It isn't good. And I know you think the ghost is protecting you, but we don't know that."

"How can we know?" I ask.

"Ask it?" Matty says. "I mean, yeah, it can lie, but at least try. We can't possibly know the truth, not really. Or maybe ask it to appear, really appear."

"Is there a way we can force it to appear?" I wonder aloud.

"I'll look into it." Matty stops at the door. "Get some salt. Put it across the doors, windows, you know. The only danger is, if the entities are already inside, the salt can trap them there."

I rub my forehead. "This got worse pretty fast."

"It was getting bad already, Ron." Matty forces a smile. "Jamaal can keep you safe."

"Even if he does believe all this stuff, he is a poor replacement for you." I feel the tears threatening.

"Just don't do anything crazy." Matty gives me a stern look and finger wag. "The haunted house isn't any safer. You shouldn't go back there until we know more."

The nodding is becoming mechanical. The second my foot crosses into the house, I feel that heaviness of the air. There are eyes on me. I try to push the image of the entities from Nana's room out of my mind, but it isn't working. Rana gives me a half hug.

"Why'd you go to that house?" she asks.

I wish I knew. I shrug. "I just felt like that was where I should be."

"I saw you leaving." She sounds hurt. "I was kinda surprised you didn't come looking for me."

"Sorry." I really mean it, even if my sorrow is focused inwardly. "I'm freaking out."

"I know." Rana tries to laugh. "I thought I'd be spending a couple quiet days with my favorite cousin. Turns out I'll be spending it with a lot of other people . . . seen and unseen."

My eyes are tearing up again. "How are we supposed to live here?"

"I don't know," Rana admits. "I'm scared, but then again, we're supposed to trust in God."

There is no "right" at the end of her sentence. It isn't a question. In a lot of religious texts, it talks about always praying, in good and bad times. I sometimes feel like I just go through the motions. I pray five times a day, I fast during the holy month, I do the required actions, but does that mean God's watching out for me? If He's watching now, what's He doing?

I think about how much my parents pray. Sometimes my mom gets up extra early to pray. During Ramadan, the holy month, she will be praying all night. It seems excessive, especially when I think about our lot in life. I could let the bitterness in, but I push it away. I should just be grateful. I'm safe. My brother's safe. My cousin is safe. It's like Marissa said, if I believe that it can hurt me, it might.

That embarrassment crops back up. I'm not sure I could have been any more ridiculous. What must she have thought? In an opening conversation with anyone you want to impress, it probably shouldn't include a discussion about ghosts. I haven't slept in ages. I don't bother to say much and pour myself into bed.

Twenty-Six

FOR THE FIRST TIME IN WHAT SEEMS LIKE ages, I really do fall asleep. I am exhausted. But a full night's rest must not be in the cards for me. The same dream from the previous night is beginning again. I think it's a dream, but I'm not sure.

My eyes are blinking open. It's still dark out. The light from the hallway is spilling into my room through the half-open door. I squint and see that between the light and the bed is a figure. Figures, I correct myself, feeling my heart begin to race. I can feel one bead of sweat, followed by others, moving down my back, dampening my shirt. The dark entity is not alone. There are five of them, I count, and suddenly I can't move. My hands and feet are stuck to my bed. I can't open my mouth. I don't feel my ghostly friend at all. Even the slightest twitch creates no movement, not an inch. I stare at my hand, willing my fingers to uncurl, but they won't budge.

The five figures are standing before my bed. I can hear them speaking, though I don't understand any of it. I'm straining against unseen chains. My body is upright in bed. But my feet aren't touching the bed. Am I floating? I can't move my head, but I can see my fingers, my toes. If I were still asleep in bed, neither of these things would seem possible. Above my door is the word "God" in Arabic. It jolts me a little.

The only thing I can do, if the cameras aren't jumping anyone into action, is to pray. I force myself to shut my eyes. I can still see the figures in my head, hear them. I repeat the words of one of the few prayers I know by heart. I don't know how long this goes on. I'm praying loudly in my head, tuning the other noise out. I wake up, jumping from the bed.

The door opens a little farther. Amanda peeks in. "Morning. You okay?"

I shake myself awake, drawing in a slow breath. "I just had a dream that five of them were at the foot of my bed." I want to be sure I'm awake now. I don't see any sign of those things, those figures. My hands are still clammy, my neck tight. I shrug my shoulders, feeling everything loosen. There's a chill in the room. I wonder if the ghost was ever here. Matty's words ring through my ears and I wonder if my assumption of a protective ghost is ill placed.

Amanda gives me a quizzical look and turns to head into the hallway. I push the comforter away, following her. She's wearing sweats. The pullover says Northwestern on it. The tablet is on the floor and she rewinds the video, using Matty's feed I notice, and the camera cuts in and out.

"Wow," Amanda marvels. "I didn't notice."

"Did you sleep?" I ask.

"We try not to." Amanda laughs. "Your sister's room is quite lush."

I nod. "I can make breakfast."

"Please don't." Amanda puts her hand up. "You guys aren't supposed to be hosting us. We never meant for this to turn into an overnighter, but I'm glad we stayed."

"Me too." I am afraid of the answer as I ask the question, "Did anything else happen?"

"Nope," she reassures me. "The feeds are mostly clear. Nothing as glaring as what happened before you went to bed."

"Blaine?" I wonder who got him home.

"Fine." Amanda laughs. "Abigail is more embarrassed than anything. It's unfortunate we get stuck with Blaine all the time. He really shouldn't have been goading the dark entities. All we want are some answers. The EVPs were interesting."

"How so?" I hear some rustling and see Rana emerging from Mom and Dad's room. It doesn't look like she slept much either.

"The voices are there." Amanda shuts her eyes for a moment. "The dark entities, as we're calling them, are not happy. I don't think they're speaking English. Your brother either wouldn't tell us or didn't know what they were saying. The ghost, I guess, is speaking English. Every time there was a dark entity near you, it appeared or reacted, and a couple times it spoke. I can't figure out how we can tell if they're all connected or not."

My mind is swirling with what all of this could mean as I head into the bathroom. The reflection in the mirror seems familiar. I'm expecting to find the same disarray as the morning after the party. The kitchen looks the same. I notice a line of salt across the entry to Nana's room. It almost makes me feel brave enough to walk by, but I don't.

I jump when I see Eric sitting in the sunroom. A huge pullover is blocking his face from me, but he turns, flashing me a smile. The morning rays made it look like someone was standing behind him. The windows are fogged up from the heat outside and the coolness inside.

"Hey." He gives me a slight wave. "Get some rest?"

"A little," I answer.

"We think the activity has died down now that Blaine is gone." Eric can't help letting a laugh escape.

I laugh. I know all too well what that feeling is like. The white kids I go to school with think we're all aberrations, like we don't belong because we're part of some weird culture. A few act like it's interesting, but they're always itching to make a break for it the second they can. To them, all of us minorities are outsiders, people that don't belong, are taking away from their perfect lives. I wish they could see that we all enrich each other's lives. I wonder if Blaine sees us that way. He was pretty rude to everyone, and he has some issue with Matty. It wouldn't surprise me at all if Blaine gives Matty a hard time for being transgender. I can't even imagine what that must be like. Matty knows who he is, and he has people around him who want him to be happy, to be himself. There will always be people who won't accept him, or more likely, want to force their values onto him.

I mean, if you really read through history, you'll see there were a lot of men who identified as women. A few hundred years later, they still just want to be themselves. Who does it hurt? No one. We'll all be judged by our faults and merits by God. I don't have time to worry about what someone else is doing. I wonder about the people who have nothing but time to worry about everyone else except themselves. As my father likes to say, keep your own house clean first, then offer to help others. I don't think that means barge into someone's house and start rearranging things as you think they should be.

My mind is wandering. Eric gives me a slight smile as he gets up and walks toward the coffee pot. I give it a sidelong look. We're Indian. We don't ever have coffee.

He laughs. "We brought our own, coffee maker and all."

"Right." I laugh and walk into the sunroom.

The computer is filled with lots of programs, and there are two larger monitors displaying some of the smaller versions of video feeds connected to the system. Eric has quite the impressive setup. I hear Amanda come downstairs, stopping and talking to Eric in the foyer. I feel something around me, that coolness again. Is my ghost here? Remembering what Matty said, I decide I should ask.

In a very quiet whisper I ask, "Are you here?"

The coolness passes through me. I shudder. The lights flicker.

I look upwards. "Is that a yes?"

The lights flicker once more. Could this be a coincidence? Am I just projecting? Hoping for a response when there really isn't one?

"Are you here to protect me?" I ask.

There's no response. Or at least no clear one. I turn, sighing. I'm such an idiot. I think of my conversation with Marissa the night before. Each detail of how stupid I am comes back into glaring focus. She was so sweet, so kind—nothing like almost everyone else I know. I prattled on about nonsense and she just obliged. Seen in another light, she might have just been patronizing me.

That thought can't hold much weight with me. I was completely losing it and she calmed me down with logic in seconds. If anything, I need more of that voice in my head. This could all just be something I'm imagining. I squeeze my eyes shut. Can I just turn that inner monologue off?

It doesn't stop. Everything from last night plays back through my head, faster than it happened. A few scenes stick out. The whole house being in chaos, Blaine being thrown through the kitchen, and Marissa's kind, comforting smile, the same one from my dreams. That last image sticks in my head for a few moments longer before I'm drawn back to the present.

Rana comes down, giving me a worried look before grabbing a bowl, or trying to. "Where are all the plates and stuff?"

This comment snaps me back to reality. "It's a long story. The disposable stuff is in the dining room."

"Should I ask or just get my cereal and go?" she asks.

I don't respond, turning to the windows. My eyes freeze as I see the words, the answer to my question, written in the condensation.

"No."

Twenty-Seven

A COUPLE OF SIMPLE QUESTIONS AND the team, once again, goes into action. Someone woke Sondra, and now she is directing the activity. Eric is rewinding through the video. Amanda is sifting through the audio, a massive pair of headphones covering her ears. Abigail and Matty won't return until later, I'm told. I just sit, staring at nothing. Did the dark entity write the response? Did my ghost? Are they one and the same? The throbbing in my head continues, and there are just way too many people in our house.

Rana has me sitting on the patio after the din dies down. There's no cacophony of noise, just the quiet nature sounds. She's eating cereal. I'm staring at a single slice of toast and a cup of tea. The only thing I want is the tea. God, I've become my mother. She'll forgo food for tea. I'm doing about the same right now. The tea is keeping me alert. I don't even want to think about going back in that house. I'm wearing my pajamas, so at some point I will need to shower and get dressed. For now, I'm just going to stare off at nothing. I notice the flowers in the garden are all wilted. The four-by-eight cement floor is really all that constitutes the patio. There is an old table with mismatched chairs around it. My dad used to grill at our old house, but we haven't done it since we moved. The corners of the patio have boxes with plants in them that are hanging on for dear life.

Since Rana is the cousin closest to me, who knows me the best, knows I prefer silence over generally anything else, she isn't pressing me for conversation. Her eyes are focused on the bowl in front of her, which is now empty. I wish I could just get on a plane and not live in this nightmare. In a couple days, she'll be home and safe. I'll still be here.

"Want anything?" Rana asks, breaking the companionable silence.

I shake my head. She gets up, leaving me alone outside. I don't feel scared. I feel like those things are only going to get me inside our house. There's no reason for me to believe this. I haven't been attacked, not really, not like Blaine. Can I live my life knowing that these things will always be there?

My eyes are shutting, even if I'm sitting, almost curled into a ball, on a chair on the patio. I hear some rustling, but I'm just too tired to turn.

"You look beat," the voice says.

I nod. "Didn't sleep much."

"You okay?" the voice asks.

I shrug, rolling my head towards the voice. I'm immediately taken aback when I see who it is. "How'd you find me, Marissa?"

She's all sunshine and a big smile. Unlike all the dark clothes I'd seen her in before, she's wearing a summer dress and flip-flops with a pair of sunglasses perched on her head. "I may have followed you after you left. The cop car is kinda hard to miss."

I nod. Once again, I look absolutely slovenly and she resembles a supermodel. It's too late to change those circumstances now. "Right."

"I feel like such an asshole about last night," she says, looking me straight in the eye as she speaks.

"I was being the ass," I argue. "I shouldn't have said anything."

Marissa leans on the edge of her chair. "No, cutie, it was me. I have met one nice person in this desolate town and I offend her in a matter of minutes. Let me apologize, at the very least."

Did she just call me "cutie"? That has got to be a first. No one has ever referred to me as attractive. "You don't need to."

"I'm sorry, Roni, really," Marissa says, her big brown eyes forcing me to look at her, to not look away. "You have every right to believe in ghosts, in demons."

"I guess." I say the words, even though I feel like she still thinks I'm nuts.

"You should trust your gut, trust that feeling that you have, the one that told you that your ghost was protecting you," she says. "It's right, even if the signs are all pointing in the other direction. You know what this is, Roni; you just need to realize the truth."

A moment or two passes and I blink myself awake. Did I just dream that? Wouldn't be the first time I've dreamed about Marissa. It didn't feel like a dream. There's no one out here. I feel really tired again. And confused. The bread has been pulled off of my plate by an enterprising bird. The tea is cold. It's getting warmer outside. I feel drained.

The team is still set up in the sunroom. Eric gives me a shy sort of smile. Sondra and Jamaal are busy chatting, or possibly flirting in the kitchen. Amanda stops me before I get too far, pointing the camera at me for several seconds.

"You okay?" she asks as she puts the camera down.

"No," I reply with a laugh. "You?"

"Never better." She laughs. "Eat something—really eat something. You're going to be fine, I promise."

I nod. "Where'd Rana go?"

"Your cousin?" Amanda asks. "I saw her about a half hour ago. Then you just sat outside for a while."

"No cameras on me?" I ask, surprised by the rare moment of solitude.

"We can't see through the condensation on the windows." Amanda is bent over the laptop.

I turn, putting a hand on her arm. "Was I alone?"

"I assume so." Amanda shrugs. "I didn't pry. Why?"

"Nothing." I feel silly all over again.

I shouldn't be suspicious of everyone and everything. It was sweet of Marissa to come and visit me. I feel like a complete fool. It didn't sound like she believed me. If I were in her shoes, I wouldn't have believed me either. I wonder if I fell asleep on her. I'm so tired, I'm liable to fall asleep standing upright. At this rate, I'm probably going to replay that conversation over and over again, not paying attention to much else, if that's possible.

Sondra comes closer, and I see Jamaal standing near Nana's room, his mouth a thin line. The tension has compounded while I napped.

"You don't look like you got any rest," Sondra says, stopping to stand in front to me.

"I feel exhausted," I admit. "I thought something happened this morning."

"Amanda told me." Sondra has a hand on my arm. "Did you fall asleep out there?"

I shrug. "Think so, yeah."

"I doubt anything will happen during the daylight hours," Sondra says, nudging me towards the sitting room. "If you're too scared to sleep, we're headed on a fact-finding mission. You could come with us."

I raise my eyebrows. "Something you can't find on the internet?"

Eric looks, his mouth wide open, pretending to be offended. "I know you did not just insinuate that I was not doing my job."

"Of course not." I laugh, feeling a little less stressed just from that action.

Amanda comes over, offering me a steaming mug of tea. "The archives at the courthouse hasn't digitized all of their files. We can do some more research on that old house. Did you ever notice anything peculiar?"

"I have been there before." Sondra motions to Eric. "We took a ton of pictures, but we didn't find anything."

"Other than what you saw in the video, no, I never saw anything." I replay the initial ghost hunt and nothing comes to mind. While I dreamt about the house, I saw something, but that wasn't real, was it? The thought of staying in this house alone, or even sort of alone, isn't appealing. "You're sure you want me to come with you?"

"Of course." Sondra puts a hand on my arm. "Ask your cousin if she wants to come too. We can pile into Eric's van."

"I might have to check in at work, for a like a second. So just stay safe if I disappear, okay?" Jamaal says, trailing after me as I head towards the stairs.

"Okay," I say, but I wonder how he could even think to leave with this going on. Although, while we're out of the house, that might be the best time to go. Nothing should happen at the courthouse, right?

Twenty-Eight

The field trip begins with me put-
ting on my nicer pair of jeans, faded blue high tops, and a
yellow flannel on over a Care Bears shirt. I shudder, wondering what Marissa would think seeing me like this, what
she could possibly ever see in me. There's a low spot in my
stomach that is doing flips just thinking about her. I drift
downstairs, following as everyone piles into Eric's van. My
eyes glaze over as I rest my head against the window in Eric's
surprisingly clean vehicle. My parents' cars are both ridiculous. I'm convinced there is something living in the trunk
of my father's car.

Orland Park, just an hour or so outside of Chicago, is
bustling this bright Friday morning. I lower my eyes from
the sunlight that feels like it's burning my retinas. I'm surprised at how easily Eric finds a parking spot. There are a
ton of cop cars around, too. Given the time of year, I'm
not surprised to see kids around, like little ones. They are
crowded around a water fountain, laughing and being generally gleeful, as parents look on. I can't imagine it would be
easy to corral a child in the confines of a boring government
building. As we trudge forward, we pass about a dozen signs
telling us not to bring cameras, cell phones, weapons, or
food, for some reason. I mean, why would they have a cafeteria in there if you couldn't bring food? Are they forcing
people to buy their food, like the movie theater?

I glance at Eric's laden bag and grab his arm. "Wait, doesn't the sign say we can't take that?"

A moment passes before Amanda, Sondra, and Eric laugh. Sondra grips both of my wrists. "You're adorable." She nods to the sign. "Yeah, but." She pulls a badge out of her bag. "I volunteer downstairs. So, you're with me. Act natural."

"I'm dying to know what normal is for you." Amanda laughs, Rana joining in.

"Sorry, buddy." Rana pats me on the back. "I didn't say bad things behind your back, but this isn't the normal you."

I try to hide the hurt I'm feeling. It's stupid to be upset that Rana would say that, or anything, really. Nothing I'm dealing with is normal. I should try to be nicer.

"I guess I am being a tad abrasive," I admit.

Amanda's expression deflates in seconds, the smile gone. "Oh my God, Roni, no. You are being the perfect host. And you're under a ton of stress. Rana just said you were usually more talkative, downright funny."

I arch an eyebrow. "I don't ever remember being funny."

"You wouldn't," Rana says as she chuckles. "Don't look so depressed. It isn't like you have to work here."

I force a smile across my face, wishing it were real. Amanda shoots me an apologetic look, following close behind Sondra. I wish I could be even half as cool as either of them.

Eric holds the door open for everyone as we file in. "Ladies first."

The deputies for the sheriff's office, the ones who are here at the metal detectors, are not intimidating at all. I try not to stare as at least two of the men look like they're expecting twins any second now. The mustard yellow shirts and dark brown pants aren't helping. Who designs these uniforms? A blind person would do a better job. Other than the two portly gentleman, the other two deputies look like they go to school with me. One is at least a half a foot shorter than me. All of them are white. The fact that none of us are white makes me uncomfortable. No matter where I go, I know people are staring at me because I'm not white. My brother is a few shades lighter than me, but I wonder how he gets treated. People probably just assume he's Hispanic.

Sondra starts a conversation up with the largest of the deputies, Rick. The man is grinning and laughing, barely paying any attention to any of us. Eric sets his bag on the conveyor belt and we all dutifully walk through. The alarm goes off a few times, but no one takes much notice.

"You brought a lot of friends today," Rick chortles as he speaks. "Interns?"

"That would be amazing," Sondra replies, affixing her badge to her belt. "Eric is still the best intern we'll ever have, except maybe Abby."

Rick nods. "Just remember you're responsible for everyone."

This is the closest to a warning we receive. The deputies let us pass without another word, laughing and joking amongst themselves. For a Friday, I think I would have expected more people. Sondra leads us down a staircase that bends to the lower level. I don't go to a lot of government buildings, but it is so stark, so white. At school, there are posters everywhere. Here there's a sign pointing to different types of archives and a pair of vending machines sitting in a corner, their lights flickering like a last gasp at life. I am imagining that all of the candies in there are expired. There's a cafeteria around the corner. A pungent fried smell is emanating from there. I breathe through my mouth, hoping to keep the scent from gluing itself into my nose.

Sondra leads us around the corner, flashing her badge at a door and punching a few numbers in. She pulls the door open. "Why don't you come in?"

Amanda hurries through. I'm surprised to see Rana close behind her. Have they become quick friends? Is that jealousy I'm feeling? I sigh, staring skyward as Eric pulls me forward.

"You sleepwalking?" Eric asks.

"No." I grimace, hoping it looks more like a smile. Any other thoughts are stopped as we enter.

The door slams shut behind us, and I hear some sort of mechanical lock sound clicking into place. The room contains rows and rows of wooden bookshelves. I take a wary step forward and see books and boxes lining everywhere. There are framed documents on the wall. I almost want to pinch myself. Am I dreaming? Is this the exact same place I dreamt about? It looks the same. It was right here that Marissa and I were, for a second. Why would I dream about a courthouse that I've never been too? I take a deep inhale. It smells kind of the same, but there's something missing, I can't quite put my finger on it.

Eric nudges me towards the closest table. "We can set up over here."

I follow, pulling the plastic chair out and sitting down. "When did I join your team?"

"You seem pretty tech savvy." Eric pulls one laptop out, then another. A couple handheld scanners emerge as well. "We'll be compiling what they give us. You don't strike me as a sit-and-read-boring-documents type."

I shake my head. "I'm having a hard time concentrating."

"That's the spirit." Eric laughs. "Something mindless might do you some good. But if you're really not down with it, take a walk around. There's a lot of really cool old stuff. Just don't steal anything."

"Uh, well, now that you told me I can't I guess I can't," I reply, rolling my eyes, once again feeling a smile breaking across my face. How is it possible that Eric is one of the only ones who can make me smile with all this going on?

I watch for a few more seconds, but it looks like Eric isn't going to be ready anytime soon. My gaze flows to Sondra, who is giving quiet instructions out to Amanda and Rana. That stab of jealousy comes back, but I try to brush it off. Everyone is here to help me. I'm not alone. I feel a twinge of loneliness, wishing someone was here for me, in a way that wasn't just friendly or familial. As expected, my thoughts bend to Marissa. God, how am I so lovesick over a girl? When did I go gay? Did I go gay? Is this just a passing fancy, as they say? Who says that? Am I now responding to questions I'm posing to myself?

I let out a slow breath. I need to get a hold of myself. I give Sondra a small smile and continue around the corner. Just like in my dream, the room seems to go on and on. I can barely see the end of the row. Each bookshelf is nearly touching the ceiling and is about ten or so feet wide. The break between them has signs with dates on them. I'm in a row for 1965. I continue, and at the next break it is 1955. The numbers continue to descend to 1905. At the end of the long row is another set of tables and chairs. I wouldn't mind being alone. And for once, in like days, I feel like nothing can touch me, hurt me.

My eyes pass across the bindings of dozens of books. There are deed books, marriage books, all of them with rows and rows of names and dates. I pull one out at random. The handwriting is difficult to read. I set the book on the table and pull a chair out. I flip through the pages, being careful as the book is ancient. The paper is thicker than what we have today. The ink is still fairly dark. I wish I could write like this. It's fancy calligraphy. My penmanship probably would never get this good, this crisp.

The boredom starts to take over. I feel antsy, like I need to go running. The tiredness is gone and now I'm left with the desire to do something, I just don't know what that something is. I set the book back, looking through the shelf and seeing a face on the other side. When I move around the long bookshelf, there's no one there. My pulse has quickened, but nothing like the last few nights. I shut my eyes. The face looked human, not demonic. A hand on my shoulder makes me jump.

"Where'd you go?" Eric puts both hands up. "We were worried you got lost."

I put my hand over my pounding heart. "Jeez, are you wearing soundless shoes?"

Eric nods. "Yes, my ninja attire for Latinos. It's all the rage. Are you just looking around back here?" He smirks. "My invitation for work wasn't enticing enough for you?"

"It's not that," I say in a rush. "Well, maybe a little."

Eric nods. "I don't want you to feel left out, chica."

I lower my eyes. How is it possible I feel invisible and yet everyone's constantly watching me? "I don't know what I'm supposed to do."

"I can't tell you that." Eric's normal smile vanishes as he looks serious, concentrating. "This is stuff I can do, but you—you need to figure out where you stand on all of this. We're bound to find something out—either about you, your family, or someone else. So be ready."

With that he turns and walks away. Well, I wanted to be alone anyway. The last thing I want to do is sit in front of a computer and scan things. I turn, passing the tables and moving around the edge of the room. Was that Eric I'd seen between the stacks? He couldn't have possibly moved that quickly. I wonder if we're alone down here.

The lights flicker above me and I stop, grabbing onto the closest bookcase. The flickering continues for a moment longer and then stops. I felt like the whole room was dark. Did no one else get scared?

A hand lands on my shoulder a second time and I'm relieved that Eric didn't wander too far. "Did you see that?"

I turn around, but there is no one there. My heart jumps to my throat.

The row goes on for quite a ways, and I take a tentative step forward, seeing a figure. I guess we aren't alone. I walk closer, slowing as I get near. The figure isn't facing me, the pullover hanging over his head. The lights begin to flicker again. I take a step back, still a good ten feet away. The lights continue to flicker and the figure is staring at me. The face is pale with deep fissures crossing it. The skin is crawling, moving, fading, turning to darkness, to nothing. I know what this is. I freeze and the lights flicker again. The figure is now halfway to me. I stumble over a box, grabbing at anything to get to my feet, papers flying. The lights begin to flicker again, and I feel a gentle tingling ripple across my skin as I take off at a full sprint.

All the years of long distance running do nothing for my ability to sprint. I take a sharp turn at a bookcase, spinning and trying to find my way forward. I'm not totally looking where I'm going and slam into someone, books flying everywhere.

"Sorry." I massage my shoulder, staring at the mess I've created. "I wasn't looking."

I can hear the other person got thrown past the bookcase, and I'm almost afraid to look. A few books are being collected and a wry smile from my dream girl is all the response I need to move a lot faster. Any thoughts of the thing that had been chasing me are fading. The lights aren't flickering either, making me think I might be safe.

"And we meet again," Marissa says, smiling.

I shake my head. "I'm really sorry." I bend down, trying to help her collect the books I've knocked over. "I thought I saw something. It doesn't matter."

"Sure it does." The sundress has been replaced with a tight pair of jeans and a button-down plaid flannel, not unlike one of my favorites, just pink and orange. I don't care for bright colors, but on Marissa, they make her radiant.

The books are being stacked into an orderly pile, one that neither of us could possibly lift. I grab a chair, stacking them there and offering her a hand. Her grip is cool and firm. I want to be bold, but I demur. Being bold isn't me.

"You know me." I laugh. "I'm always convinced something's out there, you know, something unseen."

"In here that wouldn't surprise me," she says, still not having let go of my hand, even though we're both standing. "What did you see?"

Unlike before, I don't see skepticism in her expression. Her eyes are set on me, her attention focused on me, her hand still firmly in my grasp. It makes me feel lighter, less worried. I wipe my free hand on my jeans, feeling the dust come free. "I'm not sure."

"You're sure." She leans back, almost glaring, letting go. "You just don't want to say. Look, I get it." She turns away, and it feels like the room has gotten decidedly cooler. "I am being serious, Roni, I'm . . . I want to know."

When she turns back to face me, I have no resistance left in me. "It was something. About as tall as me, but not real, not human."

The skeptic hasn't left, but she nods. "Go on."

I shut my eyes for a second. I felt stupid last night and this morning. Now I feel like I can't lose any more coolness in her eyes. "I'm not trying to be difficult. I really don't know how to describe something I've never seen before." I laugh, hoping to break the tension. "If I could draw, I'd do that." She still looks way too serious. "I was too scared to get a better look."

Despite that childish response, she seems relieved, her body language relaxing. "Why do you think it's after you?"

I shrug. "I'm not sure. The gang." I gesture to where I think the front of the room is. "They're here looking into it. I'm supposed to be helping."

"How are you helping?" She smiles, a flirty sort of smile.

Treacherous butterflies are zooming through my insides. Why am I so nervous? I know what it is, but do I need to distract myself with this inner monologue right now? Focus on the pretty girl in front of you. Stress out about anything else later. I laugh. "Me? Well, I think I cleared the area, so it's safe."

It looks like she's going to say something, but then she turns, picking up the first book on the stack. "I came here to do some research too. There's some interesting history in this place."

In a second she's stopped being flirty, being interested in me. I hide the hurt as best I can, watching as she sets the book on the table and flips through it. Her gaze beckons me closer and I take a deep breath, quieting any argument I might make.

Her fingers slide down the page, stopping at a random entry. "The house—the haunted one you're always in—it was bought and sold six times in ten years. Each sale was prompted by a death of some sort."

I nod. "Okay."

A moment passes. I'm not sure I can tear my eyes away from her. There's that soft scent of cinnamon around her. It takes me to December, the most notable holiday season in our house as we're forced to celebrate Christian holidays if we want to fit in. I'm really staring right now. Her hair is a dark brownish color with hints of blond. There is a smattering of freckles across her cheeks. She lets out a sigh, turning to look at me, seeing me stare at her.

"You're supposed to be pretty and smart." She reaches for another book. I'm too startled at the sudden switch to react. She hands me one book, taking the next one from the pile, setting it on the table. "The house also was empty for about five years after that. A bank tried to auction it, but no one would ever buy it."

I furrow my brow. "Something was wrong with the house?"

"Bingo." She smiles. "I was hoping you'd follow the bread crumbs."

"Were the deaths all similar?" My eyes tear away from Marissa to look at the books before me. There are rows of entries, deaths of people of all ages, all in the same house.

"Hard to say," She admits. "I mean, I'd argue it's weird for lots of people to die in the same place, but that's not proof. It won't help us figure out what happened."

"What about the house? I mean, before it was a house?" I correct myself. "I read somewhere there were tunnels below the house?"

She smiles at me. "Not sure where you're getting your information, but you're right. There were tunnels. Before the house was there, like a hundred years ago, it was a plantation. I guess the owner wanted an escape route or something. He built these tunnels. During a huge storm, they all caved in. When the house, the one we see now was built, they poured concrete everywhere. Whatever was there is hidden, probably forever."

"How did you know where to look?" I ask, glancing around the cavernous room. "I mean, you're not from around here, right?"

"Looking up stuff isn't nearly as time consuming as your friends are making it out to be." Marissa laughs. "You just have to know where to look."

I think about asking the question again, but stop. She called me pretty and smart. And there goes my ability to pay attention, except maybe to her. I guess not being in mortal peril is letting me just sit and enjoy all of these feelings, if enjoy is the right word.

I take a step closer, standing right next to her, our shoulders nearly touching. "So this is where you spend your Friday mornings?"

For the first time I watch her blush, a tinge of redness lightening her cheeks. "Well, not usually." She brushes her hair away from her face, that perfect smile on her face growing. "I felt really bad about not believing you, basically making fun of you, and after I crawled out of that deep hole, I thought I'd educate myself."

An impulse grabs me. I've never, ever, in my life been in a situation like this. I touch her hair, leaning closer. "Does that make you the pretty and smart one?"

Whatever might have happened next, whatever answer she might have provided is engulfed in a pervasive darkness. I grab her arm, trying to hold her close. My hand slides down her arm, and I reach for her hand. At some point she just vanishes from my grasp. The lights blind me and I see Amanda and Rana coming towards me. I feel faint and stumble towards a chair.

TWENTY-NINE

SOMEONE IS PRESSING A COLD WATER bottle to my forehead. Amanda is going through a list of questions—almost as invasive as a physical, but not quite. I'm trying to pay attention, but I'm wondering where Marissa vanished to. Did something take her? Did I dream it all? I mean, that version of me doesn't exist in reality, does it? And really, when would anyone ever find me attractive? I really need to stop getting down on myself. Even if there is a slight chance Marissa is really attracted to me, I have to believe it.

"She seems okay." Amanda shakes her head. "Were you talking to someone?"

"Yes." I sit up, feeling a pull in my neck. "Did you see her?"

"Who?" Rana asks, giving me a weird sort of look. "You seem really excited about this."

"I'm allowed to make new friends too." I cringe as soon as the words are out of my mouth.

Rana rolls her eyes. "Whatever, buddy." She nods to Eric. "He said you disappeared and then he heard something and the lights went out a couple times."

"Wait." I put a hand up. "But, you came over here; you asked me what I was doing."

Eric shakes his head, bringing the EMF closer. "Uh, no, I set the computers up and have been scanning since we got here. Sondra has been after us to work faster because we're down a volunteer."

I should feel guilty. I was supposed to be helping with research, not drawing more spooks towards us. I get up, feeling woozy. "No, I swear, right there." I point to the aisle I'd run down. When I look, it's littered with stacks of boxes and books. I turn, glance the other way, and see it is equally cluttered. Did I imagine all of it? Including Marissa? I feel a cold sweat breaking out, my back dampening, my heart plummeting. Am I losing my mind?

Sondra grabs my wrist, pushing me back to the seat. "Let's go over this again." Amanda has a camera trained on me. "You decided to explore."

I nod. "Right. I just felt, I don't know, restless."

Sondra and Amanda exchange a quick glance. "You walked down the aisle and you felt something; the lights flickered and the dark shadow person was there."

I shiver. "Yes."

"You bolt."

"Yes."

"How did you end up here?" She gestures to the tables and chairs.

I look at the cluttered aisles. "This might sound crazy."

"Oh, you have no idea." Amanda laughs. "But please, this is amazing."

"The aisles were clear, totally empty. I sprinted down and took a sharp right or left a couple times and ran into Marissa." This is the first time I've said her name. I clearly have no poker face as I see Eric snickering and Sondra giving me a very expectant look. "And then the lights when out again."

"Is this Marissa here now?" Sondra asks.

"What?" I look at her like she's crazy. "No. If she were here you'd see her."

"You're sure?" Sondra continues.

"I've touched her," I argue. "She's a real person."

"Where did she go?" Sondra presses. "How did she vanish in that ten-second blackout?"

"I don't know." I feel exhausted. More than that, I am worried about Marissa, but also weirded out that she was here, but then wasn't. I need to get a good look around, but they won't let me out of their sight. Not a chance. I set the water bottle down and press my fingers to my forehead. Am I going crazy? The looks on their faces tell me I am.

"Come on," Sondra says, gesturing for me to get up. "What's in all these books?"

I'm not sure how much to say. "I . . . I ran into Marissa, literally, when I was running away from that thing, and she had these. She said she'd been looking into the old house since we talked last."

Sondra's giving me this look like she's caught my hand in the cookie jar. It is making me very uncomfortable. "And where did you meet this Marissa?"

"At the haunted house," I answer.

"I win." Eric chuckles. "Knew it. You have that lovesick look on your face."

I want to vehemently deny it. I can't. I kind of don't want to. It may not be entirely okay to be "the gay," as my mom calls it, but I am having romantic feelings for a girl. "Guilty as charged."

Rana is just staring at the table. A moment passes and her expression changes. She looks horrified, probably how I looked when I saw those things at the house. "Buddy, no, that is not okay." And as if there weren't three people standing a foot away from us, she stage whispers, "You don't want to do that. You're going to end up in hell."

I don't want reality to ruin this, ruin how I feel—but there it is, creeping into my mind, clawing into my life. I lower my eyes. "I might be going anyway."

Rana starts to say something more, but Sondra cuts her off. "Let's just focus on what Roni's girlfriend, who may or may not be a ghost or demon, was trying to tell her."

"She is not a demon." I get up, my finger pointed at Sondra. "I told you she was real."

Amanda's grin grows. "Yes, we all heard you. But there is some debate about your dreams and what's really happening, right?"

I ease up, my shoulders lowering. "Yeah."

"Then give us, the so-called experts, the benefit of the doubt." Amanda smiles. "So, what does your girlfriend look like?"

My face is burning. "About my height, light-skinned, but not white, dark hair, dark eyes." I shut my eyes for a second. "She was wearing jeans, sneakers with pink laces, a button-down plaid flannel in pink and orange. She wears a couple rings and her ears are pierced."

I'm almost afraid to open my eyes, and as I do, I know I should be. They're all hanging on every word. I turn away, feeling my face burning even more than it was before.

If Amanda's grin could grow, it would break her face. Sondra let's out a soft laugh. "Oh, I hope for your sake she is real."

Is this really happening? Are people I hardly know referencing my crush as my girlfriend? It feels sort of weird that it doesn't feel weird. That I feel better. Like hiding who I am or who I like is wrong. I have to believe that God will be merciful, despite what Rana said. Everything our parents have told us hasn't quite been the truth, like that watermelon seed thing. They tell us things to protect us. I don't think I can protect myself from falling in love with whomever my heart desires.

I glance around. Where did she go? I don't want everyone following me. Maybe she doesn't like them? I don't even want to think about that thing I think I saw getting her. God, was any of that real? I dreamt about seeing her this morning. She didn't mention it. Does that mean I did dream it? But then, where did I get these books?

Eric is scanning the books with the EMF. "Nothing. Where did she find these? Your girl?"

"She's not my girl." I can't help the smile that still creeps across my features. They don't need to know the unimportant details, like Marissa calling me pretty and smart. "She's just a friend."

"I don't blush when I make new friends." Eric chuckles.

"Sure you do," Amanda teases. "Then you take them out and then we never see them again."

Eric stops what he's doing with the scanner. "Really? In front of the clients?"

"I think we passed the client status when we slept over." Sondra laughs. "Roni, stop daydreaming. What else did she tell you?"

I point to the books. "Just that the house had been sold a bunch of times. A lot of people had died there. That usually indicates that something was going on in the house."

Sondra just stares. Amanda takes a step closer. "That could mean anything. Any one of those spirits could have found you. Or there could be a portal letting spirits through" Her eyes land on the text. "How'd she know where to look?"

I shrug. "She didn't say exactly. Just said it was about looking."

Eric sets the scanner down. "Got what we need from here. What about the stack?"

"I'm not sure." I turn, glancing down the two sides of the row. "She didn't get a chance to tell me anything more before the lights went out.."

"Let's take everything to the front. It'll be another hour before anyone comes in to check up on us." Sondra grabs the scanner and EMF. "Roni, no more wandering around."

"But, she—" I stop, sighing. "What if that thing took her?"

"I'll go with Roni," Amanda volunteers. "Eric can work with Rana to figure out what's of value in those books."

"I have no idea what to look for," Rana exclaims. "I can scan, though. Seems simple enough."

Eric has hoisted the stack into his arms. "Vámonos, chica."

Sondra nods at the camera. "Don't take your eyes off of her."

"What if we see something?" Amanda asks, sticking her tongue out at Sondra. "We'll be safe, Mom."

Sondra throws her hands up, following Eric and nudging Rana, who gives me a worried look before continuing forward. I feel that unsettled restless feeling. It feels weird to have Amanda just standing there with the camera trained on me.

"Could you please point that somewhere else?" I ask, glaring at the floor.

"Did you not just hear what Sondra said?" Amanda counters. "Let's go find your girlfriend."

I can't make her turn the camera off. The jitters I had earlier are coming back, and I try to coax my mind to remember which way I came from. My palms are getting sweaty again. I wipe my hands on the back of my jeans, turning the corner towards the left. We walk on for a few minutes. Her footsteps are timed with mine. I can't hear the difference. I keep glancing back, but Amanda isn't saying anything.

I'm getting increasingly annoyed the farther we walk. The end of the room is right in front of us. We've seen down the rows to the end of the room. Where could she have gone? My pace quickens and I can now hear Amanda's footsteps as she hurries after me. The moment the lights flicker, I come to a dead stop. Amanda bumps into me as the lights flicker above. The camera hits me in the shoulder, the same one I slammed into Marissa with. I try to hide the pain.

"Sorry." Amanda pats me on the shoulder, taking a step back. "That was weird. I saw the lights do that earlier."

"What does it mean?" I ask.

"The power is touch and go down here," Amanda explains. "This happens all the time."

I turn, facing Amanda. "This is normal?"

"Well, no, not exactly." She winces, then shudders. "Wow, did it just get super cold?"

She hands me the camera, which I pan around the bookshelves. An EMF is out and she swaps with me, taking the camera back. I do feel colder. I don't wait for Amanda, now jogging down the row. I'm amazed she's kept up. I try to keep one eye on the EMF and one to make sure I don't fall. We reach the end of the row, a right angle that leads to the left again. When the lights go out a second time, they don't come back on immediately, but Amanda switches the light on the camera on and points it directly at me.

I put my hand up to shield my eyes. "Do you mind?"

The light lowers ever so slightly. "You know what's super weird?"

I'm afraid to ask. "What?"

"The lights are only off over here."

I drag my eyes from the blinding camera. She's right. The light is fine on the other side of the massive room. It is just here, just in this twenty-foot radius, that the power is out, the light gone.

I edge closer to Amanda, my breath shaky. "Aren't you scared?"

She nudges me with her elbow. "Don't be scared, Roni. This is something trying to communicate with us. All entities, evil or not, need energy."

"It could mean that thing is here." I shut my eyes, lowering my head, trying to slow my racing heart.

"What did it look like?" she asks.

"When I saw it here?"

"Yes."

With my eyes still shut, I feel my skin crawl just thinking about it. "At first it looked like a kid, I guess, or one of us. A person. It wasn't facing me. It wore a dark pullover, dark pants. The hood was over his face. When it turned to look at me—" I shudder before continuing, "When it looked at me, it's face was cut up, gashes snaking across his face, like something had broken free. The skin was glowing, shaking sort of. Then everything just, sort of, melted away. And I just—I just ran."

"Did it look anything like that?" Amanda asks in a surprisingly calm voice.

My eyes snap open and I back into Amanda, who's standing inches behind me. Before us is a figure just like the one I'd seen before. It isn't facing us, but it is dressed the same. Dark shoes, dark pants, hoodie covering the face. I don't want it to turn around. I'm moving backwards, but Amanda isn't letting me back up any farther.

With one hand she holds the camera steady; with the other she grabs ahold of my elbow, moving forward. "What do you want?"

My hands are shaking, but I follow her lead. "Why are you following me?" I ask.

The figure doesn't turn. The lights flicker once and it is at the next bookcase over. It moved fifteen feet in a second. I don't want to be scared. I don't want to let the fear control me. Amanda gasps, but her grip on me hasn't loosened. The light on the camera is steady.

"Show yourself!" she commands. In a softer voice, she says, "Roni, there's holy water in my pocket. If I let go of you, I need you not to run."

I nod. "No more running." I glare at the thing, feeling a tad less scared. "What did you do to her?"

I feel more than hear the response. "Who?"

Amanda has the holy water in her hand, popping the lid off. "You are not welcome here."

The water, just a few drops, arc through the air. The moment they touch the figure, the thing, an ear-splitting wailing begins. The fire alarms are going off and the lights and sounds are both blinding and deafening. Amanda, somehow, is still standing up straight, glaring at the thing that is no longer there.

She squeezes her eyes shut for a second, capping the water and sliding it back into her pocket. I feel something cool pass me, numb the sound for a moment before she grabs my wrist, pulling me forward. The farther we get from where we were, the sound seems quieter.

Eric is bounding towards us. We've stopped right where I ran into Marissa. The books are still lying on the table. My heart is beginning to ache. Where did she go? Is she okay? Is she real?

A hand grabs my elbow and we hurry outside. The sirens are still blaring in the background, but I can't hear my thoughts without feeling a deep throbbing in my head. The fresh air and green grass are a welcome sight compared to the darkness in the archives. The cold water bottle is being pressed to the back of my neck again.

"Dude, what is it with you and places?" Rana asks, laughing as she sits down, opening a bag of chips, seeming to be utterly unfazed by this latest scare.

Where did she get the chips? I don't even care as I reach into the bag. "You know me—I know how to clear a room, or building."

"We found some interesting stuff, buddy," she talks as she chomps away. "Not only was the house reported to have hauntings, some sort of dark rituals had occurred there." She waves her hands and fingers to indicate something spooky. "But that all happened like fifty years ago."

Didn't the picture that fell out of the yearbook come from the 1950s? I pull my phone out, but it's dead. I charged it this morning. How did that happen? Amanda's words play back through, a good reminder for me. Something sapped the energy out of it—possibly me.

The wind is rippling just past us. Coupled with the shade from a swaying tree, I feel cool, and more importantly, I feel safe. What does all of this mean? What can all of it mean? Rana is offering me more chips. I lean back, staring up at the sky, azure and cloudless.

THIRTY

I'M NOT SURE HOW MUCH TIME HAS passed, but Sondra and Amanda come over, Eric a few feet behind them. Sondra stops before me. Once again, Amanda has a camera trained on me. I feel like a celebrity, except I'm not famous or beautiful—even though I guess one girl finds me pretty. I blush at the memory.

"We can't take you anywhere." Sondra laughs, nudging me with her foot. "Lucky for us, no one thinks we have anything to do with this, even though I'm pretty sure we caused it."

My eyes dart to the chaos around us. The entire building has been emptied. The fire marshals are there, joking with the deputies. There isn't a hint of smoke in the air. There is no fire. Do they think it's a false alarm? I turn back around, seeing everyone still staring at me.

"What now?" I ask.

"Food." Eric laughs. "These two are going to stay put and collect the last of the data we need. Meanwhile, we, ladies, are going to grab a bite to eat."

"I'm not hungry." My stomach contradicts me, but I stare at the ground.

"You need to be clear of this place for us to finish our work," Sondra states. "Sorry, Roni. Something is messing with our investigation. And after what you and Amanda saw, which did show up on the video, you need to get clear.

We have a little more work to do. We'll meet up with you in a couple hours."

I stare up at her. "That's it? I mean, you know something, don't you?"

"Honestly," Amanda cuts in as Sondra crosses her arms, staring at me, "no. We have a lot of pieces, a lot of proof, but what little we know, you know. The house you went to was haunted. People who lived there probably messed with something they shouldn't have. How that connects to you—that we're still not sure."

"You didn't take anything from that old house, did you?" Eric asks.

I shake my head. "No."

"Are we good here?" Sondra asks, her tone curt. "We all need to be on the same page."

"I'm on the same page," I counter.

"You're not." Sondra smiles. "Girl, you are so not seeing what we're seeing, literally."

"What is that supposed to mean?" I get up, my fists clenched at my sides. The anger surprises even me, and I take a step back, wondering where the sudden fury came from. "Sorry," I say.

Amanda pats me on the arm. "Whatever it is, the demon, the djinn, it is affecting you, drawing you in. The fact that it wasn't scared to show itself in front of me says a lot. It either isn't afraid of our interference or it knows it can take you, possess you, or, well, who knows. We're worried about you, Roni. You need to see that we are not trying to hurt you."

I nod. "I'm not crazy."

"You're not acting like you, either," Rana volunteers. "This isn't like you, buddy. You don't get mad in a millisecond; you don't kiss girls."

"I did not kiss her!" I exclaim, turning to face Rana. "You know, you're a born-again Muslim, your family just discovered the faith again last year, so I'm not sure exactly how you get to be holier than me."

I can see Eric's eyebrows raise at this. Sondra shakes her head, walking back towards the building while Amanda keeps the camera on me, and now Rana too.

"Look, just because our family wasn't super religious before doesn't mean that I haven't learned from my mistakes," Rana says, trying to keep her voice even.

"And in all that learning did you miss the part about God being a teacher, being merciful?" I ask. "Isn't that in like every line in the Quran? God is the most merciful. He will forgive me and guide me wherever I've supposed to go."

"That's only if you're following Him and not the devil." Rana crumples the chip bag up, throwing it into a nearby trash can. "Even the idea of liking a girl, when you are a girl, is wrong, and you know it."

"I didn't realize you were homophobic." I regret the tone but not the words. "It is my life."

"Yeah, and I love you and I want to see you in heaven." Rana's hands are shaking at her sides. "What you're doing is wrong. You need to pray and find peace."

I take a deep breath. This is pointless. You can't argue with someone who can't see any other point of view except her own. "Fine. I'm going to hell. Want me to save you a seat? As you may recall, judging others is also a sin, and since all sins are created equally, well, there you go."

"Okay, guys," Eric pipes in, sliding between us. "At this point, I really feel like we're all going to end up in hell since we're messing with the dark arts."

"What?" I turn to Eric. "I'm not messing with anything dark."

"Eric, stop." Amanda rolls her eyes. "Roni, we have more research to do. Either you know or are unaware, but things like this don't happen just because. They don't. There is a catalyst. According to Abby, you're not totally clear on everything that's happened."

"Is this like what my brother said?" I ask. "How he thinks that it's a djinn?"

"The djinns appear to be localized to your house." Amanda narrows her eyes, pursing her lips together. "Whatever is here at the courthouse followed us, like your girlfriend."

"She's not . . ." I let the sentence remain unfinished. I wish she were my girlfriend. I wish I weren't such a coward. I should have kissed her. The mere idea of it cools whatever anger has been building.

Eric takes the opportunity to steer me and Rana towards the van. I sit silently in the back as they prattle on about music. Unlike last night, Eric has the radio quiet as we drive to a nearby sandwich shop. I didn't bring money, but Eric pays for all of us. We sit at a booth in the front. The tension is still very much there. Rana isn't even looking at me. Eric, on the other hand, is doing a fantastic job filling the silence with conversation. I'd like to say I'm listening, but I'm not.

Why is all of this happening? Did I do something to make this happen? Bhai said something about this being familiar. He knew there were djinns in the house, but how did Sondra know they hadn't followed us? How did she know that thing Amanda and I saw wasn't a djinn?

"Good Lord," Eric says, laughing as he wipes his face with a napkin. "You two could really wage war through glares. Though, truthfully, Roni's not really trying."

"What did Amanda mean?" I ask, ignoring what Eric just said. "How could she know that it wasn't a djinn?"

Eric sits up taller. "Chica, we have seen a lot. What you saw—what Amanda saw—she recognized it."

My eyes open wider. "What? Where?"

"More times than I can say." Eric lets out a nervous laugh. "It isn't the specific thing, the figure in the dark pullover—it is the darkness itself. You have yourself a demon admirer."

I shudder. "How?"

"Something in that house." Eric starts eating pretzels again. "You don't remember anything that you might have taken? Anything that might have happened when you and Matty were there?"

"Or when you have really active dreams?" Rana stares at me.

I can see the wrinkles around her eyes. She's still mad. This is not at all what she probably expected. I bet she's sorry she stayed. The anger is clawing back into my mind and I have to will it away.

"I did have a dream about the house," I start slowly. How much should I say? Whatever I withhold is only going to make it harder to figure out what's going on. "I dreamt about the old house." I sigh. "It was like the ghost investigation that Matty and I did was going in reverse. But this time, I wasn't stuck to me and him; I could move independently through the memory, tethered to nothing. I was able to walk around the house. It sort of shifted. Like, the house turned newer, less old, and then back again, maybe. I do remember seeing something etched into the ground, like a rising sun sort of. I tried to draw it when I woke up, but I can't draw."

Eric nods and pulls out a tablet, which I now see had been recording me through video and audio. I guess I should be grateful for the thoroughness.

Rana reaches across the table, offering half of her cookie to me. "No other incidents?"

"Not inside the house," I admit, taking a piece of the cookie. "But, I did dream about the courthouse, sort of."

The tablet is on the table, and Eric is once again smiling. "You did look like you'd been there before. Was she there? Your mystery girl? Are you dreaming about her?"

I stare at the ceiling with open piping and light fixtures hanging down. "Yeah, Marissa was there, in the dream, guiding me through the rows. But there was something else there then, something she tried to stop me from seeing. I know I felt scared. Then I woke up."

"The question I have, the debate we're having," Eric says, turning the tablet towards me, "is whether your girlfriend is real or not, of course—and whether she is part of this darkness that's all around you, or whether she is trying to protect you. Any thoughts?"

"She is real." I enunciate each word in turn. "I have touched her. I know she is real."

"Where does she live? Does she go to school here?" Eric starts to grin. "Has anyone else seen her? Spoken to her?"

I sip my soda, refusing to answer his question. "So what is it? The thing that I saw?"

Eric shakes his head. "I don't do the reveal part of the investigation. But can you look through these?" He taps the tablet, and there are dozens of images to sift through. "I scanned a lot of this today, some from a day back. But there is a lot to see, and if anything looks familiar, it could help a lot with answering your question."

I wipe my hands on a napkin and start swiping through the images. There are way more pentagrams than I'd expect anyone to have. Some of the images are like what you'd imagine the devil would look like: half human and half goat, or something with hooves, always with the horns. I always wonder if he just looks like a regular person. I mean, if the devil is a fallen angel, then he could look like anything. Would the evilness in him have made him hideous?

More than half of the pictures are not remotely familiar. I get to one that seems strange. It looks like an upside-down circle, a smile even. I force the image to flip, and there it is. I blink a few times, trying to force the memory of a dream come to the forefront, but it's impossible.

"This might be it." I tap the edge of the tablet. "This looks familiar."

Eric takes the tablet and presses a variety of buttons. "That was not my first guess. I was really hoping you'd pick the pentagram. We haven't had to deal with devil worshippers for a while. That's always fun."

"So now what?" I ask, going back to finishing my sandwich.

"We wait for the girls to meet us." Eric stows the tablet in his bag. "Why don't you regale us with more stories about your girlfriend?"

I set my jaw. "Funny, you're a funny guy."

"What else did she say to you? What else did you two do?" he continues. "I mean, besides making lovesick puppy eyes at you."

Rana shifts in her chair. "Yeah, what was she like that converted you from straight to gay in a minute and a half."

I could let the anger in, but I don't, letting a genuine smile cross my face. "She has the prettiest smile I've ever seen." Any worries I have are fading. "When she looks at me, I just—I don't know—I feel … lighter." I shiver, feeling cold like I'm sitting under an AC vent. "She always looks perfect and she—well, she listens to me, is sweet to me. I know, I sound like such a complete loser."

I try to laugh the discomfort off, but Eric and Rana are both staring at me. I don't want to guess at what they are thinking, but their expressions are telling. The look of disapproval is still stuck on Rana's face; her eyes are narrowed though, like she's kind of curious. We never talk about falling in love or any of that stuff, just about obligations for when we do get married. This isn't like that at all. Eric is still smiling, but it is more wistful, like he heard me, but didn't. The description is cut short as Amanda and Sondra come walking towards us.

THIRTY-ONE

THE BOOTH IS SOON BRIMMING. AMANDA slides in next to me; Rana scoots closer to Eric, even though Sondra has pulled a chair up. The equipment is out of sight. The two sit down, not really saying much, sort of nonverbal messages through glances. I arch an eyebrow at Rana, who seems equally confused. Once their sandwiches come, a grueling ten minutes later, not much has been said. I don't know that I know these people well enough to be comfortable in silence, so I've decided daydreaming is the best course of action, and I begin to replay the conversation with Marissa.

I'm not crazy. She was there. I touched her. I could smell her. That soft scent of cinnamon. Even in that dusty, moldy place, I could still smell her. The moment it went dark, she, and her scent, just vanished. Was I awake? I touched her. It was real. And I was able to read the books, so that was real. She was there. Where did she go? Amanda and I walked pretty far. We could see across the entirety of the room, and she wasn't there. The door never opened until we left. She disappeared. The fact that we're looking into something supernatural does make me worry that Eric might be right. What if I've imagined her? I mean, not that I'm saying I'm some super strong psychic that can manipulate the world, but it has been known that people can manifest poltergeists through their thoughts. But she's a living person. I know it.

I'm snapped from my thoughts by Rana shaking my arm. "Buddy, Sondra's asking you a question. You just fell asleep."

I blink a few times, realizing she was right. I had fallen asleep. "What's going on?"

"I was just explaining to you that we copied all the files we needed," Sondra says, sounding quite annoyed. "That neither your girlfriend, nor that thing, ever reappeared. We were in there alone for about an hour and nothing happened. The cause of the disturbance is tied directly to you."

Amanda cringes, trying to make this look like a smile. "What she means is that you're at the center, the nexus, if you will." She nudges Sondra before continuing, "Eric messaged us the image you saw in your dream. This put us right back where we started, sort of."

Sondra takes a deep breath. "We need you to tell us anything that happened before this ghost hunt."

"Nothing," I respond. "I never do anything really interesting."

"You just moved into this house," Amanda points out. "I mean, the boxes are kind of hard to ignore."

"I guess. But that didn't have anything to do with me," I argue.

"You sure?" Sondra asks, her eyes narrowed.

"Yes." I cross my arms across my chest, feeling cold again. "I didn't do anything. If anything, it is those djinns my brother was talking about."

"There is a lot of lore about djinns and Muslims," Rana says, coming to my defense. "I have heard all kinds of stories growing up. We both have. Isn't it possible that the dark figure thing could be related to that?"

"Possible," Eric concedes. "But why is it fixated on her?"

"Or what is it trying to tell you?" Amanda asks, leaning back in her seat. "I mean, it moved faster than light. It wanted something. I did feel scared, but I knew it didn't want me."

I shouldn't feel anger. They are trying to help me, even if I'm not being helpful. "I don't know what you think I'm hiding. But if I'm lying, then asking me straight up isn't going to give you the answer, is it?"

Sondra laughs, a really loud laugh that makes everyone in the place turn to see what is so funny that's been said. "We know you're not lying, Roni." She stops, wiping her mouth with her napkin. "I am feeling frustrated because we are making no progress and are getting way too many clues that we don't know what to do with."

"It's like a puzzle with a thousand pieces, but we have two thousand and the pieces all look the same," Eric volunteers with a laugh. "There is something, something you know or experienced that is the missing piece, the one that can make all of this work. Was the sunburst image I gave you not helpful?"

"Points us back to where we were before," Amanda crumples up the sandwich wrapper. "I think we all have one idea, but between the girlfriend that no one has ever seen and the djinns, there are too many possibilities."

The gravity of the situation is starting to weigh on me, and I feel like I just got crushed by a two-ton anvil. "What now? Do we just go home and hope it stops?"

"No." Sondra gives me a stern look. "No, we do not leave, and you do not get off the hook that easily. We are going to get to the bottom of this."

Though her resolve sounds strong, I don't feel very sure. If anything, I feel less certain that they knew what they were doing. One piece that is missing is glaring. "So, you've identified the djinn. What is the other thing? Eric wouldn't say."

Amanda and Sondra exchange a look. Sondra sighs. "You know. You have studied this long enough. You know what this is. There is only one option left, really, and it isn't a ghost. It is most likely a demon."

That feeling of plummeting, of falling from a great height with nothing left to catch me, is taking hold. Even though I'm here, sitting in this little sandwich shop, all I can feel is a great gust of wind blowing past me, tousling my hair, making me feel like a dead weight as the ground is coming closer with each passing second.

I've spaced out again because I hear Amanda saying my name. "Roni. Roni. Hello, Rana, poke her."

"Buddy, wake up." Rana shakes my arm and the feeling fades, a little.

"Sorry." I keep my eyes set on the table, a few crumbs still left over from my sandwich. "I'm awake."

"When was the last time you really slept?" Rana asks, pushing my soda cup closer.

"A week," I reply, not being sure. It has been a while.

"I was going over our next steps." Sondra looks a lot less annoyed with me than she did a few minutes ago.

How long was I zoned out? "What were those next steps?" I ask.

"We need to review the tape that you and Amanda took." Sondra pulls out a notebook and passes it to Amanda, who starts jotting this down. "We're going to do that. Eric is going to keep doing research on the image you gave us. Abby will be by later to help him. Hope Matty stops by. We could use some help. There is a lot of footage to go over, and we need to do this quickly. Rana, how do you feel about more research?"

Rana grimaces, saying with as little enthusiasm as possible, "I'd love to."

"We have a lot of work to do people," Sondra says, holding everyone's eyes for a moment before her gaze lands on me. "I need you to remain calm, Roni. If you can't keep yourself inside the house, you need to take someone with you. If you can't do that, Eric is going to attach a camera to you."

Eric grins, giving me an exaggerated wink. "I will follow you to the ends of the earth."

Heat is rising on my face once again. "Terrific."

When we get home, I'm surprised to see Jamaal sitting outside, waiting for the team. He ushers me and Rana inside, giving me a weird, suspicious sort of look. I wonder if one of his cop friends saw us at the courthouse. I'm too tired to worry about what they're talking about, deciding to lie down in the nice sitting room. If Mom isn't here, I can't get in trouble for doing this. I have been falling asleep everywhere I go. A nice dream featuring a certain dream girl would be really nice right about now.

Unlike that morning, or the night before, there are no dark figures haunting my mind. I see the house, our old house, and see myself walking around. There's a shimmer around me, a shadow, though not dark, following me—a smaller, younger version of me. I'm watching myself as if I'm not there, or I'm the camera. It isn't choppy like those terrible found footage films that I get sucked into time and again.

Something is happening in the house. There is that group, the prayer group, sitting on a white sheet. They're all focused, all reading from their holy books. I can't make the letters out, not that reading Arabic in a dream would really amount to anything I'd understand.

The other me stops outside the circle. My parents are ignoring me at first. Someone notices me. I don't know who. I'm small, barely ten—I can tell by the Tweety Bird shirt I'm wearing. It's weird. I'm the only one not wearing pure white. My grandfather has me sit next to him while he reads aloud. The image slows, like it's trapped in time. I walk around the perimeter of the room. A loud noise shakes the room, shakes the memory perhaps. I turn, though everyone in the room, except the littler me, ignores it. I can feel the fear.

Footsteps are coming. Loud footsteps. They shake everything. The paintings on the wall are teetering. The bouquet of flowers in the kitchen has been knocked over, water spilling everywhere. The littler me wants to investigate, wants to see, but is too scared to move. Nana puts a hand on my shoulder, holding me in place.

Those footsteps are now darkening the entire room. What is going on? I turn in circles. I'm not frozen, though everyone else seems to be. I do a second turn and suddenly I see it. There is a sea of faces, though not quite faces, staring back at me. We're surrounded by the dark figures. There are too many to count. Are they the djinns Jamaal spoke of?

The main religious guy is speaking louder. Everyone is speaking as one. The dark figures are closing in. They are upset about something. The man argues with them, tells them to leave. They won't. I don't know how I know this, can know this. No one is speaking English. They want something in return. In return for what? The man refuses. He wants them to leave. They don't belong here.

My skin is crawling. I feel like I'm in their midst. I try to break into the circle, to get away, but I can't. I can move anywhere else in this dream. There seems to be an invisible field around those who are praying. The room is getting tighter. What did they want? Why were they in our house?

I'm shaking, trying to escape. The movement has me rolling off of the sofa and onto the floor. Rana and Amanda are staring at me with surprise. I can't be bothered with them. I stumble to my feet, finding Jamaal in the kitchen.

"They're here because of what?" I ask. "What do they want?"

"What?" He has no idea what I'm talking about.

"What did we take from the djinns?" I am almost screaming now.

"I don't know what you're talking about." He gives me a no-nonsense glare.

The blood rushes from my face. I was the only kid in that memory. Is that why they want me?

Thirty-Two

THE SITUATION TURNS INTO QUITE THE standoff. Jamaal isn't saying anything, Rana is trying to referee and I can see Eric out of the corner of my eye, recording everything. My life has turned into one of those bad reality TV shows.

"Roni, we moved here because there was a lot of weird stuff happening." Jamaal's eyes are narrowed to slits, but I can see him stealing glances at the camera.

I know he's hiding something. "You know more, don't you? You know what's going on, don't you?"

My big brother is not the type to crack under any sort of pressure. When we were kids, he'd sneak out, going God knows where and no matter the tone my parents used, they never found out where he went or who he was with. I can feel the anger building inside. He lied to me. He's been lying to me.

His arms are folded across his chest. "The more you know, the more danger you are to yourself and everyone here."

I gesture towards Eric. "Did you tell them?"

"I told them enough," he says, his voice low.

Sondra comes up to get between us. "She has a right to know."

"This isn't your concern." Jamaal's eyes slide to her, the anger thinly veiled.

"You said you needed our help," Sondra pointed out. "She is asking you for the truth. There is something you can tell her, isn't there?"

I'm appalled that Sondra, perhaps the entire ghost hunting team, knows something about me that I don't. I stare expectantly at Jamaal, but his expression remains unchanged.

"Just stop doing crazy stuff and you'll be fine," he says.

That feeling of plummeting has returned. He isn't going to help me. More than that, he isn't going to help me protect myself. "You don't care, not even a little, do you? You and Sarah are too busy being perfect all of the time. I bet you both wish I'd never been born."

Jamaal's expression hardens somehow more. "Not for the reasons you're mentioning, but yeah, I wish you didn't have to deal with any of this."

I recoil, stepping back, feeling a cool wall of air try to hold me up, but I just turn, racing up the stairs. The last thing I want is to talk to him or anyone else right now. I can hear Rana close on my heels, but I slam my bedroom door shut, keeping her out. I curl up in a ball in my bed, squeezing my eyes shut, trying to figure out what to do next. I refuse to cry, but I can feel the hot tears sliding down my cheeks. I grab Fat Face, wishing I were smaller, that he actually covered me. I'm not sure where the afternoon goes, but I wake up feeling cold, my feet sticking out from under Fat Face.

I get up, seeing the darkness outside. I must have slept for a couple hours. I take a moment as I trudge to the bathroom. The hot shower is a quiet relief, but also a wakeup call.

I try to push away the hurtful words from Jamaal and focus on something pleasant. Was Marissa really there this morning? It felt real. I swear I touched her. But how did she vanish in an enclosed space? Even if the room is huge, she couldn't have just disappeared. I really can't be sure what's real or not, not entirely. With the state of mind I'm in, I'm not sure I can trust myself. When I emerge from the bathroom, Rana gives me a nervous look.

"They ordered pizza." She smiles. "They were nice enough not to get pepperoni or sausage."

Since we're Muslim, we don't eat pork products. It was nice of the ghost-hunting team to be aware of this.

I pull the hood from my sweatshirt over my head. The idea of facing anyone right now, especially Jamaal, isn't good. Rana grips my elbow and steers me towards my room. I toss my dirty clothes into the laundry basket. There isn't a moment of peace before Rana pushes me towards the stairs. To my surprise, no one is staring at me. The kitchen is filled with a pizza smell.

The disposable plates are stacked, and it doesn't look like anyone's touched the pizza. Eric veers to the fridge, grabbing a Coke. "We got a few different sodas. Wasn't sure if you were the girly girl type to need diet."

"I could use it." I laugh. The sound of my voice seems foreign.

"Naw," he says as he laughs. "Girls with some curves are nice."

Rana gives him a solid slap on the arm. "Roni's not fat. She's just different shaped."

"That doesn't make me feel any better." I smile.

Eric smirks. "I wonder if your girlfriend is watching and doesn't want me flirting with you."

I just turn away. The thought sits in my mind for a moment. Would she be upset if she saw me flirting? I refuse to believe that she isn't real. I know she's real. She has to be.

Sondra gets up. "Wasn't sure what kind of pizza you wanted, but for a two-day event, we thought dinner should be on us."

I nod. "Thank you."

"Don't thank us." Sondra hands me a plate. "You want to talk about it?"

I'm not sure what to say. I dart my eyes around the room. "Did he leave?"

Her smile tightens. "He stepped out. Didn't say where he was going or when he'd be back."

"He told you not to tell me anything?" I ask.

"No." She nudges me towards the pizza. "He just said that you'd been through a lot and that this might solve one issue your family hasn't been able to figure out, but it's putting a lot of pressure on you."

I feel my lips quiver. "Like he'd care about that, about pressure on me when he doesn't even want me here."

She steers me away from everyone, including Eric, who stops with just a stern look from Sondra. "Roni, look, I get we don't know one another, but trust me when I say I see this a lot. Paranormal things often look for just these situations. Whatever happened in your past, it's made you vulnerable to this, but that doesn't make you unwanted by anyone. You are loved, by your family, by your friends." She pauses and leans closer. "Your girlfriend."

I let out a sharp laugh. "I thought you said she wasn't real."

"As long as she's real to you, that's what matters." Sondra pats my arm. "It's okay to be confused."

"I can't tell what's real," I confess, fighting the tears in my eyes. My gaze is set on the pizza box.

"Roni," Sondra says and grips my wrist, "you're not crazy. Whatever is doing this, good or bad, is trying to communicate with you. It's okay to be scared. But don't doubt what you've already been through."

"But what about the memories?" I ask. "How do I know the dream was real?"

Sondra lets out a slight laugh, glancing at the door. "Your brother was hot to refute it. I'd argue that's all the

220

proof you need. He looked like you'd called him out on the biggest lie ever. Something tells me you said things that were very true."

I wipe my eyes with my sleeve like a little kid, trying my best to hold it together. "Just don't let whatever it is take me over."

"Ultimately, that will be your choice," Sondra says in a quiet tone. "A demon can't just take over your body. It needs your permission."

Somehow this doesn't comfort me. I need to stop being so afraid. It's a lot easier to hide, but I decide to sit with Amanda and Eric as they review the footage. Rana pulls a chair up from the dining room while Sondra sets a bottle of water in front of me.

My eyes sort of glaze over. The footage doesn't seem to have anything in it. I want to ask questions, but I feel like I'm intruding. It takes me a moment to realize I'm dreaming again. The plate is still firmly in my lap. This time I'm standing just behind Rana. How is this possible? Am I walking out of my body while asleep? I run my hand through myself, through the real me, but it slides right through. It has no effect. How do I get back in?

I try to sit in my own lap, but I fall through the chair. So, I can't sit down, but I'm not sinking to the center of the earth. I shake my head. The house is quiet. I wonder if I'm appearing on the cameras. It was night when I woke up from my long nap. There isn't much light in the house. The door in front of me is shut, but I can pass my hand through it without any trouble. I'm a ghost now, where should I go?

I should be more alarmed. I should be scared. The tiredness is making me feel almost calm. I guess, as long as I'm a ghost, nothing can hurt me, right? But does that mean my body is free for anything to take up residence? I glance around and see myself snoozing. I wonder where my ghost is. Is she here? I'm not dead. At least I don't think so. A soft, regular echo in my head reminds me that my heart is beating. From across the room, I can see my chest rising and falling. I must be breathing. The conversation is continuing around me, though it sounds like everything is muffled, garbled somehow.

The thought lingers and I think of the old house again. I start to turn towards the back door, everything hazy around me, when Matty and Abigail burst through the front door. He slams right through me. Abigail has enough sense to shut and lock the front door.

I know he felt it because he stops, turns, and gives me a quizzical look, his eyes then sliding to Abigail. Is this the same feeling I've gotten all over the house? The team gives him a slight nod, but he pushes Eric's setup aside and places his laptop at the center. All the expensive gear shifts at a dangerous angle and I can see a flash of panic, then anger, cross Eric's face. He must be the one who keeps all of the gear up to date and state of the art.

"Dude, have you guys been reviewing the stuff from the first night?" Matty asks.

Eric is glaring at him, the fist at his side clenched. Sondra puts a hand on Eric's arm. "Why?"

"The thing." Matty's gasping. "There's a few and they're chanting. They're reciting something. What does it mean?"

"I was reviewing this with Matty once my parents decided I could spend the evening 'studying.'" Abigail sets her bag down in the kitchen. "Not that anyone cares, but Blaine has a couple different girls doting on him. He did stick with my story, though, so Mom doesn't think anything weird is happening."

"Good," Sondra says. "The last thing we need is parental interference." She turns to Matty. "Show me."

Somehow no one has noticed that I'm not moving. Matty pulls the file up, offering a pair of headphones. Sondra shakes her head and Matty grimaces, pressing play.

It is a chant. It's something you might hear at the mosque, but not quite. Rana shudders behind me. I glance in her direction, trying to will her to nudge me or something. Everyone is transfixed by the audio. It's really hypnotic. I can feel it lull me to sleep. I'm already asleep. How is it making me tired again?

Amanda snaps her head up, turning to me. "Roni, what do you think?"

I don't respond. Sondra sits up, then jumps to her feet, as if she sees something everyone else doesn't.

"Turn it off," she demands.

Matty complies and they're all staring at me. Sondra has my face in both of her hands. The moment she touches me, I feel a jolt, like I zapped myself while dragging my socked feet across the carpet. I shake my head, the colors around me bending around the light from the kitchen. I'm watching, wondering how this might help.

"Roni, wake up." Sondra is tightening her grip. When she speaks this time, the words echo perfectly clearly through my head.

Something is pulling at me, but in the opposite direction. I turn and see outside the sunroom, surrounding every window, the figures robed in black. It isn't two or three this time; there are at least a couple dozen. I stumble, tripping over a hand protruding from the ground, and fall through the chair. I wake up on the floor.

Everyone is in the exact place they were before. Sondra is standing over me. Rana starts to move, but Sondra puts a hand up, pulling a small vial of something out of her pocket and tossing a few drops on me. I give her a confused look.

"You're still you?" Sondra asks, offering me a hand to get up.

"I think so. It was like I was sleepwalking."

"Do me a favor." Sondra searches my eyes. "Stay inside your body."

"What happened?" I ask.

"I think the chant is drawing them in," she replies.

"I thought I saw them outside." I sigh, feeling relieved that I'm awake and inside my body again.

"You did." Sondra nods to the windows. "We can see them too."

THIRTY-THREE

AT FIRST I'M TOO STUNNED TO EVEN REG-
ister what Sondra just said. But when I turn, the figures are
all there. If it were day, they would be blocking out the sun.
Rana is on her feet in seconds. Eric and Amanda are not
far behind. Instead of backing away, the figures are getting
closer, their clawed fingers scraping at the glass, though no
sound is being made. Their bodies are pressed in the windows, making them look pitch black. Sondra gives me a
hard look, pushing me towards the kitchen.

"What do you want?" Sondra says this in a very
loud voice.

There's no unified response. The chanting is all I can
hear, all any of us can hear. It's getting louder. Rana is gripping my arm; her fingers are leaving an indentation. Matty
is shaking next to us. Eric holds up the camera and we all
slide our gaze to the laptop. The screen is reflecting what
we're all seeing. I should feel reassured that it's not all in my
head, that I haven't been hallucinating, but I don't.

"You need to leave." Sondra puts both hands up, her voice
stern and calm. "You don't belong here. You must leave."

Amanda turns to me, the EMF in her hand blinking
angrily in red at us. "You need to tell them to go."

"Why me?" I utter.

"It is your house, not ours," Sondra says. "This is your
home. You tell them to leave."

225

I'm scared. I don't know that I've ever been this petri-fied before. I take a step forward, then I feel Rana squeeze my shoulder as I pass her.

"Leave. This is our house, not yours." The chanting is growing louder. It is making my head hurt. "Leave me alone."

I mean to say this with more veracity, but I'm just so scared. The words are squeaked out. I say a quiet prayer, and when I look up, the mob is fading.

Sondra turns to me, grinning. "That was unreal. You didn't hire those guys, did you?"

Eric laughs. "It is all on tape, and they were very real. I wish we could measure how creepy everything got."

"Did you fall asleep?" Amanda's staring at me.

"I don't know," I admit. "I just sort of felt like I was walking around while I was still sitting in the chair."

"For how long?" Amanda continues.

"Five minutes," I answer.

"I think that and the chanting on the audio might have drawn them in," Sondra said. "Matty, you were right about the headphones."

He nods. "I heard it at home and I felt like they were there."

"Then he called me," Abigail pulled her tablet out, run-ning a few filters over the video. "From where I stood, it looked like the entities were ice cold against the heat out-side. I've only read about stuff like this."

"We came over as fast as we could." Matty smiles. "I also left my sleeping bag and a backpack outside. I'm scared to stay at home. I wouldn't want to bring this thing home with me."

"Won't your parents worry?" I ask.

Matty shakes his head. "I spend nights at Abby's once in a while. They didn't ask any questions."

"Really?" I raise my eyebrows in surprise.

Abby winks at me. "We get each other—being looked at funny all the time, you know? Like we're not like everyone else."

I never think about how much like a minority Abby probably is treated. I nod, turning back to the sunroom. My pizza slice has fallen on the floor, cheese side down, of course. I pick it up and toss it in the garbage can. Sondra steers me towards the pizza, grabbing a couple paper towels to clean up the mess.

Amanda focuses the camera on me. "Did you feel that cold sensation at any point today?"

"I feel cold pretty much all the time," I admit. "But I can't tell anymore which is the ghost and which is the demon."

The realization saddens me. I miss it. The ghost felt safe, felt familiar. Even Marissa, who doesn't believe in any of this, told me to trust my gut. I don't think the ghost is out to get me. If it were nearby, it could have taken over my body, but it didn't. And that's assuming that anything I know about possession is true.

The quieter I get, the louder it seems to get around me. It isn't that everyone is arguing, but ideas are being debated, with a lot of explanation from Abigail and Matty to Rana, who seems more and more lost. The commotion in the kitchen and sunroom is reaching a fevered pitch. There are too many voices and I take a step back, turning to the dining room. A firm hand grasps my arm.

"They're gone," Sondra says, turning me back around. " Our friend should be here soon. Just try to be still."

I grab a slice of pizza and sit at the table. Rana sits across from me. The slice is cold, but I don't care. I do need to eat something. I sip the water as the dry bread congeals with the once warm and melted cheese. Rana isn't quite staring at me, but she has a nervous sort of twitch about her.

The earlier argument about me possibly being gay crops up and I lean across the table, saying in a quiet tone, "Well, if you're lucky, she won't be real and it won't be an issue." My heart just sinks thinking this. I feel a brush of cold. I shouldn't be getting distracted with my not-girlfriend. There were dark figures trying to break into our house. I wouldn't want Marissa to be tainted by that.

Rana yawns, sinking farther in the chair. "This is insane."

"Crazy, right?" I try to make a joke of it.

Her expression is set in stone. "I didn't expect this when I said I wanted to stay."

"I'm not doing this on purpose." I get more defensive than I probably need to be.

Eric is behind Rana, his camera trained on us. Abigail grabs a slice of pizza and a soda and comes to sit with us. I can see Matty whispering something to Sondra and Amanda. I immediately assume they're talking about me.

"I can't believe Jamaal just left." She throws her hands up in the air. "He's such a coward."

"What?" I'm not sure what to make of this. "He was mad at me for what I said."

"For what you remembered." Rana corrects me, her dark eyes narrowed. "I'm not supposed to talk about it, pretend like I haven't heard my parents—and your parents—talk about this. That happened, Roni. The thing when you were little. I've heard the story a dozen times. It's why you moved a couple years ago, and then again after school ended this year. Things started to get too active, in a weird way, at your old house. They put these special nails in the house and we thought we'd trapped them there, but they followed you here."

Once again I'm too stunned to speak. Eric's mouth is agape. The slice of pizza is frozen in midair as Abigail's eyes grow larger. Sondra is still talking with Matty, but Amanda is staring at me and Rana. I try to avoid her insistent look. If I didn't know better, it wasn't a look of "what?" so much as a "I can't believe you said that out loud" sort of look.

"Roni," Amanda says as she crosses into the dining room, "are you okay?"

My eyes are glued to Rana. "What are you saying?"

Rana lowers her eyes. "Ron, you know you're my favorite cousin, but you have some crazy stuff that happened to you before I was born. And it's all happening again."

"What's happening again?" I am on my feet, leaning across the table.

"Why don't you remember?" Rana's eyes are brimming. "They're back and they want you."

THIRTY-FOUR

AFTER EVERYTHING THAT'S HAPPENED, you'd think I'd curl up in a ball and hide in my room. Or maybe that I'd freeze and ask more questions, demand answers. None of those things happen. Faster than anyone sees, I'm gone. Matty might be the only person who knows where I'd go, but I take off. Out the front door and into the unsafe world. I know they're watching; they're after me. That doesn't matter. I just need to get outside and breathe. Get away from the chaos that's unfolding in my house and mind.

This could be, by far, the stupidest thing I've ever done. There was a house full of people who were doing everything in their power to protect me. But I didn't realize how much I'd miss the silence, and support, my brother provided. Of all the times for him to get called to work. Though, as a cop, this is pretty normal. I've sent him a couple messages with no response. I hope he's okay. The information overload was just that, and it isn't long before I'm pouring with sweat, having nearly sprinted, standing in front of the haunted house.

Why do I keep coming here? What did Rana mean? Have those things been after me my whole life? Until now, I've never noticed the presence, the feeling of eyes always on me. What's changed? What caused this to surface now? Why would they be coming to get me?

I stumble through the opening in the window, feeling hot. There is stuff in my pockets, a backup battery pack for the EMF, and a lot of lint. I pull the hood over my face, stuff my hands in my pockets, and sit on the second lowest step. I'm trying to push everything away, everything out of my mind.

That feeling returns. There are eyes on me, all around me. I say a quiet prayer in my head, but the air feels close. Even though I'm in the foyer, with nothing near me, it feels like there are walls closing in around me.

I feel like I'm having a panic attack, like a huge weight is pressing down on me from all angles, crushing me, so I take several minutes just to listen to my own breathing. There is a distinct pounding in my head and then the familiar coolness. Has my ghost returned? I jump to my feet, but there isn't a sign of the white wisp.

"Are you here?" I ask, not expecting an answer.

Just as before, the words are a quiet whisper in my ear. "Yes, but you should go."

In all of the ghost hunting videos I've seen, not once has a spirit been able to speak clearly. Does that mean this is the demon? The dark entities? The djinns?

"Are you going to take over my body?" I ask the question not knowing if I'll get an honest answer.

A soft sound of laughter—kind, not mean-spirited—begins, and my gut tells me to relax. There is no danger here, not yet.

The response continues. "You aren't safe here. I can't protect you."

"Why do I keep coming back here?" I ask, my eyes searching for some sign of my ghostly friend.

"Go. Now." The voice is urgent.

I don't feel scared, even though I know I should be. "I don't see anything."

"They're coming." The voice falters.

That wary feeling returns and I turn. There is always darkness in the neighborhood. Now it looks like the darkness is moving, like a wave, growing taller and more menacing as it draws near. I blink a few times, frozen in place by the fear that should have been here all along. In an instant, the wave crashes and clears. There's nothing there. I want to breathe a sigh of relief, but the coldness takes a partial solid form as two hands firmly grasp my shoulders.

"They're outside." The voice urges, "You have to go, now."

I turn and freeze, staring the ghostly entity in the face, or what would be the face. The white wisp is there, a mass of moving smoke. It has a form, it just isn't anything I can relate to. It isn't until I step back that I see what I couldn't see before, the ghost moving right with me, and we pass under the gaping hole above, slivers of moonlight leaking in.

"Marissa?" My mind is trying to process, and I'm staring at my friend, who's looking scared. "What?"

She shakes her head. "Now, Roni. Go."

"But?" I'm too stunned to move. "Marissa?"

"Roni, I can't stop them," she says, lowering her eyes. "I couldn't help you earlier. I'm sorry. Coming during the day, while you were dreaming, was hard enough."

I'm still not moving, despite the dread creeping in. "But how can you be . . ."

I can't finish the thought when she smiles that soft smile I've grown accustomed to. "Dead? I've been dead a while, sweetie. We can talk about this later. You need to go."

I should feel scared, like I did at the house, but I don't. She turns away, and I see the shadows moving in the kitchen. There's some courage burrowing inside me and I take a step closer, but Marissa pushes me back, her cool hands on my shoulders.

"This isn't your house," she warns. "You can't just send them away."

"I can help you." I don't know how, but I feel like I can.

"I'm not going to risk hurting you." Her hair falls across her face as she speaks. "Move it. I'll catch up with you later."

I'm scared, but not for myself—for her. How can she possibly deal with djinns? How is it possible this girl I was possibly crushing on isn't alive? I never would have imagined I could have, like, a serious relationship, but the idea is fading and my hope with it. The one person I connect with . . . and she isn't even alive. I'm doomed to be alone. I don't understand how I can see her. How did I not notice this? Was I the only one who ever saw her? My gut is telling me to stay. I don't move.

"You told me to do what I thought was right." I move closer. "I can't leave you. Come on."

Marissa shakes her head. "I will be fine, Roni. Besides, looks like the cavalry is here."

Her eyes shift to the window and I follow her gaze. On my bike, I see Matty coming at breakneck speed. I'm torn. Do I stay or go?

A rush of darkness covers us and Marissa pushes me back, knocking me down, away from the reach of the hands that are clawing out for me. I stare up in horror. The darkness is like a layer of thick black smoke, but there are hands—reaching and grabbing—from everywhere. I scramble on my hands and knees, jumping through the window, feeling glass crunch underneath me as I roll out of the way.

I stare into the house. The darkness is draining, suffocating Marissa. I lean forward, but I know I'll only be more of a hindrance. My mind stops as I reach into my pocket, feeling the brand new battery pack. I'm not sure what I'm thinking, but I throw the battery pack and it slides to a stop a few inches away from Marissa. My eyes widen as I watch her burn brighter, and the darkness backs away.

Matty has jumped off the bike, running towards me. "What are you thinking?"

I shake my head. "Do you have any batteries on you?"

"What?" Matty is staring at me with confusion.

I don't have time to be polite, so I turn Matty around and rifle through the bag, searching through each compartment. I grab three packs of batteries and hurl them into the house. The bright light flashes even more and Marissa shakes her head, looking tired.

"What are you looking at?" Matty asks.

"Didn't you see?" I don't take my eyes off of Marissa. "Can't you see her?"

"Who?" Matty is gripping my arm. "We need to get back to the house."

"You're coming, right?" I'm looking worriedly at Marissa, who is walking gingerly towards me.

"That was cute." She laughs. "He can't see me, Ron. You're the only one who sees me."

The darkness is circling, gaining strength. I can feel that oppressive energy that Amanda spoke of. Outside, it feels like it isn't as suffocating. I need to go, but I don't want to leave Marissa. If she is a ghost, can she go wherever she likes? I give her a questioning look, but it's Matty who pulls me back into the moment.

"We have to go, now." Matty grabs my wrist, pulling me forward.

My feet are moving, but my eyes are set on Marissa, who is fading from sight. The dark mass is regrouping. There isn't time to falter, and we run out of the neighborhood.

THIRTY-FIVE

I'M EXPECTING EVERYONE TO BE UPSET, to be angry with me, but it looks like the team was more worried about safeguarding the house than being angry at anyone. My eyes are downcast as I enter. A cool rush moves past me and my eyes dart up. She's here. She's safe.

Sondra gives me a slight smile. "Didn't realize you could run that fast."

"I surprise myself sometimes," I say, my eyes scanning the room. Where did she go? And where's Jamaal? How is he still not back?

"Can you try to stay inside the house?" Amanda comes forward, a box of salt in hand. "Keep this nearby."

"I'm on a low-sodium diet," I quip.

"I'd laugh if it were the first time I'd heard that." Amanda rolls her eyes. "We are still reviewing all the footage. "

I grimace, staring at the laptop. "I'm not sure how long I can stay awake."

"No worries." Eric comes into view, focusing the camera on me. "I brewed a pot of coffee. Tea isn't strong enough."

I groan. I'm dying to get somewhere private, to find Marissa and ask her a thousand questions. Now isn't the time. Rana is looking mega-guilty, her eyes on the table in front of her. I know I need to talk to her, but I just don't know that I care.

"What did you tell them?" I ask, sitting down across from her.

The entire team is watching, and Matty is on the fringe, Abby giving him a consoling smile. The two are close friends. When Matty first started to be open about his gender identity, it never phased Abby like it did the rest of us. The memory is biting. I was not as kind as I should have been. I acted weird, kind of like Rana did. In hindsight, I feel ashamed. I should have been a better friend. Matty is putting his life in danger for me now, and it took me years to finally see that he was the same person. Since I'm going through some sort of thing now, I guess I see how important it is not to judge others.

Rana looks up, her face drained. "I don't have much to tell, Roni. My parents always talked about something crazy happening a long time ago, that we had to be careful around you, but I never needed to."

"You said they were after me," I say pointedly.

Rana squeezes her eyes shut. "Look, Robia told me the story. Well, I heard her and Sara talking about it. Right before you moved into this house."

"And?" I know she's stalling.

Rana has the team's undivided attention. She fusses with her hair, trying to avoid the looks. There are at least two cameras on. The EMF and REM-POD are set on the table. I roll my eyes at this.

"All I know is that you did something, by accident, when you were really little and it caused them—the djinns—to want you to replace whomever you got rid of," she says these words with quiet resolve.

"That's it?" I glare. "No, Rana, you know more. Spit it out."

This time she's wringing her hands, making a strange sort of face, like she's doing long division without a calculator. "We've always been told that we shouldn't bring it up, unless there's some sort of emergency. You know how we are. We don't talk about bad stuff, just gloss over it."

"This doesn't qualify as an emergency?" I gesture to the windows. "What did I do?"

The floodgates finally open and the words come out in a rush. "You were riding your bike or something—a tricycle maybe—inside the house, and you knocked into a bookshelf and the whole thing came down. No one seemed to be hurt, but then like two or three days later, there was all this knocking or banging on your doors and there was no one ever there. Your parents never opened the door, but they went to the Imam and he read at your house for like two days and told them you'd killed a little djinn girl who thought you were her friend, and they wanted you as a replacement. They finally sent them away, but a year ago, things started picking up, so you moved."

The whole room is silent. I don't even know how to process this. A quiet voice whispers in my ear, "No, I'm not a djinn, just a regular ghost. It's a long story."

I try not to react, but the EMF and REM-POD go off. Eric is on his feet in a second, panning the camera towards me. I don't see anything. At this point, I've only seen Marissa by myself. Will she show up on the camera as the white wisp? In a few cases, I've seen it with my naked eye. I'm not sure that'll happen now.

Amanda brings her handheld EMF right next to me. "About ten degrees cooler. Did you find your ghost?"

I feel the blood rushing to my face. Eric and Sondra are laughing at me. Rana looks stricken from across the table.

"Maybe." The word tumbles out. I feel the brush of cool and then she's gone.

Amanda raises her eyebrows at me. "Warming up now. Must not like me."

"I'm sure that isn't it," I argue. I stop myself, for once. I have no idea what they're going to say or do to her. I need to know her story. How on earth does she piece into all of this? "Is that it, Rana?"

My cousin is turning pale. "Yeah. That's it. That's enough."

Sondra clears her throat. "Wow, this is a lot of information. How can we verify any of it?"

Eric nudges Sondra. "Thomas should be here once the sun is up."

"Thomas?" Is there another part of this team? How many more people are going to invade my house?

"He's a local professor of the occult," Eric says this as he makes his body stiff, walking like a vampire.

Amanda pushes him in the back. "Dude, she is scared enough. Stop that."

"I'm okay," I say, and I mean it. I do feel okay. Knowing that my ghost is someone I sort of already know and have a soft spot for makes me a lot more at ease.

Sondra glances at her teal and black watch. "Think you can sleep and not have nightmares, for once?"

"I can try." There is absolutely no way I'll be able to sleep.

Rana gives me a sad look. "I'm sorry, Roni. I didn't want to upset you."

A twinge of indignation is boiling up, but something cool passes by me, setting the EMF off again. "I get it, Rana. That doesn't make it okay, but I get it. And where's Jamaal?"

She shrugs. "Don't know. He hasn't responded to calls or messages. Must be something crazy going on. Are you sure you're okay in your room alone?"

I nod. "I'll just pour salt around the doors and windows to stop anything bad from coming in."

"But anything bad also can't get out once you do that." Rana grimaces.

"We'll be watching." Eric points to the laptop. "No worries, chica. You'll be fine."

There is no doubt in my mind that I'll be fine. I almost feel relieved as I climb the steps, feeling the familiar cool air all around me. Matty is hovering by the door, Abby staring at me, past me, almost.

Abigail takes a step closer. "Are you okay, Roni?"

I nod. "Hope this isn't too much for your first investigation."

I meant it as a joke, sort of. She doesn't laugh. "This is way scarier than I would have ever guessed. I've always seen, felt stuff, but this is another level."

"Wait, you can see things?" I take a step down from the staircase, even if I feel the cooling calm from Marissa beckoning me upstairs.

"I don't need the tablet," Abigail confesses. "I can see your friend, the outline of her."

I turn, my eyes scanning the stairs. Marissa doesn't come into focus, but I know she's there. "You can see her?"

"Any relation to your girlfriend?" Matty asks, starting to raise his camera.

"Stop that." Abigail knocks his arm down. "There are enough cameras on Roni and her friend."

A wave of relief washes over me. "Thanks, Abigail." I don't want to tell them more about her, about Marissa, not yet.

"You can just call me Abby," she says. "Everyone does."

I muster the courage and ask one of many questions, "When did you and Matty get so close?"

Matty starts to turn away, but Abigail turns him forward. "Blaine, if you can believe it."

"Blaine?" I raise my eyebrows.

"Blaine hates Matty, torments him through gym and the weight room," Abby explains, gesturing lifting weights with her hands. "When I saw it happening, I gave my little brother something to think about."

Matty cut in, "Yeah, Abby told him that what he was doing was what all her bullies had done to her. The same bullies that Blaine had beaten back. He still kinda hates me, but he doesn't call me a tranny or anything."

"Matty!" Abigail balks, swatting his arm. "Don't ever use that word. That's like me calling myself a retard. Those words aren't okay. If we use them, other people think it's okay to use them. Normalization."

And then it hit me. Society spends so much time trying to dictate to everyone what is and isn't proper. The world tries to force values down our throats and we're all just trying to be ourselves. Why is that so hard? I'm seriously crushing on a ghost who is a gorgeous girl and that should be okay. Being perceived as gay is probably just as awful as being perceived as disabled; people harboring pre-conceived notions about you before you open your mouth. When I look at both Matty and Abigail, I realize they can't hide who they are, and they shouldn't. Neither should I.

"Those words don't define either of you," I say, feeling a coolness draw near. It wraps a phantom arm around my chest and rests a cold chin on my shoulder, making me shiver. "I'm glad you both are here, for me, for each other. I can use all the friends I can get right now."

The arms let go and I turn, following the unseen figure up the stairs.

THIRTY-SIX

I PLACE A TOWEL AT THE BASE OF THE door and pour salt on it. In Islam, for reasons I never thought to ask, it's sinful to waste salt. I always assumed it was because salt preserved food back in the day. Makes sense to me. I pour salt on the windowsill itself and the room somehow seems more open. I try not to jump as I see Marissa siting on my bed, her long legs stretched out in front of her. She's barefoot, wearing jeans and a loose-fitting T-shirt. I feel butterflies in my stomach.

"Be careful." She wags a finger at me. "They're going to think you're talking to yourself."

I sit down at my laptop, pulling the hood over my head. "Am I talking to myself?"

"You're not crazy, Ron." Marissa slides forward. I glance at the laptop, seeing the sheets on my bed move ever so slightly, bunching up, with no apparent cause.

"I'm not sure what to think," I admit. "Who are you? What are you doing? Are you attached to me?"

There is some lore that ghosts attach, are anchored, to places or things, but rarely people. Do I have something of hers? My mind flies straight to the picture. I gave it to Matty, didn't I? The book isn't on the shelf anymore. What was the significance of it?

"You look beat, darlin'," she drawls. "We can talk about this whenever."

I narrow my eyes, not quite glaring. "I got a good nap."

Her eyebrows raise and she says, "Should I get your blankie out?"

I can feel the blood rushing to my face, the heat rising. "At least I don't have to admit that to you." I try to force a laugh. "He usually stays in the bureau. Did you take him out?"

She smiles, a warm, inviting sort of smile. "Yeah. Though, I have seen you talk to him, is it? Why is he a guy, exactly?"

I grit my teeth. There's normal teenage awkwardness and then there's this. "I don't know."

Her smile broadens to a grin as she slides closer to me. I can't take my eyes off of her, even though I'm ridiculously embarrassed. She's teasing me and I'm still completely smitten.

"Where did you get him?" There are slight dimples in her cheeks as she continues, doing her best to not laugh. "Does he have a name?"

Do I say more or less? At least she does already know, so I can't be more embarrassed, can I? "Fat Face."

The eruption of laughter has me breaking eye contact, but only for a second. It is a really silly name. I should have outgrown the blanket, but I never really did. A moment passes as she tries to catch her breath. Can ghosts breath? Probably not a question worth asking,

"I'm sorry." She wipes the tears from her face. "I didn't think you could be any more adorable."

I blink in surprise. "Adorable?"

"Absolutely." She holds my gaze for a moment, the smile locking me in place. "Does Fat Face have more of a backstory?"

I stare at the ceiling. "And here I was hoping we'd stop at you thinking I was adorable."

"Later." She sets her hand on the back of my chair. "Go on."

I set my jaw. "Oh boy." I press my lips together tightly. "I guess my sister didn't want him, Fat Face, and so my mom gave him to me when I was born. I've had him ever since."

Marissa leans closer, brushing a stray piece of hair away from my face, the coolness around her making me feel slightly less embarrassed. "That is so cute. And you had, what, like adventures with him?"

I want to be annoyed or angry. I feel nothing except the desire to kiss the mystery girl in my bed. That's something that I don't think I've ever thought in my entire life. "Maybe. You got your answer, stop teasing me."

A soft laugh escapes. "Fair enough. Should I go get Fat Face? You do seem to sleep better with him around."

I arch an eyebrow. "I'm sure we can find a replacement."

Marissa smirks, sliding back to her original position, patting the space next to her. "Turn the lights off and it'll look like you're just sitting in the dark."

I know she's right about the camera, and I close the lid of the laptop, pull my sweatshirt off, and turn the light off. The moment I touch the bed, I do feel really tired. She gives me a playful smile.

"If you're tired, go to sleep," she urges. "I can keep watch. I promise nothing will bother you."

"Can you even promise that?" I ask, sitting down next to her.

Unlike before, her hands aren't like ice, just cool. Her palm is pressed to my cheek. "I can promise you the world, if you'd let me."

A chill runs down my back. "Why are you protecting me?"

"Because you saved me," she answers.

I blink at her, unable to process the words. I rest my chin on my knees as I fold myself into a tighter ball. "Didn't you hear? I killed some kid."

"Yeah, and that kid was a djinn, one I crossed a long, long time ago." Her hand is at my back. "When you killed her, you freed me."

"That's why you're here?" I ask.

"Sort of." She smiles. In the moonlight, I can see the darkness to her eyes.

"Come on, Marissa," I urge. "You saved my life a few times over. Why are you staying? Not that I want you to leave."

"I did something really stupid a long time ago," she confesses. "God, just lie down, Roni. I promise I won't leave."

"Even if the gang downstairs tries to get rid of you?" I ask. Our faces are way too close together. When did that happen?

She brushes a tuft of hair out of my face. "Then I'd have to go."

"You can't just hide?" I feel my heart begin to race.

"Relax." She's trying to sooth me. "If they get rid of the djinns, you won't need my help anymore."

"It isn't your help that I might miss." I hear the words replay in my head. God, I'm such a dork. I should just say it. No, that'd be stupid. I don't know what I feel.

She's watching me, scrutinizing my reaction. "I'll miss you too."

Sleep is getting the better of me and I sink into the bed, letting Marissa lie down next to me. In this tiny twin bed, the two of us shouldn't fit. I should be cold, but she pulls the covers up, over me, not her. I glance over, realizing she isn't feeling cold or hot.

A soft laugh escapes. "I assume you're going to get colder the longer I stay."

"So what happened?" Real smooth, Roni, I chide myself.

I'm lying on my back and she rolls over to face the ceiling. "You're so stubborn."

"No, I'm not," I laugh.

"Okay, you're right." She sticks her tongue out at me. "I won't tell you how long ago it was, but I guess djinns don't age like we do. Anyway, I was being haunted—a lot like you are now—but back then, there were no ghost hunters. You just went to an asylum."

"They got rid of asylums in the 1960s or 1970s." I'm searching my brain for history facts. Being Indian, history was not one of my most studied subjects, even if I found it quite interesting. You can't get a good job from studying history, as my father likes to say.

Marissa lets out a loud sigh. "This happened in 1952."

"Wow." A moment passes, like she's waiting for me to process this. "The picture. That house. Is it yours?"

"No." Marissa shakes her head. "I wanted you to have it, so I found a way to get it into that old yearbook. A different house used to be there. I'm wondering if the connection between us keeps drawing you there."

"So, wait, the house in the picture, that isn't the gutted house we see today?" I ask.

"That haunted house was burned to the ground," Marissa confirms. "I think that was their house, their place— the djinns. The plots got sold, built on, and then things got spooky."

"Is there something still there?" In all the research we'd done, Matty and I were never able to confirm anything more than some tunnels.

"I don't know." She lets out a slow sigh. "I think it's just got a lot of traffic, not unlike your house now."

"Is that how you ended up there?" I ask. "How you got stuck there?"

Her eyes lower. "No."

I wait a second, hoping she'll elaborate. The silence doesn't seem as heavy as it would with anyone else. It almost feels nice. I take in all her features as she sits there, eyes downcast, not noticing me staring. The way her fingers are curled around my sleeve. The way her legs are tucked underneath her. It's all so remarkably cute.

She lets go of my sleeve, bringing her eyes up. "No, Ron, I ended up there because I thought I was helping someone. I lost my life because I didn't realize what I was doing, what I was agreeing to."

"I don't understand," I say, sliding closer, wishing I could comfort her, seeing her grow less solid.

"I hope you never understand." She tries to smile. "The house is pretty evil. Your friend Eric might get his wish with the devil worshippers, or something. They were up to something, someone, a long time ago, long before even I got there. I was hoping your friends would have told you by now."

I lean closer, resting a hand next to her knee. "I'm not the one they're talking to."

"I don't get why they're hiding things from you." She shakes her head, her hair falling around her face.

"Nice try." I smile, seeing her face redden. "Don't change the subject. I can handle it."

Her smile is more reassuring than I expect. "I know you can. I wish they knew that."

"Go on." I want to be cool and aloof, but I also really want to know what she knows.

She takes a deep breath. "There's something there, Ron, something evil. I always thought it was just the djinns. Someone might have summoned something. Are you sure you don't have anything you accidentally took from there?"

I blink at her, gesturing to the yearbook. "Just the picture."

She laughs. "Right, besides that?"

"Nothing." I laugh. "So, 1952, huh?"

Marissa pokes me. "You're not going to comment on how old I am?"

"You look the same age as me," I say.

"Close." She turns to look at me. "Seventeen."

I reach out to touch her, surprised when I feel something solid under my fingertips. "Are you sure I'm not crazy?"

"Pretty sure." Marissa laughs. "Takes a little more energy to be solid than not."

"Sorry." I pull my hand back.

"It's nice to just be almost human again." She turns back to the ceiling. "To almost be a part of this world."

"You're a big reason I'm still a part of this world." These lines are getting worse and worse. How do boys talk to girls? Why can't I talk to one specific girl?

"The only reason I'm able to even be myself now is because of you." Marissa sits up. "I didn't know who I was talking to. I thought it was some little kid trapped in between being a ghost and moving on. I wanted to help. We did a séance, which is stupid, so don't agree to that or speaking to the entities. The thing asked me for help and I said I would do whatever I could. That's an open invitation for taking me over. I lost control of myself, of my body, of everything. I thought it was the djinn, but maybe it wasn't." Her voice wavers as she continues, "I wonder if your friends can shed some light on what happened. I'm not even sure how long I've been like this. I thought I'd been watching you for years, but now I just don't know. And I'm worried that I don't even know who I am anymore."

"I know who you are," I say this, feeling my heart lightening, like I'm making a huge admission without actually saying it.

Marissa turns to me, a soft smile on her face. "You're pretty much the only one."

There's that urge again. That desire to kiss her. I still have so many questions. Why can't I ever turn my brain off?

"Wait." I stop myself from sitting up, realizing they're watching. I roll over onto my side, facing her. "You were trapped for fifty years?"

"Your math needs some work." Marissa laughs. "Close enough. Yeah, and then—boom—I was just me, but ghost me. It took me years to just adjust to walking through things, not being seen by anyone, except you."

"I don't recognize you," I admit.

"You wouldn't." She slides her hand near mine. It's icy cold now. "I didn't know me until a few months ago. I was there, but this physical form you see, it took me a long time to remember. I was just that white smoke for a long long time."

"When we moved?" I ask.

She furrows her brow. "I hadn't thought about it. It's hard to know exactly. At first I followed you around, like a stalker, I guess." She laughs. "Not unlike now. But at the time, I just kept being drawn to you, to the house. I think you or Matty might have uncovered something. I remember it, but I can't find it, or haven't been able to. The image of it just vanishes from my mind. I wonder if it used to be mine, like something of mine that's jolted all these memories loose. It might be tying me here, besides you, to this time and place. I guess I could use that computer to look some stuff up."

I smile. "How many hours have you watched me waste looking at that thing?"

"A lot." She laughs. "But you do study an awful lot, so I won't harp on the time you waste with this kind of dangerous hobby."

I feel my face redden. She's scared for me. I can hear it in her tone. It might be the first moment I realize that our feelings might be mutual. I'm not sure how to handle that. "So, you have a ghostly attachment to me?" Another really nerdy response. How is she still talking to me?

Her laugh softens my anger at myself. "Yeah, actually. I can get away from you, but I seem to just keep snapping back. I do wonder why those entities aren't leaving. And why I'm able to fend them off. I've never been able to manifest powers, or never needed to."

"You could only just start that?" I'm struggling with what words are really capturing what I'm trying to say.

She nods, her hair falling across her face. "I just got scared for you," she adds this last part in a rush. "Something was always following you, besides me. As soon as you moved into this house, I noticed. It didn't start to get anyone else's attention until a month ago. Are you sure you didn't find something and bring it here? Something that that thing might be looking for? I had something it wanted, that's how it found me."

"What?" I wonder aloud.

"A brooch," She says. "It was an antique. I found it a thrift shop. Cute, but was not worth this."

"Who else noticed the activity?" I ask, feeling my eyes growing heavier.

"Your mom," she answers, looking skyward. "You think she hates you, but she doesn't. She's trying to protect you."

"They haven't told me anything," I argue. "How can you side with them?"

"Roni," she says with exasperation in her voice, "she is praying nonstop. I'm surprised whatever she's doing isn't keeping me away. But it is keeping those djinns away, and whatever else they have with them."

"There aren't just djinns?" I feel foolish even asking this question.

"No." She slides down next to me. "That thing you saw, in your grandfather's room, that's a demon. It sucked the life out of him, but he'd been trying to fight it off for a week. It just overpowered him. It would have gotten you too."

"If you hadn't gotten in the way." I stare at her, this time not being embarrassed about it. "You saved me."

"Yeah," she says with a smirk. "So, next time I tell you to move, do it, huh?"

I nod. "Aye, aye, captain."

Marissa pats the comforter. "You look beat, cutie. I don't sleep, so you get some rest, okay?"

I have so many questions. The entire day, or week, is catching up to me. I drift off at some point, not being plagued by any scary entities for an entire night.

Thirty-Seven

THE SUN IS SPILLING INTO THE ROOM. I can feel a pair of very cold arms around me. I rub my eyes, turning and seeing Marissa fast asleep beside me.

"Ghosts don't sleep, huh?" I say this stifling a laugh.

It's gotten super cold and I grab my sweatshirt from the chair at my desk, pulling it on. The salt is still layered on the windowsill and the towel hasn't shifted. I pull the door open, careful not to move the towel. Will this lock Marissa into the room? The moment the door is open, I feel the darkness surface. The salt must be keeping whatever it is out. My mind slows to the admission from Marissa. There are djinns and a demon here, plus my ghost. The house is getting more and more crowded.

I take a deep breath, knowing I really have to go to the bathroom. The house is cold, much colder than it should be. I hustle to the bathroom, rushing through using the bathroom and brushing my teeth. I peek into my room. Marissa is still sound asleep. I feel bad waking her up, but then again, I don't want anything to happen without her around.

It's hard to make it not look like I'm waking someone up. I open the closet and try to throw a few things in her general direction. This has no effect. I let out a loud sigh and slide across the bed, feeling the chill as I get closer to her. I stare at the ceiling, my eyes darting to the camera in the corner.

"Marissa," I say her name as quietly as possible.

My patience isn't great, and I run a hand across my face before waving it in her general direction, expecting my hand to stop at her body. It slides right through a block of frozen air, slamming into the wall. The sound alerts her and she shakes herself awake.

"What was that you were telling me about sleeping?" I ask, massaging my hand.

The playful smirk has returned. "I don't sleep often." She holds her hand out. "I can apply some ice for you."

I don't hesitate, sliding closer to her. "It's the least you can do."

"Of course." She laughs, covering my hand with both of hers, the slight pain fading in seconds. "I don't know if I can leave the room with the salt. But if you move it, that might be weird."

"Right." I'm not facing the camera, not worried about anyone watching. "I can nudge it with my foot. Also, it did feel super creepy outside."

"In the hallways?" She arches an eyebrow.

I nod, getting up and stretching, my stomach grumbling. "I should probably eat something."

Marissa nods, following as I fold a small corner of the towel with my foot, allowing her to come out. I can tell she's behind me. I feel a lot more confident with my own personal protector in tow. I expected everyone to be up, but now embarking on the third day of this misadventure, I'm not surprised to see most of the team asleep.

The sun is out, but the rooms are still dark. I pull the blinds back in the sitting room, finding Matty and Amanda stretched out on two different sofas. Sondra is in the sunroom. I can see her hunched over the laptop, headphones covering her ears. Rana must be sleeping upstairs. There's a sleeping bag that looks like a cocoon in the dining room. That must be Abigail. I almost jump as Marissa speaks.

"They've earned a little bit of rest," she comments. "Looks like they've salted the doors. But then, where's the heaviness coming from?"

I shrug. "Kept it in, maybe?"

"Maybe." She doesn't sound very sure. "Can we watch whatever Sondra was watching?"

The fact that no one can hear Marissa is making me feel weird. Will her voice come up on the recorders? Will it look like I'm just talking aloud?

She pokes me. "I'm talking to you."

"I know," I whisper. "Everyone else is going to think I'm talking aloud."

Marissa laughs. "Make it look good."

I bite back a smart comment, shaking my head. Sondra is leaning over the laptop, but it isn't too tough to wrestle it out from under her elbow. I pick it up, disconnecting the power cord, and move to the dining room and nice sitting room area. I set the laptop on the low table, crossing my legs and booting it up. The password is taped to the top right-hand corner on a yellow Post-it Note. Marissa scoots in next to me, her shoulder brushing mine. I get a slight chill, but it's quickly gone by the rush of heat on my face.

There are a zillion things on the desktop. Open, above everything else, is a document. It looks like a map. At the center is a crude drawing of a house. The caption labels it as "main haunted house." Scattered across the image are stick figures representing different people. Under the haunted house is one labeled for me—right next to it, one for Marissa. Her stick figure has a box around it. Farther across the page are a group of figures, labeled "djinns," and another labeled "demon." There are notes scrawled in tight print. The arrows seem to be moving in all directions, but a bright pink line is drawn between the demons and then between Marissa and the old house. I glance at Marissa, who gives me a slight shrug in response. Does this mean the demons and Marissa are linked to the old house? She said as much just a few hours ago. Maybe the team is better than I'm giving them credit for. It looks like the map points to another document. When I hover the mouse over it, the text changes color. I think about pressing it, but Marissa gives me a slight nudge and instead I scan through the most recently used programs list. The video player is at the top of the list. I pop it open and look through the queued videos. In addition to that list, there is a currently recording option. For fun, I turn it on, scanning through the various feeds until I find the one on me. I study the image, not seeing even a hint of Marissa on the screen. I'm starting to really wonder what's true and what's fake about all the ghost hunting books and shows I've watched. Is any of it based on fact? Has anyone ever developed an actual relationship with a ghost?

A cold finger pokes me. "Are we viewing the feed from last night or just staring at ourselves? Well, just you—I'm not even there."

"This is crazy," I admit. "How is this even possible?"

Marissa lets out a loud sigh, moving my hair against my shoulder. "My expert opinion is that when I'm in solid form, then I don't appear as anything, but when I'm not solid, then I do appear. Not sure what the physics are on that. I was a girl growing up in the forties—I didn't get a whole lot of science."

"No?" I ask. "No experiments with oversize goggles and some dreamy boy?"

"Like that idiot Blaine?" she says with an icy tone.

"Hey, I have eyes. I can look," I argue. There's a sense of pride burning inside.

Growing up in a conservative Indian family doesn't afford me any chances to date. I wonder if this is what it feels like to be infatuated with someone, to know they're into you, and to know they don't want you to be into anyone else. I'm not sure how to describe it except to say that I have a nice, fuzzy feeling all around me, with a hint of winter.

The tapes from last night are uneventful. It isn't until midnight passes, and everyone is beginning to fall asleep, that the house starts to reflect some strange activity. The lights are flickering on and off in all of the rooms. One by one, I see the dark mass move from room to room. There appears to only be one, but the movement is hard to gauge. Like Marissa, the entities could be moving as fast as they please.

Each member in the house is fast asleep and then the entity stops. A transfer of light blinds the camera for a fraction of a second. It doesn't look like anything's changed, but something has. Their bodies are limp. I glance at Sondra sitting in the sunroom. Her body doesn't even appear to be moving to take in air. Marissa gives me a warning look. In a flash, she's across the room.

Her eyes betray her worry. "Where's the salt?"

I give her a questioning look, remembering I left it upstairs. The kitchen is right there. I'm on my feet in a moment, finding a box near the stove. I wait for Marissa to join me in the dining room before pouring it over the entrance and then rushing to the windows and other entrance from the sitting room, sealing the room from any dark entities. The heavy feeling is receding. We're safe now. Nothing can get in here, that isn't already here, like Marissa.

"Was she breathing?" I ask.

"Faintly," she confirms. "I couldn't jolt her awake with my hand. Let's keep watching. Maybe we can figure out what they're doing."

I furrow my brow. "It looked like they were sucking the life out of them."

Marissa's cool hand is on my arm. "The tapes, Roni. We can guess all we want, but there has to be something there, right?"

I hop over the salt, grab the headphones from Sondra's limp body, and hurry back to the safety of the dining room. The hop back in reminds me of the lava game from a when I was a kid, jumping from surface to surface without touching the floor. I shudder, feeling like an intruder in my own house, my own mind.

Marissa grabs me firmly, her cold hands like ice. "Snap out if it."

With a quick, firm shake of my head, the presence is gone. "Is it trying to grab me?"

"Seems that way." Marissa lets go, nodding to the laptop. "Come on."

The dark feeling has faded, but I still feel uncomfortable. I shiver, sitting down, feeling like there are eyes on me. I look up and the sun is out, yet the hallway and rooms beyond are black. The hands are reaching, reaching for me, reaching and stopping at the salt-covered entryways.

"Ignore it, Ron," Marissa says. "We can't make them go away."

"You can't?" I ask.

She lowers her eyes. "I am running on empty, doll. I'd have to drain a car battery to get enough juice to do what I did last night."

A thought starts and I blink at her. "What happened at the courthouse? I didn't dream that, did I?"

"No." Her smile tightens. "I don't know what was there. It didn't want me there. I was scared that it might hurt you, but I had to run. I was afraid it would follow you, so I hoped to lure it away. I think it worked, for a little while."

"How does that work?" I ask. "I mean, can you just run from place to place?"

She laughs. "Not like you, no. I just move and the world around me sort of stands still. It isn't like I can think of a place and be there, but pretty close. Like last night. I knew I needed to get from here to that haunted house before you."

"There are so many really nerdy questions I have for you." I laugh, feeling carefree for just a second. "I hope we get the chance to get those answers after all of this."

"We will." Her scent is intoxicating, distracting.

There's something nagging at me, a strange warning, but I can't place it. I'm too unnerved by the hands that are reaching for me, the malice and hate that stretches across the expanse. Marissa wraps an arm around my shoulders, and it feels like a cold buffer is there.

"Can they see you?" I ask, leaning closer, feeling safer, wishing she would wrap both her arms around me and tell me everything is going to be okay. She can't know that. Neither can I.

She nods. "Oh yeah, and they are not fans."

I try to laugh, letting out a shaky breath instead. We both turn back to the footage. I don't see the room Rana is in. Is she still asleep upstairs? I knit my brow, receiving a firm shake of the head from Marissa, as if she knows what I'm thinking.

"Not a chance, Ron," she says. "I can't protect you. God knows what they'll do if they get their hands on you."

A thought starts and I begin to wonder. What if they're not a danger? That seems impossible. I'm scared to death. The dream I had about when I was little should be enough. I turn back to the video, not wanting to reveal that I'm filled with doubt.

The djinns move from room to room, person to person. There's no telling what they're doing. It doesn't appear like they're taking over those bodies. A strange scrabbling noise starts, stopping me from watching the video. It's followed by a low thump, then another. I see Eric lurch towards us and I know I'm wrong. The invisible barrier stops him from getting closer.

Any fear or terror I was feeling before is now rising exponentially. It isn't normal for a human to walk in the manner he's walking. The feet are touching the ground, but his upper body looks like it is attached to at least a dozen strings. His arms are stiff, but the hands and fingers are splayed out as if there's a wire on each digit. It's unnatural. Eric bares his teeth and a low-pitched growl begins.

I lean back, staring at his face. Marissa is leaning forward, a second away from getting on her feet. It dawns on me that we are trapped in this room. I can't leave. She can't leave. They can't get in. An idea starts in my head, and I know it's our only chance.

"If you flare like you did last night, will it get rid of them?" I ask, setting the laptop down.

"I don't have that energy." Marissa is giving me a wary look. "I don't think I can grab enough from the power in the house. They've tapped it out."

It occurs to me that the lights are on in all the rooms, but nothing is lit. After watching the videos, I know the lights were never turned off, but the power was sapped from them. The familiar hum from the refrigerator is gone. The EMF and REM-POD are in the hallway, silent and dark. All of our tools look like toys. They're of no use now. We don't have one thing that can really save us, protect us, from all these things we've sought out.

I get up, and I know what I have to do. I'm just hoping not to get too much of a fight out of Marissa. I shake my head. "We are going to be trapped here forever if you don't do something."

She sets her jaw, her face scrunched into a mix of hurt and anger. "No. Absolutely not."

"We don't have a choice, Marissa," I argue. "I'll recover. I did before."

She balks. "I barely touched you earlier. I just needed a quick jumpstart to get moving. And I was right—a few minutes later you were fine. What you're asking me to do now is something entirely different."

"I know you won't let me die." I feel this in my heart. Marissa won't let anything happen to me, despite any doubts that are in my mind.

Her eyes glisten. Can ghosts cry? I guess they can. I feel the dampness on my cheeks. This is our only play.

"I would never let anything happen to you," she says earnestly.

"I know." I shut my eyes. "Go ahead."

A moment passes and nothing happens. I open my eyes. She's staring at the hoard in front of us. What other option could she be debating?

Her eyes turn back to me. "I'll be here when you wake up, okay?"

I don't know if I can ever describe exactly what it feels like to have the energy, the life, sucked out of you. My limbs grow immensely heavy. My eyes are shutting. I can see Marissa getting more solid, less see through. She pats my arm, giving me a saucy look before kissing me on the cheek.

"We're going to talk about this later." Her voice is distant.

I can see the darkness shift. The light around her is forcing them back. It takes a couple seconds, and the whole room is bathed in white light. Eric thuds to the ground. The darkness is gone and I'm slowly losing consciousness. Marissa is back in front of me, in focus but somewhat transparent.

"Let's see if I can give any excess energy back," she says as she smiles.

I feel achy all over, but I let out a deep sigh, feeling tired. "You did it."

"For now," she warns. "They'll be back."

I swing my feet to the floor. "We better wake the rest of the team."

I start to get up, but I slump back down. Marissa's cold hand is trying to keep me upright, but I tilt over onto my side, my eyes closing as I pass out.

Thirty-Eight

When I wake up, I'm confronted with far more faces than I expected, and one furious girlfriend. Oh God, did I say that in my head? Please let no one be able to hear my thoughts. I don't think I'm allowed to be gay. I can feel my face scrunch up, like my head is pounding.

"What does that face even mean?" Rana asks. "Are you okay?"

I nod, easing up, squeezing my eyes shut for a second. "Yeah, what happened?"

Sondra is holding a glass of water out to me. "Well, where should I begin?"

"I woke up and saw the footage." I try to smile at Marissa as I reach for the glass and take a sip. "What did they do to you?"

The room grows quiet. Matty and Amanda are sitting at the table. Eric isn't there. Abigail is in the back, with a tall man. The tweed jacket makes him look like a teacher or something.

His eyes catch mine. A sheepish smile crosses his face. "I should introduce myself." He sets his glasses down on the table, his dark hair accented with shots of gray. "I'm Professor Thomas. I study the occult . . . but what you have here is quite something else."

I smile. "Hi."

This is the best response I can think of. Unlike the rest of the team, this guy looks old, like he can get discounts on movie tickets or goes to bed by eight. Knowing that no one else can see Marissa makes it harder for me to watch her. Out of the corner of my eye, I can see she's keeping her distance, but also she looks ready, like poised to move in a second. It's making me feel on edge. Balance is still very much an issue as I try to get up, and I feel pretty lightheaded from even this little movement.

Rana offers an arm. "How are you feeling?"

"Okay." I shake my head. "We—I mean *I*—hid in here once I started watching the tapes."

No one notices the slipup except Marissa. "I was here. You could just admit your ghostly friend almost killed you while trying to save everyone. Wonder how that'd go over."

"Those things, they did something to all of us," Sondra says this with disgust in her voice. "I didn't even think to protect anyone. Luckily Eric's girlfriend picked him up. He should be okay. Blaine was almost smart getting out of here when he did."

"I doubt my dad would agree." Abigail chuckles. "Maybe it'll teach Blaine a lesson about disrespecting the supernatural."

I don't realize I'm staring at the professor until I feel a very cold hand pushing my shoulder. "Hey, eyes on the prize, princess."

The rush of cold jolts me. "What are you doing here, Professor Thomas?"

"I'm the expert." He laughs as he sits down. "I feel vastly out of my depth, but I can tell you're all under a lot of stress and you're not making any of this up."

"We are definitely not making this up." I feel the heat rising on my neck. How can this guy even imply that we're making this up?

"Simmer down, hun," Marissa drawls. "You're going to have a heart attack if you let every Poindexter get the better of you."

I shake my head. If I didn't know better, it looked like the good professor was laughing, too. But at what? He can't hear her, can he? I glance at Marissa, who seems to have noticed the same thing.

"Maybe he's sensitive, like you?" Marissa says, getting closer.

Professor Thomas is on his feet in a second, moving around the long edge of the table, as far away from me—from Marissa—as possible. "The salt is an effective tool. But what we really need here is a cleansing."

"Remove the spirits from the house," Abigail explains.

The professor wipes the sweat beading on his forehead. "I've never performed an exorcism, but blessing or cleansing the house is the best way to go. I have some sage in my car. I can go room to room and try to clear the spirits."

"The ones attached to the house, right?" I ask.

"Yes." His eyes are on the ground.

Marissa looks angry. The look is one that would terrify me even if she were human. As a ghost, the look is that much more menacing. "I don't like him."

This is a surprisingly controlled comment. I nod, not daring to voice my agreement with her. "Are you sure?" I ask the professor.

"As sure as I can be," he replies.

Sondra puts a hand up. "I don't know."

I glance at Marissa, not arguing, not wanting him to cleanse the house, not yet, not until I'm sure. "Can we find out what they're doing here first?"

"I find it extraordinarily dangerous to use ghost boxes or anything like that." Once again he's fiddling with his glasses.

Abigail smiles at Rana. "A ghost box might allow a spirit to speak through it and use the already existing words to get a message across."

"What?" Rana asks.

I turn to Rana. "It's like a small radio. Theoretically a ghost can change the channels or use them to get words or phrases out. There are other, more dangerous methods available."

"Such as?" Rana crosses her arms. "God, please tell me you're done with this stupid hobby."

"Probably not," I admit, feeling the cool rush get closer. I say under my breath, "Not hardly."

"Better not be." Marissa smiles, leaning closer.

"An Ouija board." Professor Thomas stands up taller, clearing his throat. "Those items are unbelievably dangerous. You can't control whom you're speaking to. It could be an open invitation to anything that is around."

"My brother said there were djinns here," I start the thought. "Is there anything else here?"

"A ghost." Professor Thomas is staring at Marissa.

"Nothing else?" I press.

"Like what?"

"A demon?"

The room grows tight. Sondra lowers her eyes. Matty and Amanda are still not saying anything. Abigail flips through her notebook, scribbling something down. Rana laughs, but stops, seeing how serious everyone has become.

"That's a possibility." Professor Thomas takes a step closer. "Is the ghost under control?"

Before I can say anything, Marissa advances. "What? Am I what? I'm not a puppet."

No one else is seeing this, except maybe Abigail. Professor Thomas moves around the table, but this won't stop Marissa. She walks right through the table.

"Stop," I say this aloud and everyone stares at me. "Please, you're scaring the man."

All eyes are on me. Marissa has her arms crossed, her disembodied form halfway through the table. The discussion would continue, but the house groans and creeks. The sound makes my skin crawl. A second later, Marissa is again next to me, her anger gone, replaced with worry.

Matty is up, the EMF in his hand. The REM-POD in the hallway is blinking, but the alarm hasn't gone off. Something is coming.

THIRTY-NINE

THE SALT ACROSS THE DOORWAYS IS STILL
in place. The power has returned, but now everything is
flickering. It's like a wave. One after the other, each light in
the hallway and room leading to the dining room is bright-
ening and then popping. The sound is jarring each and
every time. Thomas, the supposed expert, looks absolutely
frozen in place. The rest of the team is hustling around, save
Abigail, who has moved to the dining room table. Matty is
looking over her shoulder; his body tenses, the EMF out-
stretched towards the kitchen.

Sondra cuts through all the commotion. "Guys . . .
everyone . . . stop."

The activity within the safety of the salted doors grinds
to a halt. Marissa is trying to grab a hold of me, her ghostly
hand finding no purchase. Matty drops the EMF he's
holding. The REM-POD in the hallway is wailing and then
groaning as something crushes it. The noise makes everyone
jump. I hear someone yelp. I think it's Rana, but I can't pull
my eyes away from the doorway.

"It can't get in here," Sondra says, taking a deep breath.
"Let's all just relax, okay?"

"Are you sure?" Rana asks, her voice quivering.

Marissa's voice is soft in my ear. "No, of course not. A
pile of salt is not really going to keep something out. If it
wants to get in, it will find a way. But it is a nice thought,
and it kept me in."

I give her a quizzical look. Is that just an old wives' tale? A way for people to believe they have some control? Is there something in the salt that might repel a spirit? The air is growing heavy, even within the salted room. Amanda grabs a cross. I stare at the piece of wood, wondering how anyone can derive some sort of confidence from it. In a way, I guess it is no more outlandish than the salt. My mother always preached having faith, believing. I guess now is the time to display a whole lot of faith.

A pocket Bible is produced and Thomas is speaking very quietly—too quietly for me, or anyone, to hear. Marissa is standing in front of me. She's more transparent than usual. I think about holding onto her, realizing how strange that would look. A slow creak begins as the entity shifts its weight to the other foot. From the hallway, the lights flicker and vanish. We're in a mostly dark room. The night fell while I was passed out, I guess. The only light is from the hand-crank flashlight that Matty is holding and the street-lights outside.

I feel the wall as I bump into it. The glass in the front door is pouring a shallow square of light into the hallway. The square is soon being filled with something dark. There is a foot, a hooved sort of foot. It breaks the tense silence as it slams to the ground, forcing cracks and splinters to form in the linoleum floor.

"It is just trying to scare you." Marissa is leaning close. "Look at me. You're okay. It can't hurt you."

"You said it could still get in here," I say. I feel tired—like I don't have an ounce of energy to give her.

Sondra turns to me. "No, I said it couldn't get in here."

"It's just salt." I look through Marissa who has moved to the doorway. "It isn't going to stop whatever that is."

"It's just trying to scare us." Sondra takes a step closer, moving around Amanda, who has the camera pointed at the hallway. "Scare you, really. Tell it to leave and it will."

"I don't think it likes having all these people here," Marissa comments, leaning around Amanda, who jumps at Marissa's closeness.

"What was that?" Amanda's eyes blink wildly as the light from the camera is spinning around the room.

Marissa rolls her eyes. "I guess I'm not part of the team, huh?"

I shake my head. "Come over here."

Now everyone's looking at me. I let out a loud sigh. Marissa passes everyone, all of them jumping as she draws closer to me, hopefully ending the discussion of whom I might be talking to.

"Only 'cause you asked so nicely." Marissa shoots me a playful smile. "Maybe ask it to leave again?"

"Think that'll work?" I say this as quietly as possible, knowing everyone's watching me.

"No." Marissa lets out a very, very cold breath. "But I am optimistic one of these characters can do something."

The foot pivots, and the sound of fingernails digging into the linoleum floor vibrates in my ears. A cool hand presses to my cheek. I don't want to look. I have seen too much. The entities from my dreams are bad enough, but this is like all of my fears made whole. Despite the salt, a hand reaches around the wall, the fingers curling to grip it more tightly. The black hands taper into long claws. The form isn't really a form at all. The places where there should be defined body parts are only masses of black smoke. The only solid things I can see and hear are the claws or hooves, the very edges of the entities' arms and legs.

A dark hole appears above a set of shoulders, or where shoulders should be. There aren't eyes, but the absence of anything at all. I shiver, and not from the cool presence of Marissa standing in front of me. Can she see this? Is everyone else seeing this? I can't tear my eyes away. It isn't until the hooved foot plants firmly through the salt that whatever quiet reverie we're all feeling crumbles.

The room turns into chaos. Any doubt I had as to whether anyone else could see or hear what I saw is gone in seconds. Much to my surprise, Thomas is at the forefront, cross in hand, denouncing the demon and telling it to leave. I can hardly understand what he's saying. I don't think I've ever been this scared in my life.

Marissa's semisolid form grabs my attention. "We have to go."

"Where?" I ask, gasping for breath. I must have been holding it in for at least a minute.

"The house?" Marissa doesn't sound too sure.

"Don't move." Sondra is inching closer to me. "It is manifesting your fear. Don't be afraid."

I stare at Sondra incredulously. How can she ask me not to be afraid? With Marissa so close, I'm getting cold. I can see my breath coming out in short, quick puffs. I'm beginning to hyperventilate. My brain is saying this is a rationale response. I am trying to remember something, anything, to pray, to hold onto. Even my ghostly girlfriend isn't solid, isn't someone I can grab and hold onto and never let go.

Sondra looks calm and composed. The entity doesn't advance, though it is tilting its head to one side, like a dog would when it doesn't understand what you're asking it to do. The look gives me pause and makes me worry for Thomas, who's standing way too close to the thing for my taste. A moment passes. Does it understand? The arm solidifies from gas to solid and it slams through Thomas, slamming him across the room, through the dining room table, and out the windows that lead into the backyard. A shriek erupts from Abigail, who I see is shaking in the corner. Matty has both arms wrapped around her, trying to protect her with his slight frame.

If the entity had eyes, they would be glued to me, holding me in place. One clawed finger is pointed at me before the hand rotates, the finger curling back to the entity, beckoning me to come closer. I don't dare move. But if I don't, who will get it next? I'm pressed to the wall. Tears are sliding down my cheeks as I push myself upright. I start to take a step forward as a solid wall of ice stops me and I stumble, hitting the wall on my way down. I can't see her, but I know Marissa used what little energy she had left to stop me.

Everyone else is just stunned. Matty throws an electronic something at the entity and it snarls; a blood-curdling bellow erupts. This time the salt slows it. As it passes through, a burning courses over its gas-like form. The entity sets its sights on Matty, who presses a remote, and the thing he threw pops open, flooding the room with light and something else, something in the air. It isn't a pleasant smell, but the demon crumples and writhes. Soon it turns into nothing but a dark puddle on the floor.

I feel the coolness next to me. Marissa doesn't have time to say anything, or to even take shape, but I feel the cool hand over mine, even if I can't see it. The lights are beginning to flicker back on.

"Is it gone?" Rana is the first to speak.

"No." Sondra turns grimly to Matty. "But you stopped it for now, and made it twice as angry."

FORTY

THOMAS LIMPS BACK INTO THE ROOM, A gash running down the side of his face, blood trickling through a hole in the arm of his shirt. Somehow, he doesn't look completely beaten. His glasses are cracked and he gives them an annoyed look, tossing them onto what's left of the dining room table.

"That could have gone better," he admits, smiling. "Wow, I've never been thrown through anything with such force."

Sondra opens a first aid kit. "You've looked worse."

"I bet." Thomas laughs. "Wow, Roni, what is going on in this house?" He consults the laptop. "We have a full view of nothing that just threw me through a window. How is that even possible? It manifested enough to get into the room and throw me through the window, but then it vanished after a salt and silver bomb went off."

"A bomb?" Rana asks. "You have bombs?"

"Not the ones that hurt humans." Thomas raises a hand, letting Sondra apply some gauze. "Just hurt them." His eyes stray to me. "How's your friend?"

I'm sitting in the small space between the nice sitting room and the dining room. Marissa is kneeling in front of me, a worried look on her face. "Hun, he's talking to you."

My eyes are set on the floor. "He's asking about you, Mar. Were you affected by that thing?"

Marissa grips my knee. "Seem fine."

"She's okay," I answer, keeping my eyes down.

"I'm not into the sullen look." Marissa sits down next to me. "Just so we're clear. Though, the snoring you, that's a sight."

I can't help the laugh that escapes. "At least I didn't lie about not sleeping." I nudge her, thankful there's a solid, albeit cold, person sitting next to me.

The fear is keeping me locked in place. I want to curl up into a ball and pretend like none of this is happening. Marissa's icy hand rubs my back, her fingers leaving a light trail of goosebumps. Our conversation could have continued, but the rooms outside begin to creak and groan anew. Amanda pulls a bottle of holy water from her bag. Then she quickly sets it on the table, grabs a tall jar, and begins to spill purple powder from the jar across the doorways and under the windows. Marissa bristles next to me.

"What is it?" I ask.

Sondra turns at hearing me. "A different mixture, something a little more potent. Is it bothering your ghost?"

"She has a name," I say in a bit of an exaggerated huff.

Sondra gives a theatrical nod. "Marissa, did it bother you?"

"No." Marissa smiles.

I smile, shaking my head "no". Sondra turns back to what she and Amanda are doing. Matty is consoling Abigail, who looks about ready to burst into tears. Rana is looking just as upset. All three of them are hanging together. A soft stab of guilt cuts my heart as I realize I let this happen to Rana, to Matty, to Abigail. I could have left all of them out. If not for Matty's quick thinking just now, I'm not sure how that scene would have played out.

I let the thought fade as Marissa pulls me closer, latching both arms around me as we sit closer and closer together. It feels a lot like it did that morning. There is a definite chill, but I'm not freezing; I'm not as cold as I feel like I should be. Marissa isn't aware of my thoughts, pulling me closer.

"I am losing confidence in this group." She rests her chin on my shoulder as she speaks.

I nod, not wanting to agree with her aloud. "Any ideas?"

Marissa shrugs. "I'm just trying to make sure they don't get you killed."

"Right." I feel my mind wandering. Would it really be that bad? I've finally found someone who gets me, and I can't ever be with her, in any serious way, unless I'm dead. I shrug, feeling Marissa sit up taller. "You seem pretty okay being not alive."

"That isn't an option," her voice is stern. "I want to see you live a long, happy life."

"I want you to be around to see it," I whisper, hoping the rest of the room isn't listening to our increasingly intimate conversation.

Marissa presses her lips to the side of my head, right on my cheekbone. "Let's just get through tonight, huh?"

An argument is beginning in my head, but the sounds around the house quiet my thoughts. This is not the place, and absolutely not the time, to have this conversation. I just hope there is a later when we can both sit down and just talk, like we did last night. The idea starts to fade as the darkness begins to creep into the room.

Matty grabs the hand-crank flashlight. The shadows are moving like waves, like they did last night. Marissa starts to move, but I pull her back, nodding at Thomas and Sondra. The two are pulling some sort of net out. The net is sparking a little, which seems a tad dangerous, but I shrug it off after learning a bomb went off in the house. Long poles are deployed, covering the entrance from the kitchen. A second net is set up in the other entrance. Amanda has a similar setup, but she hangs the net from the curtain rods at each window. The room starts to return to a normal temperature, save for the fact that I'm sitting next to a block of ice.

"That should keep them at bay," Thomas says, wincing. "At least I'm able to get online. I have a colleague in Seattle who's getting a bunch of Wiccans together across the country to help create a virtual circle. Their chanting should coax anything outside of this room to leave."

I sigh, relieved that this means that Marissa should be safe. "How long will that take?"

Everyone turns at the sound of my voice. Thomas gets up, keeping several feet away from me, showing me the screen of his tablet. "The idea is to do this shortly. They will coordinate to start and stop at precise times. It will bind the djinns to an item of our choosing." He points to the table where there's a regular brick sitting. "I brought a brick that we can use to bind the darkness to. It can be buried or discarded at sea. All of the entities should be drawn into it, if everything works the way it should. In the past, we've been able to trap powerful beings, supernatural beings, in this way . . . stop them from escaping and doing further harm. The current running through the net, through a battery, keeps a sort of resistance to the supernatural. Think of it like a force field, but for demons and such. Not without excruciating pain can something not of this world pass through it."

Matty stares at me, his eyes wary. "If it works the way it should?"

Thomas pivots. "We can't be sure of any of this. Not really. I'd love more certainty—trust me, I would. But with what you've all witnessed, especially that possession with Eric, we need to be proactive, be ready to take the fight to them."

"He does know they can hear all of this, right?" Marissa asks me.

I furrow my brow. "Good point." I lean forward. "Uh, Professor Thomas, you do realize they can hear all of this, right?"

He shrugs, as if this is of little importance. "Of course, but they can't stop us."

"Says who?" Marissa laughs. "If not for all the salt and webbing, I could be almost anywhere I wanted to be in seconds. And if this is one clan or group of djinns, I'm sure they know others."

None of this occurred to me until Marissa said it. "But wait—how many can there be? Especially ones interested in what's going on here?"

"No, hun, that's not the point." Marissa turns to face me. "They can talk to anyone as quickly as they like. I have no one to communicate with. They're all connected. I think that's how they became one big thing, that hooved demon thing. Does this make sense?"

"Too much." I get up, feeling Marissa right at my side as I try to catch everyone's gaze. "She's right. I mean, Marissa was just saying, what if they can talk, can communicate with other djinns? Are you putting all of your friends in danger? What if the djinns or demons or whatever go after them?"

Thomas scoffs at this. "We've been doing this a long time, sweetie."

The condescension isn't lost on Marissa, who pushes Thomas hard in the shoulder. "Don't talk to her like that."

"He can't hear you." I smirk, feeling warmed by her defensiveness.

"I get the picture, Roni." Thomas glares at Marissa, as if he knows exactly where she is, and rubs his shoulder. "They took precautions."

"How'd that work out for you? Your precautions threw you through a window." Marissa is inching closer to Thomas.

I slide a hand in front of her. "Stop. Come on, this isn't helping. Let's just see what happens."

I'm trying to convey that we need an alternative plan. Marissa eases back, but she's staring daggers at Thomas. Matty clears his throat and I move towards him, beckoning Marissa to follow. Sondra and Thomas start talking as Amanda pans the camera around the room.

"We need another plan," Matty says this under his breath.

"Professor Thomas means well," Abigail says, her eyes red. "But I'm scared. I didn't expect this. I don't want to die."

"Agreed." I sit down next to Matty, feeling Marissa lean over the back of my chair.

"Ideas?" I ask.

"Exorcism."

The word chills me. I feel Marissa bristle behind me, setting both hands on my shoulders. "I absolutely won't let you even try, Roni."

I glance back, thankful for her unerring support. "Then who? None of us even know where to begin."

"No." Matty shakes his head. "That is the most intense cleansing we can do."

Abigail opens her notebook, flipping through pages and pages of elaborate drawings of everything, including one of Marissa. The paper stops as Marissa leans closer. Abigail's eyes follow the movement.

"She has a good eye." Marissa smiles, gesturing towards the sketchbook.

"You can see her?" I ask Abigail.

"Sort of." Abigail flushes. "I saw her for a second when we were upstairs earlier. I can see parts of her, like a white smoke now. I know she's holding onto you pretty tightly."

Marissa gives both of my shoulders a gentle squeeze. "Can you hear me?"

Abigail doesn't respond, going back to her notebook. "Is there anything less extreme we could do without, I don't know, dying?"

"Guess not," Marissa whispers in my ear.

"I'd like everyone to live through this." I scoot closer to Matty, feeling Marissa staying close. "I don't like our chances with this professor."

"We're stuck with them." Matty massages his forehead. "I'm sorry, Roni. I thought they'd know what to do."

"Me too." I admit.

Any discussion is cut short as the netting to the kitchen begins to bend inwards. Something is pushing against it. Marissa grabs my arm, pulling me up, back towards the wall. Matty and Abigail are close behind us. The netting is sparking. The purple dust is swirling, flying upwards into the net. The swirl is forming into something solid. The shape of the entities at the foot of my bed flashes to the front of my mind. The darkness is forming shapes, bodies. I'm backing into the wall, and there's nowhere to go.

The body is solidifying. Right as this one is taking shape, the other net is bending inwards. The windows are glowing purple and black. The dust or powder, or whatever it is, has created some sort of buffer. It's also forcing those entities, who are bold enough, to be caught.

Marissa has a firm grip on my arm. She's now in a much more solid form, but she seems to be shifting from solid to smoke in seconds. "This is not safe. What happens if they pull the nets off the poles?"

I shrug. "I have no idea."

Thomas seems untroubled by this. He uncaps a small bottle, reciting the beginnings of an exorcism, if everything I've read is true. I'm tuning the words out, watching as the entities are writhing in pain, either from the powder, the net, or his words. The clawed fingers poke through the holes in the net, a low growl echoing throughout the room. The lights flicker above, and then everything is bathed in white light.

My eyes are burning from the quick switch from dark to light. The only one not blinking in discomfort is Marissa, who's wrapping her icy arms around me. I can hear her muttering something under her breath. When my eyes return to normal, I realize why she's scared.

The entities are everywhere. None have broken into the room, but that isn't for lack of trying. The ones stationed in front of the nets are burning—the purple powder is electrified by the net, singeing anything it touches. Their faces, if you can call them that, are hollow and blank. There's nothing there. The body is loosely formed: legs, torso, arms, and head in the appropriate places. There is little definition, save for the feet and hands. Just like the demon, it tapers to hooves and claws. Even though there are no eyes, I can feel them on me—deadly, unfriendly, ready to take me . . . for what, I still don't know.

"I won't let them near you." Marissa's voice is a quiet whisper in my ear.

I can feel her, but she's starting to fade from my sight. "Are you okay?" I ask, worry and dread growing.

"Fine," she says soothingly. "Just marshalling my strength, in case we need another white out."

"You'll come find me if I have to run, right?" I can feel the cold, but I can't see her. "Mar?"

"Of course." Her voice is getting distant.

"Don't leave. Not yet," I beg.

"I'm right here." The whisper echoes through my head. "I'm not going anywhere."

FORTY-ONE

ANY DISSIPATION OF ENERGY HAS stopped. I can feel Marissa still right next to me, or maybe behind me. The wall of cold in human form is all I want. After everything that has already happened, it's silly that all I want is to see Marissa for a second longer. My thoughts don't have time to settle as the nets yawn away from the doors, tumbling to the ground. The purple powder is creating a haze. I can see a shape. The figures are turning into black smoke again.

There's nowhere to run. I squeeze my eyes shut, feeling a cold hand touch my cheek. "Don't be afraid, Roni."

Where is the courage I had when I started all of this? It never once occurred to me that I'd be in danger—not like this. The worst I ever expected was a scratch or scare. This—this is something far more advanced and terrifying than I could have possibly imagined. It's a nightmare come to life, with me at the center of attention. I'm praying again, a short surah playing through my head. The words are getting jumbled.

The room is frozen, save for me. Even Marissa seems to have stopped moving. Thomas is stock still, drops of the holy water suspended in mid-air, as if there were hundreds of invisible strings holding each drop in the air. The fog is stuck in place; the closest dark figure is moving through it like a great wind, pushing it backward. I lean back into the wall, sliding out of Marissa's grasp. I don't mean to, so now I'm struggling to find her again.

"Child, you must come."

I don't need to turn to see the source of the command. The voice is booming through the room, though I can't see it, I can feel it. The nets are scattered. The powder has been rendered useless. All the people here, including my ghostly friend, are unable to withstand this power. I don't know what I'm supposed to do.

"I will never come with you," I say crossly. Nice comeback, Roni. That's sure to do it.

A soft laugh begins. "You are not of this world. Not anymore. You were promised to us, and there is no negotiation. There is no bargain. We have found you once again."

"Bargain?" I can't help asking.

"The attempt to change locations, to mask your presence with an undead presence, has not worked."

"Masked?" I search for Marissa, seeing the cool, white wisp nearby. I'm trying to will her to move, to unfreeze. "I didn't ask her to mask me."

"Her?" The laughter grows. "She is not of your world."

"She isn't of yours either." I am getting a little too entitled for my own good. "You don't own her and you don't own me."

"Yes."

I stare at nothing. "Yes, what?"

"We own you both." The room shakes. "You will come or I will kill all of them."

What choice do I have? I look around at all of the gadgets. None of them is going to help. Is this it? Will I be with Marissa? If we're together, that won't be so awful. Will it?

Her warning rings through my head and I continue praying, hoping that God will strike this thing down or send an army of angels to fight it. Or strike me down before it can take me to whatever ungodly places it plans to take me. Nothing happens. I've never been one to question religion. I just do it out of habit because I know I should. Maybe that was the mistake. Conviction might have made a difference. Now there's no time to make up for that, no last second reprieve. I let my fingers slide through the ice cold of Marissa's body as I pass her, doubting I'll see her again. . . truly feel her again.

"You promise to leave everyone alone? Including my family?" I ask, my voice quivering. "Marissa too?"

I don't need to hear the answer to know it, to feel it. There is nothing stopping the onslaught now. The moment the darkness surrounds me, shutting any signs of light out, the whole room reanimates. Thomas is throwing holy water at me. Marissa jumps at me, solid and whole, and both of us crash into the sofa I was sleeping on earlier, breaking through the bubble I'd been enclosed in. The wind is knocked out of me, and I don't notice the front door opening as I'm struggling to catch my breath.

The darkness begins to fade and I stare up from the sofa. Marissa is pinning me down so I won't move. I blink a few times, wondering if it's just me. My mother is standing there with my brother right behind her. The two of them are reciting something from the Quran. A *tasbih* (the Islamic version of a rosary) is hanging from one of my mother's hands, the other hand clutching the Quran to her chest. Wherever the voice has gone, it is fading, fast.

I feel like I'm falling, the icy coldness of Marissa, holds me in place. "Don't ever do that again."

I glance over my shoulder, seeing Marissa's eyes brimming. "I didn't know what else to do."

"You are not permitted to sacrifice yourself for anything," she chokes the words out, her lower lip quivering. "Do you hear me?"

I try to nod, but I'm frozen, my insides melting into a great puddle of nothing. Guilt is something my mother has always used well against me, but in this instance, the guilt is coming from some unseen well and I feel dreadful, sick to my stomach, knowing I've caused someone I care about to be this upset. Those tears are entirely my fault.

I play for some slight humor. "I hear you loud and clear."

The very edges of her lips curl upwards as she wipes her face with the back of her hand. "Don't do that again."

"Never." I take her hand, finding comfort in her icy touch.

The moment of quiet is gone in an instant and I tear my eyes away, seeing the thing, the growing darkness solidify. All of the visions, all of the shadows I thought I'd seen could never prepare me for this. I'm trying to remember to take a breath as this creature, this monster, comes out from the shadow of the room, the outline forming from the scant light filtering through the window. Marissa is grabbing my wrist, pulling me away.

There isn't time for pleasantries. There's time for moving. A great clawed hand comes dangerously close to me, but Marissa drags me backwards with great force, more than I'd expect her to be able to exert on me. I feel like my feet are glued to the ground, but I drag myself after her.

Matty grabs my other free hand. "Why are you moving so slowly?"

I can see the camera in his hand, see the display, see Marissa almost clearly in it. He knew she had my other wrist. I feel tired all of a sudden and I don't muster much of a response. The moment Matty drags me towards the kitchen, Marissa knocks him backwards.

"I can't." I exhale loudly. "Outside the dining room the djinns might get me, like they got you all earlier."

"That, that isn't what's happening." Matty throws his hands up. "That thing, that thing is all that we need to worry about."

I nod dumbly. Marissa creates a wall between me and the dining room doorway. "I can't go with you."

I furrow my brow for a second before kicking the salt away. To my surprise, the djinns, the reaching, searching, clawing arms, don't appear. I turn to the scene in the dining room, feeling both of Marissa's arms wrap around me, trying to turn me from the scene.

The action in the nice sitting room is devolving into all out violence. The thing has it's dark eyes set on me. I can feel them, almost hear the voice in my head. Marissa is pressing her freezing hand to the side of my head, forcing me to look away. I see enough.

The beast, the entity, the creature is moving, slowly. The hands, the arms, the djinns, are formed into one being, like a box, surrounding it. My mother and brother are still praying. Thomas and the team are clamoring to throw something, a net that's sparking, around the box. I feel like I'm watching a confusing piece of performance art.

Another moment passes and Marissa drags me to the kitchen. "God, stop looking, Roni."

It is more exasperation than anger in her voice and I let her lead me away. Matty lays the salt back on the floor. Abby, not far off, is busy drawing. Her eyes dart to mine, then Marissa. She sees her.

A smirk crosses Abby's face. "She's prettier than I can draw."

Amid all this chaos, it's like a normal teen thing to say. "Thanks."

Marissa jostles me. "We need to move."

Matty nods, not hearing Marissa. "You need to go."

"Where?" I ask, my eyes wildly shifting from one to the other.

Abby pulls on my arm. "Go upstairs. They can handle this."

"It can't pass through the floor?" I feel my hands shake, feeling Marissa's cool fingers intertwine with mine, reassuring me.

"We'll be safe," she whispers.

Matty and Abby turn back to the fray. I skirt through the kitchen and up the stairs to my room, feeling Marissa's hand firmly in mine. I can hear the crash, hear the shouting, hear what I can only ever say sounds like a roar. I shut the door and it's like a vacuum.

Marissa pulls me back to the door. "The towel."

I slide it back across the doorway and the room feels lighter. "Not sure how it can't go through the floor."

"Don't worry," Marissa says.

A loud crash and the house shakes, contradicting her words. I wrap my arms around her, pressing my face into the coolness of her neck, inhaling the soft scent of cinnamon. I feel her fingers slide through my messy hair. God, what must I even look like right now? I try to push the thought away, but I feel those butterflies in my stomach again and pull away, an inch, maybe less.

All the worry, all the fear, all the despair are spilling away as I stare at her, up close. The freckles dusting her cheeks in the low light of the moon, her dark eyes with a touch of green in them, holding me in place. I felt uncertain, maybe nervous even, but I don't feel scared now, I feel safe, I feel like I belong, like I am being my true self.

I lean forward, feeling jittery, feeling bold, I place the tips of my fingers on Marissa's face, expecting her to pull away. She doesn't. We're frozen, both of us, a little unsure, maybe. After my near-possession downstairs, I push the worry away, tilting her face towards me with the lightest of touches, pressing my lips to hers. I've never kissed anyone. I've thought about it, but never done it. I'm not even sure if I'm doing it right.

Despite the fact that my girlfriend (there, I said it!), is basically frozen, I don't feel cold, I feel warm all over. Everything tingles, from my head to my toes. The floor outside creaks, but the door remains closed, from what little I can see, as I blink, feeling Marissa caressing my cheek in a way I've never felt someone touch me before. Her hand is soft, reassuring, as it slides into my tangled hair. There is so much chaos going on around us, yet I still feel safe, in her arms.

I want to get lost in this feeling. I am sure, deep down, I know how many people love me. But right now, right here, the only person I know for certain cares about me, deeply, is Marissa, and I just want to have this moment last for an eternity, even though I know it won't.

The house shakes, the windows rattle. I'm already pressed up against the bed, but I lose my balance, and we tumble over onto the bed, a soft laugh escaping. The bed cushions our fall, and I turn, feeling breathless, a smile reaching from ear-to-ear.

I can see the same sort of smile reflected on her face. "Hey."

"Hey," I reply, feeling weirdly embarrassed. "Hope I wasn't too forward—"

"Don't." She is sitting up, giving me an annoyed look. "For one second, can you just not think so much?"

I arch an eyebrow, feeling the room getting closer. I rest a hand on her knee. "Have you met me?"

She laughs, her hair falling around her face. "Yeah. Known you for a while, so just, relax."

Her icy fingers slide up my arm as she leans over me, her hair falling around my face. I reach up, tracing her cheekbone, easing up on my elbows, our foreheads nudging. I tilt closer, but another crash rocks the room. Marissa pulls away, turning to the door, as it glows on its hinges. Another stolen kiss would be nice, but I'm feeling that familiar panic setting in.

"It can't get in here," Marissa says this with far less conviction than I'd hoped. "The salt should keep it out."

I try to move, but once again I feel frozen, but not from fear. "I can't move."

Marissa blinks, grabbing my hand, pulling on it. I feel like I'm stuck, sinking through the bed. A wild look crosses Marissa's face. "I don't have enough energy."

I nod at the desk. "I have batteries for all the gadgets Matty makes, everywhere."

This is surreal. The bed feels deep, like I can fall and fall and fall. I've never much liked feeling weightless, but it feels like my eyes are shutting, my body relaxing. My eyes dart to Marissa, seeing the panic in her eyes, makes me try to move again, to fight my way out.

The room is bathed in white light and I know Marissa has found the batteries. She gives me a slight smirk, grabbing both of my elbows, bracing her foot on the bed, and pulls. The room white washes again, but I'm not sinking. I tip over, bumping into the desk.

"You okay?" she asks, squeezing my hand.

"Thanks to you, yes." I don't hesitate, kissing her on the cheek. "I thought I was falling through the bed."

"All those experts and what do we know?" she asks, her face reddening just a touch.

"Will we be any safer outside?" I ask.

She sits on my desk as it teeters, things falling all over the floor. "Oh, wow, I'm sorry."

I laugh, feeling the smile ease the tension. "Don't worry about it."

She's busy picking things up off of the floor, turning a rock over in her hand. "When did you start collecting rocks?"

It looks familiar. I saw it recently. My mind is blanking, but I reach for it anyway. She drops the stone in my hand and it feels heavy, heavier than it should. I turn it over, feeling something clawing my brain, from the inside out. I drop the rock on the floor, feeling a splitting headache stab through me.

Marissa's cool hands grip my face. "Roni? What is it?"

The longer her hands are there, the quicker the pain is fading. "Don't know."

My eyes are scrunched shut, but I can feel the room growing darker. Marissa wraps her arms across my shoulders, shielding my body from the darkness. "You're making me worry."

I feel the cool fabric of her shirt as I slide my hand up her back. Once again I feel the pressure from everything ease. "I'm okay."

She pulls away, staring into my eyes. "You sure? Should we make a break for it?"

"Go where?" I arch an eyebrow. "The haunted house won't be safe."

From here, it almost looks like the rock is glowing. The texture is coarse, as I pick it up. In the dark room, it seems whiter than anything else. I press on it and bits of it start to come off. How old is this thing?

"Now is not the time for this, Ron," Marissa says, pulling on my arm. "Besides, you're making even more of a mess."

I look around my desk, finding a screwdriver and place the rock on the desk, slamming the end of the screwdriver into the rock. It crumbles, revealing a broach, rusted and broken. I pick it up, showing it to Marissa, but she's gone. Was she tied to the rock? Did she recognize it?

Time feels like it is dwindling into nothing. "Marissa?"

She's not here. I dart around the room, stumbling over boxes and junk I've just never put away. She's not here. The cold spot is gone. The door begins to glow anew and I stare at it before it blows off of the hinges. Something stops it in midair. I see the familiar smirk and then she fades as the thing slams through the doorway, roaring. The windows rattle.

I stand my ground. "Get out."

It doesn't seem to understand, or maybe it doesn't care. The prayers are ringing in my head, through the whole house. Everything is glowing. I want to know Marissa is okay, but there's basically nothing between me and this thing.

It reaches a clawed hand towards me, stopping short. What is it waiting for?

"What do you want?" I shout. "There is nothing for you here."

In a lot of ghost hunting shows I've seen, destroying the object that ties the ghost to a location will set it free. But does that mean it will set it loose? My mind is reeling as the beast is standing before me.

"Too scared to speak a second time?" I ask, backing into the desk.

If there were defined facial features, I would say it is smiling, laughing, maybe, at me. The room fills with this low growl. I feel two icy hands on my shoulders, but it isn't Marissa, I can tell by the size of the hands. A moment passes and I'm across the tiny room in a second. I'm gasping for air as I feel books falling all around me. Through blurry eyes I see not one but two of those huge beasts standing at my desk. They aren't even looking at me now. They never wanted me? Who was talking to me earlier?

I try to sit up, but in quick fashion the thing is there, grabbing me by the throat, lifting me up. I grab at the hand, but there's nothing there. I reach behind me, trying to find something that can double as a weapon and the best I have is an old science textbook, which is cut in half the second I lift it.

"Where is it?" The voice comes out like gravel, but I dart my eyes between the two things.

"Where's what?" I try to say.

I get slammed into the wall for my response. There are stars in my eyes. It isn't quite panic anymore that I'm feeling. I was so quick to give up just fifteen minutes ago. Now, now I'm fighting, praying in my head, though this doesn't seem to be doing much.

There are growls going back and forth across the room. The sound is grating. I'm struggling to free myself, but I can feel my whole body getting cold. Is this what it's like to lose consciousness? My eyes are growing heavier and it reminds me of when Marissa sapped me of energy just last night.

I'm fighting to stay conscious, to keep them from taking me. Black spots are floating through my vision, but I can't tell if that's from a lack of oxygen or the evil spirits in my room. How did they get past the salt? I wrench my eyes to the door and see the hands, dozens, maybe more, reaching, grasping. Neither of the beasts has noticed them. I'm praying for them to come to help me, and the moment I think it, they are grabbing the beast that has me by the throat.

I crash to the ground, coughing and gasping for air. The second beast stomps towards me, the walls shaking, but it stops. Now I know where Marissa went.

Before me, glowing like an angel, is Marissa, a human shield. "You will not touch her again."

I'm struck by how beautiful my girlfriend is. Saying it a second time makes me feel warm all over. I ease up on one elbow, trying not to be a further distraction. I feel safe. I know I'm safe as long as Marissa is there.

"Roni, are you okay?" Marissa asks, not turning. "Babe?"

The term of affection almost has me frozen. I nod, getting to one knee. "I'm okay. Where did you go?"

"Had to get more energy." She smirks. "Can't leave you alone for a second."

"I wish you wouldn't." I hear the words come out of my mouth, stunned by my own courage.

"I don't know how long I can keep this guy away." Marissa's face is turning into a grimace. She's turning a little less solid, a lot more see through.

"What can I do?" I ask.

"Give me the broach." A voice calls from the hallway.

I turn, seeing Sondra, Thomas, and further down, my mother. I look to the desk, but it isn't there. I'm searching from the safety behind Marissa, knowing I need to hurry.

"Ron," she says my name softly. "Behind you. It got tossed with you. I can feel it."

"Will this do something to you?" I ask, edging closer.

"This needs to stop." Her voice is flat.

"That's not what I asked." I put a hand on her shoulder, relaxing when I feel her under my touch.

"I don't know," she admits. "They need to do this. Whatever happens, you know I love you, right?"

"Yes." I feel the weight of the decision on me. "I love you."

"I know," she turns slightly, smiling. "Oh, I've known."

I squeeze her shoulder, staring at the broach. Time seems to slow. I don't want to lose her. I don't want to be the reason she ceases to exist. I wouldn't call this death. She's already dead. I wish I could be with her. I would never squander my life. I've never seriously thought about suicide. That is one of the greatest sins in Islam. I let out a shaky breath, tossing the broach to Sondra. I slide both arms around Marissa, pressing my face into her hair, hoping I can hold onto her forever.

Whatever they do, the thing, the beast, begins to fade from sight. Marissa doesn't let up, both hands up, a near blinding light keeping the beast at bay. A moment passes and both she and the thing are gone. I slump to the ground, feeling tears sliding down my cheeks.

Epilogue

FALL CAN COME ON PRETTY QUICKLY here outside Chicago. I have the window cracked open. School starts in about two weeks. I need the distraction. All of my summer reading has been done. I've spent every waking moment, when not plagued by recurring night-mares, doing research. What was that thing? How did it find me? Why did it go away? What was the significance of the brooch? What happened to Marissa? Is it dead? It isn't like we can speak to the djinns, not directly. I know they're still here. I've removed all the salt and any other objects to ward them off. Yet I still I feel them. Every time I leave my room, the darkness—it's always there.

The occult book in front of me was printed about fifty years ago. I stare at the pictures, trying to match any to the one I saw in my vision. My memory is still a little choppy. The creature should be embedded into my brain. It isn't. I think of it and it flashes into my mind and then it's gone. I wonder if all of Mom's praying has it out of my mind. She has, under no uncertain terms, forbidden me to look for Marissa or ghost hunt ever again. This book had to be smuggled in, hidden among a bunch of other books. My ghostly girlfriend is a topic I can't even think about without bursting into unending tears.

There's a sharp knock on my door. I pull my notebook over the book and start tapping it with a nearby pencil. "Come in," I say.

My mother is dressed in a dark blue sari with a floral print. She and my father are going to a party. This will be the first night in a long time that they are leaving me to my own devices. I haven't been in the mood to socialize all summer. Sara has started college. Jamaal, as always, is a phone call away.

"You are staying in tonight?" she asks.

"Yep."

After the whole ordeal, I don't even bring up Matty's name. Sondra and Amanda came by a week later. My mother chased them away with a broom in hand. If not for Jamaal, I'm pretty sure she would have hit one or both of them. Anyone who was there, was in the house when this happened, has been deemed unwelcome or compromised. I'm still trying to figure out what the issue is. Asking directly has not proved fruitful.

"You will stay inside?" she persists.

I shut my eyes, not daring to meet her gaze. This is basically house arrest. While I ranted and raved the first two weeks, now I don't have the energy to mount any sort of argument or discussion.

"I was going to eat dinner on the patio," I answer.

Her expression doesn't change. "Are you wearing your necklace?"

"Yes." My fingers glance the locket, shaped like a tiny book. Inside, I'm told, there is a *surah*, written on a small piece of paper, rolled up and sealed inside. The etchings on the outside of the locket are the words God in Arabic.

"Have you prayed today?"

"Three times."

"We'll be home after ten."

"Okay."

A second later she's gone and I'm by myself again. I prop open my laptop, checking the most recent sites and finding a demonic site that Thomas had recommended. I have sifted through it again and again. Just like all the books, I can't find anything. Even if I'm not allowed to see Sondra, Amanda, or anyone else, that hasn't stopped me from messaging them. Thomas's not nearly as pretentious as I'd first thought. He's still recovering.

From my room, I can still hear my parents. I stare at my computer, jotting down notes and drawing crude outlines of what I see online, hoping to find one that matches my tormentor. I wish I had the skill Abigail has. What I wouldn't give to get my hands on her notebook. It takes another fifteen minutes, much of that with my mother repeating herself to my father, before they finally leave. I sigh with relief once the front door is locked. It'll take at least five minutes for them to clear the neighborhood. Jamaal won't be home or check in until after seven. I have about an hour and a half before anyone will be around.

I get dressed in a flash, changing from my pajamas into jeans, a white T-shirt, and a red pullover. I grab my backpack as I stuff my feet into my sneakers and slide my window open farther. The habit hasn't died. I swing over the edge, climbing down the trellises to the garage. My old bike is leaning against it and I grab it, careful of the rust on the frame, and start pedaling.

The trip to Matty's house is pretty quiet. It isn't until I turn that final corner that I realize this is the big party Matty's been talking about for months. I slow down, uncertainty stabbing at me. I've come all this way. I'd hate to turn back now. I get off the bike and lean it against the mailbox. There are tons of people, all of them Matty's parents' friends. I pull the hood over my head even though it isn't that cold. I don't need to attract too much more attention. I tried to avoid a ton of human contact in the past two months. It was a challenge. I keep my head down as I walk quickly to the open garage door.

I see two people in the room between the kitchen and the garage. It's sort of like a cubby. The two are mincing something, making a salad maybe. I ease around the luxury cars parked in the garage and knock on the doorframe.

"Hi," I say, feeling stupid as I say it. "Is Matty home?"

Both girls look up. I'm surprised to see one is Amanda. I give her a quizzical look until I realize Matty is the one standing next to her. There's no way to school my features at this, and my eyes grow wider than possible. I can't remember the last time I saw Matty in a dress.

A deep maroon is spreading across Matty's features. "Good to see you out, Ron."

Amanda cuts through my awkwardness. "How's your mom?"

I can't help laughing at this. "Well, she hasn't tried to attack anyone with a broom recently, so I think we're doing good."

Amanda picks up the bowl. "Let me put this in the kitchen."

"Roni . . ." Matty slides a hand down his dress. "My parents let me be who I want to be at school, you know, most of the time, but my great grandfather is here. They say that would be too much for him."

"I get it." I try to force a laugh. My features haven't shifted to a smile in ages. "It's been a while since I've seen you in a dress."

A flash of red darkens his cheeks. "I really don't feel like myself, though. One day I'm hoping I won't have to indulge my parents this. I'd prefer something less formal."

"Well, you'd look nice in a suit and tie, I'm sure," I say, pulling the hood from my face. "I probably should have called first."

"No worries." Matty takes a step closer. "I know this must be weird."

I put both hands up. "Stop, really. You'll always be Matty to me."

"Thanks, Roni." His eyes glisten. "I have the files. But I'm not sure you should be looking at them."

"Your mom was pretty clear about all of this." Amanda comes up behind Matty, holding an overstuffed file folder she pulled out of her nearby bag. "I think she's right. You're sensitive to all of this. You proved it time and again."

My eyes are locked on the folder. "I just want to know."

Matty waves a hand in front of my eyes. "You can't go near any of this stuff. We almost watched you die, Roni."

I furrow my brow. "I need to know."

"You *want* to know." Amanda shakes her head.

Matty stares skyward. "Give me a sec. I have the video files on an external drive." He hurries out of the room. I can hear the high heels clacking off of the wooden floor.

"Roni, seriously," Amanda begins as she takes a step closer, "Sondra told me that you're asking Thomas all sorts of questions."

I set my jaw, furious that he'd tell them. "He owes me some answers."

"He doesn't have any that are going to tell you where Marissa is." Amanda sighs. "The folder has a lot of stuff in it. We didn't find Marissa's name, exactly, but we found an incomplete police report. Since none of us know exactly what she looks like, we can only assume it's her. Seems like she got sucked into some supernatural something. Sondra and I have been doing research on the brooch. Looks like it was an antique, from like a hundred years ago. I don't know how it's connected to Marissa, but one of the leaders of whatever cult that called that thing forward wore it, so that makes some sense."

"Yeah." My eyes grow distant.

"I'm sorry, Roni. I am." Amanda leans closer. "We all are. She saved you, protected you. We all did what we thought was best. We had to send that demon packing, and without the protection around her, we couldn't differentiate between Marissa and it. I'm sorry."

My eyes are brimming, but I push it back. "It doesn't matter now."

"It does matter." Amanda takes a step down into the garage as she grips my hand firmly. "I'm sorry, Roni. I know you loved her and I know she loved you."

I take several long, slow breaths. "Right."

Thankfully, Matty comes into the room. His eyes slide from me to Amanda and back. "Roni, please don't use this." In his hand is the external hard drive. With it, to my surprise, is what appears to be Abigail's notebook. Matty notices my look. "She made a copy for you."

The sun isn't even close to setting, but I open my bag and stuff everything in. "I'll call you before school."

I don't wait for more of a response and ride as fast as I can. With the cooler temperature, I'm not pouring with sweat, but my heart is pounding. It is exhilarating to just weave through parked cars, kids playing ball, tuning all of it out and just powering home. I make it back in record time, under ten minutes. I situate my bike exactly how I found it.

The bag feels extra heavy as I climb the trellises to my room. My hands are shaking as I pull the folder and hard drive out. While my laptop is booting up, I set that and the hard drive to one side and open the folder, feeling like I'd been struck in the face when the image staring up at me is Marissa, in full color. It takes my breath away.

The image of her is ingrained in my mind. It's always that first time I met her in the haunted house. She looked normal—human, I should say. Dark hair, dark eyes, sassy smile, maybe an inch or two taller than me. The pictures is a four-by-six, perfect for an empty frame I have sitting on the bookshelf. I don't worry about how I'll explain this to my mom. I just slide the picture in, grateful to have something to look at. My fingers slide across the bottom of the frame, and I feel an involuntary chill, one I'd grown accustomed to.

I could stare at the picture all day, but I turn back to the file and flip through the documents. It looks like someone may have taken copies from the courthouse. I see an official police report from Marissa's disappearance. Her parents' testimony is graphic and depressing. They had initially found Marissa's things—her bag, a scarf, a shoe—but that was all. Days passed before the police turned the investigation from a missing person to a missing body. I stop reading at this. I don't want to know this. She didn't want me to know. I set the report aside, finding a newspaper clipping from her school newspaper. The full-length picture doesn't do her justice. It never will.

There is nothing but the past to be found in these files. I know what I need to about her. I need to learn about the thing that attacked us both, that almost killed me. I close the file, glancing at Marissa's smiling face, unable to hide the smile that I return. The memories begin, our time together far too short, and I shake my head, hoping to get back to business.

My laptop thrums to life. I plug the external hard drive in. There are a few folders. One is marked "demon." I love that Matty knows that I don't have time to guess. I double-click the folder, but the screen blacks out, the power on the battery light gone. The laptop has shut itself off.

I let out a loud huff. "Come on."

"You come on." The response is quick and annoyed.

I clench my jaw. "I need to figure this out."

"We talked about this." A cool breeze comes through the open window, accompanied by a very translucent hand resting on the keyboard. "I don't want you reading any of that. The demon is gone."

"We don't know that." I swivel in my chair, finding Marissa sitting on my bed, not quite solid. She hasn't been solid since I woke up after the incident. The exorcism did something to her. I don't know what. It's my fault. "I can fix this."

"Darlin'," she drawls, "please stop. You've been at this for months. I may have all the time in the world, but you don't. Your friends are worried about you. Your mom would take you with her everywhere if she could, just to be sure you're okay. I'm already dead, Roni."

I fight the tears that are threatening. "What happened was my fault."

"You don't know that." Marissa slides closer. "I'll be fine."

"You haven't been the same since." I feel a treacherous tear sliding down my cheek.

"Honey," Marissa says as she inches closer. There's no solid hand to stop the tear from falling. She's truly become a ghost. There is no solid form, just cold.

I turn away, wiping my face with the back of my hand. "It doesn't matter. I can figure this out."

The cool wall comes up behind me. She tends to disappear when she gets this close. It's hard to both appear and make her presence known through the cold. Her voice is still in my ear. "It won't change anything. I sucked a car battery dry and I still can't be here. It's okay."

"It isn't." I'm on my feet in a second. "Just let me do this, please."

She's semisolid again, sitting on my desk, on my laptop specifically. "I hate to see you like this, Ron. This isn't your fault."

"I wish people would stop saying that." I sink onto my bed. "I'm so tired of all of this. I just want, like, a second of what we had."

"We've had that second." Marissa laughs. "Remember when you woke up that one day?"

A small smile breaks at the corners of my mouth. "Yeah."

The pleasant memory calms me. I was still feeling sick about a week or so after everything that had happened. I was limping back from the bathroom and curled up in bed. It got cold, like winter in my room. At first I didn't understand it, but I sat up, calling her name. I couldn't see her, but I knew she was there. It was a huge relief to know that she hadn't been banished to some other place, or forced out of this world. That relief was tempered by the realization that she wasn't part of this world almost at all. We couldn't touch each other. Her hand slid right through me. Since then, I've been a lot more adamant about figuring out what was going on, what I could do to help. If she hadn't been so close to me, none of this would have happened.

"Go eat something, doll," Marissa says, nodding to the door. "I know you skipped lunch and you didn't eat breakfast really."

I give her a wary look. "Mar, I miss you."

"I miss you," she replies. "We're here, and that has to count for something." A moment passes and neither of us have moved. "Please, please don't start crying." Her voice breaks. "We can make this work, we can, but I need you to be strong for me, for you, for your family. I'm here and I'm not going anywhere."

I squeeze my eyes shut, trying to force the tears back. "I know."

She vanishes from sight, but I feel the soft, cool presence right next to me—a half-embrace, as it were. I can't refuse her, even if I want to believe I'm not hungry. I trudge down the stairs, leaving the files, the computer, the clues behind. It can wait for another day.

AFTERWORD

WELL, READER, YOU MIGHT SAY TO YOUR-self, *Hina, why on earth did you write this book?* Picture it . . . Sicily, 1942. I'm kidding. I just love the *Golden Girls*, and I did get Sophia on a Buzzfeed quiz, which is highly scientific. But seriously, picture it, July 2016, living just outside of Washington, DC, overlooking a set of train tracks. Some of you may remember exactly where you were when a certain person got up on stage in Cleveland, Ohio, to spout lies and mock people of all types. At the time, I was working in a heavily Republican-controlled office, surrounded by the base that supports a certain Nazi in Chief, and I couldn't speak my mind for fear of losing my job, which happened anyway, under the watch of a so-called Democrat three years later, but I digress. I sat quietly in my office, listening to the latest album by Tegan and Sara (the absolute best Canadian band), called *Love You to Death*, on repeat, wondering what I, a lowly IT manager, could do about the hate that was spreading, even just in my own sphere of influence.

I had dabbled with writing for about ten years, having received about sixty or so rejections for the first book I wrote. I shelved it, along with about eleven other books, and started the writing process anew. I thought to myself, *What kind of story could I possibly write that would make a difference?* I could go for a heavy-handed approach, writing about politics, how wrongheaded people were, or I could do what authors are supposed to do: show, not tell. And so I put together the most diverse group of people I could think of (characters) and set about making them normal—and everyone is normal, I realize, but certain people don't see people of my ilk as normal. We're different because we're not the right color, don't worship the right God, come from crap-hole countries, whatever. And so, that's how you, hopefully, ended up reading this book. I wanted to do something that I knew (love horror movies and, truthfully, one of the scary scenes did happen to me, but was it a dream? I'm not sure) that lots of people could relate to. I mean, how many of us love to guiltily watch horror movies? I got about one hundred rejections for this book, but decided—you know what, why not self-publish? What's the worst that could happen? And on the flipside, what's the best that could happen?

Acknowledgements

WHERE TO BEGIN? THERE ARE SO MANY people who have played varying roles in my quest to write and publish a novel. This list is really in no particular order, or it isn't intended to be.

To my friend, Lay Bragg. You were the first person to read any of my work, and your unbridled acceptance and enthusiasm encouraged me to keep writing, to keep plugging away. While the book you read has yet to see the light of day, if I hadn't written that, I would never have written this. So, thank you.

To my friend, Michelle Prieto. You've always encouraged me to keep trying, to never get discouraged, and to always believe in myself and believe that people will want to read this book. If you're wrong, you owe me an iced tea (unsweet) from DD!

To Erin Servais, my editor. Erin, I would not be in this position if not for you. You've been more than an editor in this process, and, having read more than one of my books, you probably know me better than most. I will be forever grateful for your ability to give me tough love and encouragement in equal measure. You never gave up on me and my work, and I thank you for that.

To Luke Tolvaj, my sensitivity reader. Luke, you opened my eyes to things I could have never seen myself or ever understood without your insight. Thank you for joining me in this journey.

To my stylist, Liz Kalipi. Thank you for listening to me talk about publishing a book for more than a decade. Your support, and styling tips, are always on point!

To my mom, dad, and sister (who didn't know I was even writing a book), thanks for keeping me sane and grounded.

To my family and friends not mentioned by name, your support has meant the world to me.

To all the LGBTQ kids out there—you are heard, you are valuable, and you are loved. Don't ever forget that. In a large part, I wrote this book for you. Don't listen to the haters. Love is love, and yours is valid, as are you.